Also By Cathryn Grant

Cathryn Grant

THE WOMAN
IN THE MIRROR

An Alexandra Mallory Novel

D2C Perspectives

ISBN: 978-1-943142-25-5

1

Aptos, California

The ad said a *sweet and responsible* woman was looking for housemates to share her cottage.

The ad did not mention that the cottage was perched rather too close to the edge of a cliff overlooking Monterey Bay. It would seem easy to rent spare rooms in a house with a glistening ocean view, but the house was really, *really* close to the edge of a sandstone cliff that was eroding ever so slowly onto the boulders and crumbled rock forming the shore below. Nail biting territory on a stormy night when trees bowed under the wind, and rain whipped at the windows like a woman with a cat-o-nine-tails.

Noreen Palmer told me that everyone who responded to her ad stepped inside the front door, caught a glimpse of the ocean through the back doors, and couldn't believe their good fortune, or the below-market rent. Once they were standing on that faintly sagging deck, wondering how much rot had infested the soft planks beneath their feet, with nothing but empty space below, the flesh of their faces turned to pudding. They bolted for solid ground, calling back to her that the house wasn't a good fit after all.

The disturbing aspect of the ad itself was this — if a woman feels compelled to emphasize that she's sweet and responsible, it's a red flag. But the thing is, she did seem sweet. And the tidiness of her house, her clipboard and paperwork with forms for providing information about myself, all appeared very responsible.

And I was desperate. I had a new job at a small high tech company based in Aptos. Nearly all of my connections in Silicon Valley on the other side of the foothills had been severed recently — murder has a way of orchestrating an abrupt change in relationships. Living at a Santa Cruz motor inn, eating meals at taquerias and burger stands, aside from the supplemental yogurt or cup of noodles, was blasting through my minimalist savings account. Desperate was an understatement. I needed a place to live, I needed a responsible landlord taking care of utilities, asking nothing from me but my monthly contribution. Cash was fine, she said.

It didn't occur to Noreen Palmer to ask whether *I* was sweet. She had her own kind of desperation — needing income from rooms in a house that might not survive the next El Niño deluge pouring down cliffs weakened by years of drought.

I would never describe myself as sweet. It's not that I'm horrid, I'm not an axe murderer, but I'm not sweet. In fact, I would never describe any woman as *sweet*. I find that word condescending and somewhat misogynistic. Sweet is for cookies and ice cream, not women.

Noreen led me to the pine dining table surrounded by

three chairs. She placed a clipboard with several forms on the table and handed me a pen. I sat down and wrote my name at the top of the first form. I looked up and smiled. I twisted my ponytail around my finger. After reading her ad, I'd had my hair cut into thick bangs, a blunt shoulder length style on which I used a curling iron to give it a slight wave. I put the pen between my teeth for a moment, then pulled it away and smiled. "Isn't it better to chat and get to know each other instead of relying on a bunch of forms? You can miss so many things in a form. All the subtleties. All the things that really matter."

"That's a very good point." She ran her fingers through her hair, mostly dirty blonde with a few glints of a pale red that had revealed themselves when she'd stood in direct sunlight on the back deck. The gesture emphasized her slightly larger than average nose and a mouth that settled naturally into an expression between sadness and worry.

"Tell me who you are, Noreen. Girl chat." I put the pen down.

She giggled. "I like to run."

It was an interesting introduction, not usually the first thing someone tells you about herself. I grinned. "Me too!"

"Maybe we can run together!" she said.

I held her gaze, smiling eagerly.

After a few seconds, she glanced away. "You're in better shape than I am. You look really strong."

"I lift weights."

"I should try that. I think about it, but never do."

"You should. It feels great."

She adjusted the strap on her tank top, settling it over her shoulder bone. She was thin and small, elfin, and her long, silky fine, un-styled hair added to the impression. She was currently unattached, she said. I was currently unattached. We both loved vodka martinis and pasta.

"If you love pasta as much as I do," she said, "You'd better be a runner."

I laughed. "Totally agree."

She bit the nail of her index finger and tilted her head to the left, expecting more from me. When I didn't speak, she yanked her finger away from her mouth as if I'd slapped her hand.

I filled out the forms anyway because I could see it was important to her peace of mind — Alexandra Mallory (middle name and last name), age twenty-seven (I can't say why, exactly, but it seemed wise to be closer to Noreen's age), employer Macy's Department Store (I prefer to keep work and home separate and the best way is if work is an unknown), job title sales manager (the manager part was correct), non-smoker (I would never smoke inside her house, so the white lie wasn't important), no pets (true!). I filled in the lines asking for years with my current employer (less than one, but that didn't bother Noreen and she didn't ask how much less than one), previous employers, personal references, job references. Those slots were filled with names of a handful of people from the less recent past who owed me, even if they didn't want anything to do with me. Noreen wouldn't bother to check anyway. We'd *bonded* — *kindred spirits*. Besides, her nervous, eager smile said she needed two bodies in those spare rooms, and money coming in. It was a perfect place for me — a desperate renter and a desperate landlord, no important questions asked.

The candidate for the other unoccupied bedroom was male.

Are you okay with that? she said.

Absolutely, I replied.

The three bedrooms were on one side of the open floor plan living and dining area. Noreen's room had an adjoining bathroom and was on one side of the short hallway. The doors to the second and third bedrooms were side by side across from hers. The guy and I would share the second bathroom off the same short hallway. She didn't ask whether that was okay.

The kitchen counter opened into the living and dining area, and there was an alcove off the living room with French doors giving access to that treacherous back deck. The floors throughout the house were sand-colored tile, the grout chipped in a few spots. The tile would be easy to keep clean, but on foggy mornings, it turned cold as a gravestone. The garage had space for a single car, Noreen's Jetta would be parked there. I'd only been told my share of the rent and utilities, not the total cost, and I began to wonder if this was a profit making deal for her despite the low rent. It wasn't the first time I'd run into such an arrangement.

The house was adobe with a red, glass-paned front door. The front yard was slightly barren with dying grass and a Japanese maple holding its own against years of drought. An eight-foot fence surrounded the side yard. It contained a dead vegetable garden, a small lemon tree, and a metal shed.

"When does the guy move in?" I said.

"Jared. Jared Wellington. I'm not sure. He already paid the deposit and first month's rent, so he can take his time."

It was another two weeks before I met Jared. The man knew how to create an aura of mystery around himself. Who has money to pay rent and not move into a place right away? If he had money to burn, why was he renting a room in — let's face it — a sagging bungalow? The window frames needed scraping and repainting. The tile floor was nice, but the bathroom had a vague hint of mildew, despite looking spotless. And there was no covered parking, which became more surprising when Jared pulled up in a brand new white BMW. He climbed out and closed the door with obvious care. In my experience, a guy that good looking would somehow end up with the only covered parking for his Beemer, but Noreen didn't offer to park her faded Jetta in the driveway, and he didn't ask.

When he climbed out of the car, Noreen's lips parted slightly and she ran her fingers through her hair, separating it into chunks. Hitting on a tenant is generally not a good idea. But a woman who advertises her sweetness might be a tiny bit naive. She snuck a glance at me as he walked around the car.

Jared was six-one. He had dark, almost black hair, longish but not grubby and stringy like some kind of beach bum. He removed his sunglasses, revealing dark brown eyes with thick lashes. He had a perfect nose, and teeth that had been well-cared for by an orthodontist.

As it turned out, Jared was not attracted to elfin women.

And it only took a moment for him to express his opinion of my appearance. He did it with an exaggerated wink. Unfortunately, he didn't have the discretion to hide that wink from Noreen. A grimace crossed her face, tight with rage, complete with red streaks on the pale skin of her forehead. Her fists tightened and her knuckles turned chalk white. It was clear, no matter how confidently she advertised her sweetness, she was fully capable of putting a knife through my ribs if I followed that wink to its natural conclusion.

2

Jared Wellington fell in love with Alexandra the moment he saw her. It wasn't something he'd admit because it sounded trite, and he would never trivialize her like that.

He'd climbed out of his car and looked at the two women standing near the edge of the rough, faded lawn. They couldn't have been more different.

Noreen smiled and took a step forward, eager to wrap the warm arms of her home around him. She raked her fingers through her pale, oddly colored hair and deepened the smile.

Alexandra remained where she was, a look on her face that said she couldn't care less whether he stayed, or climbed back in his car and drove away, no longer willing to live in a house that was ready to slide down the cliff into the Pacific Ocean. She seemed to be more taken with his car than she was with him, gazing at it as if she wanted to stroke its sleek, white haunches. He shut the door and walked toward them. He took off his sunglasses.

Fog was blowing in from the ocean, and behind the two women, the house looked like it was fading out of existence with its beige stucco walls, thirsty tree, and the grayed worn boards of the fence surrounding the side yard. All that stood out was the red frame surrounding the glass panes of the front door.

Noreen grabbed his wrist and pulled him onto the dead lawn. He tried to slide his wrist out of her grip, but it was too strong. Wrenching violently away would hurt her feelings, and she looked like a woman whose feelings were easily hurt. Alexandra did not.

Noreen introduced them, finally releasing his wrist so he could shake Alexandra's hand. Alexandra still didn't smile, but she managed to look pleasant and mildly welcoming without a smile. Her hand was cool and soft, her grip firm.

He couldn't stop looking at her. She was gorgeous. Not perfect — her ass was smaller than he liked and she had a narrow nose that ended in a sharp tip — yet she seemed as close to perfection as any woman he'd seen. She held herself separate in a way that made him long to find out what was going on behind her cool gaze.

The fog did nothing to disturb her sleek dark hair that hung over her shoulders, covering the straps of a white top and framing her round, firm breasts. She was slim with long legs. Her eyes were dark and looked at him as if she knew everything about him. Bangs covered her eyebrows, making her eyes appear larger. She wore faded jeans with a tear in the left knee. The tear looked real, not one of those phony rips that comes from the factory. Her feet were bare and she had gold rings on the second and third toes of each foot.

He'd decided to move to Aptos after his sudden departure from Cisco, dreaming of weekends lying on the sand, swimming in the ocean, and a live-and-let-live culture. No more over-eager women with long, reinforced nails and sharply pointed shoes, clawing their way to ever higher salaries, twisting your balls into withered mice in the process. No more working until seven at night and checking email when you woke up to take a piss. No airports and meetings and hotels, no expense reports and performance reviews and PowerPoint slides.

The magic of Silicon Valley had turned into a circus for him, with terrifying grins painted in grease on the faces of the clowns who led the show.

His abrupt departure was viewed as an act of bravery by some and stupidity by others.

He'd stood up in the middle of a product readiness review meeting. He'd closed his laptop and walked around the U-shaped arrangement of tables, passing behind men and women hunched over their computers, simultaneously tapping on smart phones and glancing at the slides displayed at the front of the room. They looked like gargoyles, curled shoulders and twisted faces under the panels of florescent lights. He'd paused at the bottom of the U where Michelle Oliveri, the Vice President of marketing sat with her arms folded across breasts that looked to be as empty of life as his balls. He placed his laptop beside hers.

Without looking at him, she said, "What's this for?"

"I quit."

She laughed. "Don't be so impatient. Your section will be up in twenty minutes. I promise. I know we're running behind, but Mel will make up the lost time, and then it's your turn."

"No," Jared said. "I quit. I'm resigning."

"You can't resign. We're two weeks from the most important launch event in three years."

"Everything's on the laptop." He turned and walked toward the door at the back of the conference room. He paused at the door, lifted up first one foot, then the other, removing his shoes. He tucked them under his arm and waved at his colleagues. Only half of them had even noticed the interruption, the others continued typing and tapping and scowling at screens.

Michelle laughed. "Okay, you made your point, Jared. You can go next and leave the meeting early if you have to be somewhere."

"Ms. Oliveri, I no longer want to spend my life sitting in meetings re-doing every project thirteen times because of some arbitrary change in strategy. I'm not leaving the meeting, I'm leaving the company. The industry. Now." He opened the door and stepped into the hallway. In his stocking feet, he ran along the corridor, turning left twice, until he reached the lobby. He unclipped his badge. He took his corporate credit card out of his wallet and left both on the receptionist's desk. Then he peeled off his socks and walked outside.

He'd always liked the beach. It seemed like a good place to start looking for housing.

Fortunately, the condo he'd lived in for the past four years had his roommate's name on the lease. Ray was more easy going than most. Or maybe it was that he was one of the few who believed Jared had committed an act of bravery. "I always wanted to live near the beach. Maybe someday."

Jared decided not to drive a virtual sword through his friend's heart. Instead of informing Ray that *someday* was now, another someday might not arrive if he never looked up from his desk, he grinned and said *thanks for understanding*.

The ad for a bungalow overlooking the ocean, with its emphasis on *sweet* and *responsible*, struck him as just the sort of thing you would expect in Aptos. Despite his dramatic exit from the five story office building, among a sea of similar buildings, it took him a week or so to take care of exit forms and rolling his 401k out of the company coffers and into his own IRA, packing and selling most of his furniture, and cheerfully agreeing to a farewell bash.

They thought his sudden race for the door was just that — sudden, but it had been coming for almost half a year. After seeing his doctor for insomnia, and then seeing her again two months later for a madly twitching eyelid, and two weeks after that for a ringing in his left ear, she suggested he try meditation. *You're showing symptoms of stress. A lot of people find meditation helps.*

In his typical hard driving fashion, he'd purchased fifteen books on the subject, a set of MP3 lessons, and taken a class at the New Age Nirvana Center in Santa Cruz. During the third class, he'd felt his brain float out of his skull, rise up to the rafters of the re-purposed church, and stretch into a thin film that then descended over him and his fellow meditators. The experience was both frightening and beyond blissful. It was better than getting high, which he didn't do often. Better than a few drinks, better than driving a hundred and ten miles on dark, curving, deserted Highway 280 at three o'clock in the morning. He was still debating whether it was better than sex. Probably not all sex, but a lot.

Now, standing a few feet from Alexandra Mallory, he regretted his vow that he would steer clear of sex and drinking while he continued to explore the hidden corridors of his mind, the universe, and the nature of life.

She wasn't just hot. She was transcendent.

It went beyond her extremely pleasing body, her serene face, and her thick, silky hair. A presence emanated from her that seemed to burn beneath her skin, a strength that said she was in charge of every situation, impervious to the insecurities and self doubts and neuroses that lived in most people to varying degrees. She held his gaze without looking away, not staring, not challenging him, not trying to get his attention. Just looking. Like a cat looks at you, unthinking, unperturbed, simply observing. He would gladly yield his soul to those eyes.

Without thinking, as if it had a mind of his own, his eyelid moved in an exaggerated wink.

From the corner of his eye, he saw Noreen scowl. Alexandra's expression didn't change.

3

On the Saturday that Jared moved into the bungalow with us, he stacked his four boxes in the corner of his room, and informed us he was going out for the evening. He didn't share the details and was vague about what time he'd be back. The implication was that he might not be sleeping in his newly occupied room that night.

The minute the front door closed behind him, Noreen clicked her playlist of 90s tunes and pulled a bottle of Smirnoff out of the refrigerator. She filled a shaker with ice, poured vodka into a shot glass, and then over the ice. With the second pour, vodka spilled on the counter. She didn't seem to notice it was there. She splashed in vermouth. "I'm crushing so bad," she said. "Isn't he cute?"

"Be careful," I said.

"Why?" She blinked rapidly, then turned and began shaking ice and alcohol. The racket of ice against metal prevented her from hearing when I pointed out the obvious. The rattling stopped. "Why should I be careful?"

"You're his landlord," I repeated.

"So?"

"It's not a good idea to mix business transactions with romance."

"I'm not."

"You absolutely are."

"I like him so much. He's gorgeous. And such a gentleman."

I flopped on the couch and put my feet on the coffee table. I sat up again and unzipped my boots. I tugged them off and nudged them under the table before putting my feet on top again. "I'm not blind, but I would be careful."

She shook the metal container more vigorously. Ice slamming against metal made me feel as if my brain was slamming against my skull. I put my hands over my ears to muffle the sound. The racket didn't faze Noreen. She stopped shaking, poured the drinks into glasses, and added two enormous olives to each one. She picked up the glasses and walked by sliding her stocking feet across the tile, cross-eyed as she watched the liquid waver close to the edge. She carefully lowered the drinks to the table and pushed one in my direction. I leaned forward and took a delicate slurp from the stationary glass. Then I picked it up. "Very nice."

She smiled. "Cheers."

We didn't touch our glasses in a toast. The liquid was still too close to the rim. The olives bobbed like decapitated heads, the red tongues pushing to escape the round, surprised mouths. I took another sip.

She settled beside me, cradling her martini in both hands. "Maybe we should have eaten first."

"Plenty of time for that."

"Leftover pizza?" she said.

I nodded. After that brief look of rage when she'd caught

Jared winking at me, she'd reclaimed her chummy self, but the look nagged at me.

Still, it was nice having someone to chat with. I liked living in a house again. In an apartment or condo complex, you're smashed up against each other all the time. When you approach the building from a distance, walking home from the train every evening, you see that there are far too many people contained in a rectangular box. It wouldn't take much to set them against each other. A hundred people with a hundred different religious beliefs, political viewpoints, food preferences, music preferences, and varying tolerance for noise. It's amazing there isn't more violence in apartment complexes. The sheer number of people per square foot is enough to stretch nerves until they feel more like strips of wire than human flesh.

Noreen pulled her knees up to her collarbone and hugged her lower legs. She laced her fingers between the toes of her left foot and mumbled into her kneecaps. "How am I mixing money and romance?"

It wasn't clear whether she wasn't very bright, or so in the grip of Jared's beauty she was willfully not understanding the problem. I put my glass on the table and flicked down the volume on her phone.

"I like that song." She reached across me and turned it up.

And *that's* what I mean about too many people living too close together. If infringement on your space and psyche happens enough times, or at the wrong time, perpetrated by the wrong person, some would be driven to murder. Killing a human being shuts a person out of the mainstream for good.

It can never be undone. It shocks and horrifies most normal people. Although the shock and horror depend on the circumstances. Far fewer people are shocked by murder under the guise of war, and many are actually pleased when the perpetrator of a heinous crime is executed by the state.

Passion over musical tastes and political views, sex and love and religion, make for murderous feelings. If it happens enough — having the music you love turned down, or any other slight that is normally insignificant — so-called moral rules are drowned quickly. Little things have a way of turning into something huge, given the right set of circumstances.

I took a large swallow of my drink. "He's paying you to live here." I set my glass on the table. "Let's say you start up a relationship. Then, let's say he's late with the rent. You don't want to hassle him and introduce a thorn into the romantic bliss. A week later, you mention the late rent. He laughs it off. Seven or eight days later, you remind him again that he owes you. He says you're acting like you care more about money than him. You see where it could end up, don't you?"

She sipped her drink. Her eyes were watery. She took another sip.

"It's not worth crying about."

She batted her eyes. "I'm not crying."

I picked up my glass, took a sip, and touched the edge of my glass to hers. "Cheers. If the attraction is mutual, you should do what you want."

She sighed. "I just...he seems so nice. I can't see him being that way. About money."

"You don't even know him. Except for his paperwork."

She took a long swallow of her drink. "I feel like I *do* know him. It's one of those instant connections. It seems like I've known him forever. And the way he looks at me, I think there's something there. He was so eager to pay the rent even though he wasn't moving in yet. So I really don't think he'd take advantage of me like that."

"A gentleman."

"Exactly." She gave me a watery smile.

I'd been wrong to assume a woman who liked martinis was a certain kind of person. It seems to me, a woman who likes martinis is tough at the core. She's less sentimental than most, knows what she wants, doesn't get all gooey over the idea that she can let go of protecting her interests and trust a man to be nice, just because.

I took a deep breath and a long sip of my drink. It was important to be friendly, to be nice…sweet, even. "Should we watch a movie?" I said.

She shook her head and scooted closer to me. "Let's just talk and get to know each other."

I poked my tongue at the bobbing olives. Why hadn't she put them on a stick?

"We're almost total strangers," Noreen said.

"You don't feel like you've known me forever?"

"That's mean."

"Why?"

She stood up and walked across the room. She turned out the overhead light. She picked up a butane lighter and lit two fat, gardenia-scented candles that were sitting on a table next to the armchair. "There, that's better." She smiled.

"It was a joke," I said. I suppose it was a joke, but with an old style, double-edged razor blade hidden inside.

"Jared is a guy," she said.

"Well, yes."

"It's completely different, connecting with a man, than it is with a woman."

I picked out one of my olives, sucked out the pimento, ate the olive, and licked the vodka off my fingertips.

"Why does everyone do that?" Noreen said.

"Do what?"

"Suck out the pimento?"

I shrugged.

"It's weird."

"Not really. Like you said, everyone does it."

"I don't." She returned to the couch, sitting farther away again. "Tell me about your last boyfriend."

"What's the point of that? It's not a happy story."

"I guess no former boyfriend is a happy story," she said.

I ate my other olive and finished my drink.

"Do you want another?"

"Let's eat first."

We heated four slices of tomato and onion pizza. Noreen took a pitcher of iced water out of the fridge and filled two glasses. We put down cushions on the tile and sat side-by-side on the living room floor, setting our plates and water on the coffee table. We ate and watched a comedy news show. "Hey, I was thinking." I smiled warmly. "I don't have a streaming account. Do you mind if I tap into yours? I'll pay half, of course."

She giggled. "Don't be silly. I'm already paying, it doesn't matter."

After she finished her second slice of pizza, she turned toward me. "Why won't you tell me about your boyfriend?"

"He's not my boyfriend any more, why would I want to talk about him?"

"Do you still love him?"

"Do you love your ex?" I stuffed the last of my pizza into my mouth. I stood up and carried the plates to the kitchen and put them in the dishwasher.

Noreen washed the martini glasses and started mixing a second round. Two is usually my limit but they're so damn good, I break that rule more than I should. It was only seven-thirty. I vowed to take this one more slowly. Much more slowly. It's easy to get tempted for a third, and once I have a third, my tongue takes off on its own. I didn't want to go blabbing all kinds of things about my life to Noreen.

"Of course I don't love my ex," she said. "I wouldn't be thinking about Jared if I did."

I returned to the couch. I wanted a cigarette. That's the other thing martinis do to me. To distract myself, I picked up my discarded boots and carried them to my bedroom. I changed into leggings and when I returned to the living room, I sat on the large, soft pillow again and arranged my legs in a lotus position to further suppress the smoking impulse.

When Noreen was finished mixing the martinis, she proceeded to tell me about her ex-boyfriend. She'd met him when she was fifteen and they were together forever. I asked how long, exactly, and she repeated — for-*ever*.

They'd bought the house together. For her share, Noreen had used a *very generous* inheritance from her grandmother. They were *so, so* happy, and then he left. He practically *disappeared*, walking away from his share. He was that eager to get out.

It wasn't hard to see how that would hurt. A lot. A guy is so anxious to get away from you, he walks away from half a million dollars? Probably more? Not to mention the years invested in his share of the mortgage payments? What was to keep him from coming back and demanding they sell it, telling us we had no right to live there? Surely he'd wake up one day and realize how stupid he'd been.

Asking her why he was so eager to get away from her would have implied there was something terribly wrong with her. So I didn't, to be nice. To be thoughtful and sweet.

And then she volunteered the information. A horror story of misguided love.

4

When Noreen and Brian got together, she was fifteen and Brian was nineteen, so right from the get-go, there was a problem — her parents forbade her to see him. It was practically pedophilia, they said. This enraged Noreen who, despite her sweetness, said she has quite a temper.

Keeping her temper in check, she proceeded to climb out of her bedroom window at night and meet up with Brian. When they discovered their daughter's empty bed, her parents nailed the window shut. Who does that in the twenty-first century? After labeling your daughter's crush a pedophile? They might have taken a wait-and-see approach, but many parents lose their sanity when their daughters start having sex. The woman they see remains a baby girl in their imaginations. All they can think of is their daughter's naked body ravished by a man, her heart tugging away from theirs, filling up with experiences and feelings they know nothing about. Devotion to mommy and daddy are replaced by another — a complete stranger.

In Noreen's eyes, Brian was charming and good and kind. He was funny and attentive. He made her feel important and cherished. He was the love of her life. His smile melted her heart. That smile froze the hearts of Mr. and Mrs. Palmer.

With the window nailed shut, Noreen found ways to meet up with Brian during the day. She cut class, forging notes from her mother. Her approach was quite clever. She wrote that she was in therapy with twice weekly sessions. Of course twice a week for two hours wasn't enough to fill her aching need for Brian. She added more free hours by informing her parents she was trying out for the track team. Instead of running with other kids around the sports field or along nearby open space trails, she did the obvious with Brian.

This went on until several months after her sixteenth birthday when someone at the school became concerned that bi-weekly therapy wasn't resulting in better classroom behavior. Her parents were called. Noreen was immediately enrolled in a Catholic school where kids didn't leave campus unless mom or dad showed up at the school office and escorted their teenager out to her appointment.

Noreen ran away.

Brian's mother welcomed Noreen into her house, perfectly comfortable with Noreen sharing Brian's bed. Noreen returned to the public school and Brian dropped out of Junior College. He found a position with a landscaper who had a lucrative contract looking after Silicon Valley companies who needed gorgeous, drought-friendly landscaping to enhance the altruistic side of their public image.

When Noreen graduated from high school, her parents showed up at the ceremony and everything got smoothed over. They were no longer willing to let the *pedophile* cut their daughter out of their lives. Besides, Noreen was eighteen. It was time to bury that ugly word in the drawer where family secrets are kept and never looked at again. Noreen's grandmother had some influence in the reconciliation. She loved Noreen to death — Noreen's words, not mine — and she'd kept in close contact with Noreen during the years she and her parents were estranged. Grandma was very tech-savvy, with an email account and a Facebook profile that gave her complete access to Noreen's life.

Noreen's grandmother died suddenly from a stroke when Noreen was only nineteen. Grandma left everything to Noreen. The substantial inheritance severed Noreen's already fragile relationship with her brother because Noreen felt no obligation to include her brother in her good fortune — he'd sided with her parents' opinion of Brian. So she cashed the check from her grandma's estate and went house shopping with Brian near the ocean. Brian was a motorcycle aficionado who liked the twisting, turning highway through the Santa Cruz mountains and didn't consider the commute from the ocean to Silicon Valley a burden. Noreen stayed home taking care of their funky new home. She grew vegetables in the side yard and made jam with fruit from local orchards, transforming herself into an earth mother type.

I closed my eyes and tried to imagine an earth mother who was a hard-core runner and martini drinker. It didn't quite fit, but I guess we all have our inconsistencies. "It sounds very cozy," I said. "Why didn't you get married?"

"It didn't come up."

"Did you want to?"

She shrugged. "I guess if we decided to have kids."

"Did you think about kids?"

She shook her head. "We had Terry."

"Terry?"

"Our beagle."

"Aw. Beagles are cute. I love beagles."

"Me too. So does Brian."

Her words sent a light shiver down my arms. Usually, when you're talking about someone you were in a relationship with, you say he *was* like this or that, he *used to do* this or that, not in the present tense, as if he's still part of your thought process. "Do you still see him?"

"No."

"When was the last time?"

She shrugged.

Fully embracing the earth mother role, Noreen took up knitting. She got into it big time. She signed up for knitting classes and formed a knitting group. The group took trips to Marin County and down to Santa Barbara, pursuing unusual yarns in quaint shops. It seems like it would be easy to find unique yarn all over the world with the internet, and she did a bit of that too, but she and her knitting companions liked the road trips. "Besides," she said, "sometimes you have to touch something, and see the color in real life."

The knitting group met at Noreen's house once a week. They talked and knitted and helped each other with complicated stitches and patterns. It was a small group — three women besides Noreen, because the other knitters Noreen knew couldn't stomach sitting on that back deck where she insisted they meet on balmy, cloudless summer evenings. The sheer cliff beneath the deck made them shiver even with silky warm air on their arms. The deck sloped ever so gently toward the railing. Not enough that a knitting needle would roll off, but enough to make you feel uncertain about your balance. Just beyond the left corner of the deck was a large pine tree. That portion of the cliff was so badly eroded, half the tree roots were exposed, sticking out into space like the tree wanted to change its location and was sending out feelers.

Naturally, Noreen knitted scarves and hats and blankets for every family member, friend, and casual acquaintance. After a while, Brian suggested that ten scarves and eight hats were more than he'd need in a lifetime, so along with sweaters and scarves for herself, she began knitting jackets for the beagle. Brian said the fluffy pastel sweaters humiliated the dog, which led Noreen to the conclusion that Brian found the scarves and hats she'd knitted for him humiliating. He insisted it wasn't the case, but that dogs weren't meant to wear clothing, especially such un-masculine clothing. There was something feminine about a hand-knitted sweater, even if it was a studly navy blue.

I was on Brian's side, but I nodded and kept my mouth shut.

Their arguments turned into fights that gathered increasing ferocity.

Another example of little things turning huge.

Soon, those knitted dog sweaters came to represent Noreen's soul, her artistic contribution to the world, her love for their dog. To Brian, they reflected an attempt to control him — her refusal to let the dog be a dog, and by implication, to let a man be a man.

He began to make rude comments about the girly way she'd decorated their house and the cloying smell of gardenia that filled the bedroom, wafting out of her candles, and spritzed on their comforter. She accused him of dismissing everything feminine and female as inherently inferior. She came to believe he'd chosen to ride a motorcycle simply because they terrified her. Her refusal to get on the back allowed him to drive off alone whenever he felt like it, leaving her behind as if she was an insignificant part of his life, no more important than his backpack.

The dog was caught in the middle.

All day long Terry wore Noreen's knitted sweaters, unless the weather was too warm, and a house perched on a cliff above the ocean doesn't get hot very often.

When Brian came home from work, he removed the sweater, and he wasn't very gentle with the knitted garments. Often Terry's toenails snagged on the carefully constructed stitches. After Brian went to sleep at night, Noreen put the sweater back on the dog.

Listening to this, I wasn't sure whether to laugh or cry. It was a good thing that they'd delayed addressing the parenthood question. The dog started showing signs of stress. He barked constantly and peed on the floor. Neighbors left angry notes in their mailbox, complaining about the incessant noise. Noreen tore up the notes.

Late one afternoon during a violent storm, a seagull landed on the railing of the back deck. Terry went nuts over this invasion of his territory. He barked more wildly than

Noreen had ever heard him. The gull was unperturbed. Terry started flinging himself at the railing, barking maniacally, saliva flying out of his mouth. Noreen stood in the doorway, begging Terry to calm down. She held out biscuits and even a chunk of leftover steak trying to lure him back into the house. She didn't want to go out there, certain the dog was angering the gull and it would fly at Noreen, digging its talons into her scalp, pecking at her eyeballs in the mistaken belief they were sand crabs meant to be dug out of her skull.

The gull hopped along the railing, and then flapped its wings and flew a few yards to one of the lower branches of the pine tree. Terry leaped. He cleared the railing, but the little knitted belt that secured the sweater around his ribs caught on an exposed nail. The force of the turtleneck sweater yanking on his throat broke his neck.

"Oh." I put my hands over my mouth. "Oh, that's so brutal." It was sickening, knowing how her ridiculous outfits killed the poor thing. I wanted to rush out and adopt a dog right that minute. Maybe two. I felt if I could save at least one dog from a stupid human being, I would be doing the world more good than I had in my life so far.

Brian couldn't forgive her.

But still, I wondered…he was so eager to escape her passive contribution to the dog's death that he walked away from a million dollar cottage?

"*Why*, exactly, did he leave?" I said.

"I told you. He wouldn't speak to me. He slept on the couch. Then his mother died, and he didn't cope well with that at all."

"Lots of people can't deal with it when a parent dies, especially at our age. You don't expect it to happen when we're this young."

She nodded and sipped her drink. "He fell apart."

"And he didn't care about his investment in the house?"

She shook her head. Her eyes grew red, brimming with tears. She put the glass to her lips and took hurried little sips.

It was a horrifying story, and yet, it seemed as if a piece was missing. Maybe more than one. Someone like me, who has lied when necessary, recognizes when the truth is being reformatted to appear like something different, but I couldn't get a sense of where the story had been twisted to cover up the real horror. I felt as if I was standing on the edge of an abyss, looking into utter darkness, while Terry's barking shrieks pierced my skull, preventing me from making out the words of a voice that was screaming right beside me.

5

It was embarrassing — watching Noreen brush up against Jared, put her hand on his arm, his leg, his back. Instead of the loose, flowing tops she'd worn over skinny jeans, now she squeezed her torso into t-shirts that looked as if they'd been purchased in the children's department. When she wasn't wearing a skin-hugging shirt, exposing the dip of her navel above the low-slung waist of her jeans, she chose spaghetti strap shirts, displaying an average amount of cleavage. She found every excuse imaginable to bend over in front of him, offering a more complete view.

He rarely looked.

One night, I heard her knock on his bedroom door. The first knock was so soft, I wasn't sure what I was hearing. When there was no response, she rapped more firmly — a pleasant thunk of bone on wood. The third time, it sounded awfully close to a fist on his door. He still didn't answer.

I sensed her lingering, a few feet from my door, for a long time. I felt her breath in the small space between our rooms. I envisioned her face — eyes squinting in the darkness, lips parted as if he might feel her desire and suddenly wake up to his own. I pictured her squashing her ear against his door, trying to determine from whatever quiet sounds he was making what he might be up to. I imagined her turning and pressing her breasts against the door, as if she could melt through the wood and fall into his arms. Or straight into his bed.

It was at least twenty minutes before she walked away, bare feet slapping softly on the tile floor.

Sleep took a long time coming, even after she was gone. I'd felt her staring at my closed door, thinking about me, worrying that I was a competitor she was going to have to remove from the contest. Starting with his aggressive wink the first time we met, he seemed to want to rub it in her face that he was drawn to me, not her. But after a while, I didn't understand why she didn't take the hint and move on. Who wants to be with a guy who has his eye on someone else?

Ignoring advice isn't a flaw unique to Noreen, but part of the reason she found it easy to ignore my advice was that I hadn't been strong enough in my warning. I should have told her how I knew it was a terrible idea to mix a financial power imbalance with sex — I lived through it with roommates in my very first apartment.

After two years of college, I'd reached my limit with dorm life. It was nothing but a factory for cliques and cat fights. Claymore Hall was a six-story building that looked like a shoebox. So many tiny rooms formed by cinderblock walls, filled with women who were paired based on the untruthful answers they gave in their dorm applications. What woman admits she snores? And what eighteen-year-old writes on a dorm application that she prefers peace and quiet? It makes her seem unfriendly, dull, a loser, a poor candidate for dormitory life altogether. And those were the minor mismatches. There were also the predators who failed to mention they would destroy a woman's reputation if she chose to wear plain white underpants instead of a thong. The days were filled with gossip and betrayals. By the age of twenty, I needed a change of scenery.

The apartment I wound up in was only two years old, twenty-two-hundred square feet with lots of windows and a sleek kitchen. Lucky me.

Dianne Whitaker, a woman who lived on my floor at Claymore Hall, invited me to share the place. Her mother was subsidizing the rent on the palatial apartment one block from campus on a tree-lined street. Mrs. Whitaker had paid the deposit, hired a housekeeper, and told Dianne to pick two friends to share the second bedroom. Dianne was installed in the master suite, complete with an oversized jacuzzi tub. But even the shared bedroom awarded to me and Lisa Allen, also from our floor at Claymore, was large enough for two beds, two dressers, and two desks. We had a walk-in closet and our bathroom featured two sinks, a long counter, and a shower large enough for all three of us, if we desired. Dianne's mother picked up the entire tab for the utilities and paid half the rent while Lisa and I paid a quarter each. It was more than fair. A very generous woman, but it turned out, not generous enough, in Dianne's opinion.

The first month went smoothly. On September thirtieth, Lisa and I handed over our checks for the second month's rent, made out to Dianne's mother.

On October third, Randy Flynn moved in.

Randy was Dianne's boyfriend. He was not on her mother's approved list of boys Dianne should be dating. He'd been a student at UCLA for nine years because he was having difficulty pinning down a major that would launch him into a satisfying, profitable career. Randy liked to smoke pot, drive his motorcycle at ninety miles an hour, and didn't show the proper respect to Dianne's mother. The last was what doomed him. Randy was also hot, which meant nothing to Mrs. W, but apparently Mrs. Whitaker thought that moving her daughter out of the co-ed dorm where *anyone* was allowed to live, and into a nice apartment, would curtail the amount of time Dianne and Randy spent together. Mrs. W thought the relationship would die a natural death if she didn't fight too aggressively to split them up.

In the middle of October, Lisa, Dianne, and I were sitting in the living room drinking beer and planning a Halloween party. Lisa put her bare feet with their pointy toenails on the coffee table and crossed her ankles. "Is Randy going to stay here more or less permanently?"

"Yes," Dianne said.

"Shouldn't he be sharing the rent?" Lisa wiggled her toes to show she was asking a friendly question.

"You only pay a quarter, so it wouldn't change your share." Dianne's voice was hard and slightly louder than her normal speech, an echo of Mrs. Whitaker's tone.

That night, when Dianne closed her bedroom door, Lisa and I whispered about the unfairness of this deal, although we could not explain why it wasn't right. It just wasn't.

Time passed. Once in a while, Lisa and I whispered about it, wondering what Dianne would do if we alerted Mrs. W to the arrangement, but knowing it was equally possible such a move would jeopardize our invitation to stay in the lovely apartment.

In January, Dianne broke up with Randy, but there was a catch — she felt sorry for him. *He's trying so hard to focus on his education. He thinks architecture is for sure the right choice. I feel bad that I dumped him and he can't find housing mid-year, so he'll stay with us.*

Lisa and I glanced at each other. We both knew in the same moment that it was unlikely Randy would be staying in Dianne's bed.

"You two can sleep in my room," Dianne said. "Randy can take your room."

"And we still pay seven hundred bucks a month?" Lisa said. "I don't think so."

"Would you rather look for a new place? You'll never find anything mid-year."

"It's not right," I said.

"There are no other options," Dianne said.

"What if we leave and your mother finds out he's here?" I said.

"You'll be in the same position. No place to live."

She was right, and we knew it. Apartments were almost impossible to find anywhere within a five-mile radius of the school even a month before classes started in the Fall. Neither of us had a car, so even if we found a room to rent farther away, we were stuck.

"You can trade off sleeping in my bed with me," Dianne said. "Every other week, or whatever — you two work it out."

In a king-sized bed, that was a doable situation. The odd one out would use a sleeping bag. The carpets were thick with nice padding so it wasn't awful. And we still had a first class kitchen, a huge dining and living area with a state-of-the-art TV, the luxurious bathroom, now shared by three, and a balcony custom designed for nice parties.

We swapped rooms with Randy.

On Valentine's Day, Lisa went to a *girls without guys, let's love ourselves* dinner. Dianne went to a very expensive restaurant with her expensive new guy — a charming guy who treated Mrs. W with respect.

Randy and I hooked up. After all, it was Valentine's Day and neither of us had a Valentine.

Dianne came home from dinner, heard Randy and me in the bedroom, and threw a fit. It appeared as if she was still in love with him, and the worries about feeling sorry for him weren't that at all. Or something like that. Her fury was a little confusing. Maybe she just didn't want me to have him. She screamed so loud I thought the neighbors might call the police. Through her screaming about my whorishness and Randy's betrayal, it came out that she'd been collecting seven hundred dollars a month from him as well — her own secret nest egg.

When she finally calmed down, she ordered us to sweep up the broken glass from the wine glasses she'd hurled on the kitchen floor, to never so much as look at each other again, and to start writing our monthly checks for nine hundred dollars each.

Once she received the first eighteen hundred dollar installment, she *fell out of love* once again. Money of her own, hidden from her mother, eased all her pain. I moved into the second bedroom with Randy, and Lisa continued to share Dianne's room. For the time being.

During the final months of the school year, Lisa, Randy, and I sat on the balcony on balmy evenings, which is pretty much every evening in LA. While Dianne was wined and dined by her new guy, the victims of extortion and Lisa passed around a joint and devised ways to be rid of her. It was a mind-twisting game of course — without Dianne, there would be no apartment. We couldn't really be rid of her.

On April first, we were doing the same, and Randy started laughing. He laughed so hard we thought he was going to puke on us. "We should kill her. She only communicates with her mother through text messages — it would be months before her mother figured out she was dead."

I laughed. Lisa looked at me, guilty. Each of us picked up our bottle of beer and took a very long swallow, our throats pulsing in unison.

It became a game. We would go out on the balcony, light up a joint, and the first person to take a hit had to describe a method of murder. Throughout the spring, we considered car accidents, fires, staircases, guns, knives, poison, razor blades, ropes, and the swimming pool.

When I came home to the apartment after my Shakespeare final exam and saw Dianne face down in the swimming pool, I laughed. It was only an illusion induced by repeated fantasy, too much thought given to the matter. Too much dope. Randy was playing games with my head.

Dianne's body, clothed in a navy blue bikini, a sheer white coverup clinging to her wet skin, drifted close to the edge of the pool. The partially deflated pink plastic raft prevented her from bumping against the side. I put out my hand and pushed her onto her back. It was no illusion.

I told the police I had no idea how it happened. I had been locked in a room writing about King Lear. It was easy to verify, so there weren't too many questions. Then, I held my hands over my mouth, afraid I'd vomit, as they lifted her out of the water and placed her body on the concrete, covering her with a thick, black tarp.

6

Jared had decided to resurrect Noreen's dead vegetable garden in the side yard. The section of the eight-foot fence facing the front yard was actually a large gate. The whole fence could be opened, exposing the garden. Two sides of the fence were covered with thick vines that looked as if they were swallowing the wood. The back edge of the fence ran along the cliff with only a few feet of earth between the fence and the drop-off to the rocks below.

It was a sunny, clear Saturday afternoon. Noreen had driven over the hill to visit her parents in the East Bay. I guessed they were making up for lost time now that Brian was out of her life. She certainly seemed to be looking forward to spending the afternoon and eating dinner with them. Her willingness to take her eyes off Jared for most of the day was surprising, but she informed me that absence makes the heart grow fonder. She also advised me to leave him alone so he could focus on his gardening.

I went out to the front porch and pulled out a cigarette. I lit it and took a long, pleasing drag.

"Noreen's rule list says no smoking," Jared said. He drove

the blade of the hoe into the dirt.

"In the house," I said.

"I think she meant no smoking at all. She doesn't care for smokers."

"I'm not a smoker. It's an occasional thing."

He stabbed the hoe into the ground again.

I sat on the edge of the porch. "So what brought you to Aptos?"

"I'm trying to make some changes in my life."

"What sort of changes?" I tapped my ash on the ground under a shrub and shoved my heel in the soil to cover the evidence of my rule-breaking.

He dragged the hoe in a straight line, angling the blade so it made a small furrow. Then he dropped the hoe and squatted on his heels. He plucked out a few small weeds and tossed them to the side of the garden area. "I'm investigating Buddhism. Living in harmony with the earth and its inhabitants. Detaching from the endless quest for more."

"So that's why you have a new BMW?"

He had the dignity to blush.

I took another drag on the cigarette, feeling mildly anxious that it was shrinking so fast. I didn't want it to reach the end of its life too quickly, and I didn't want to light another and sink into old habits.

"It's a process," he said.

"Why not a studio apartment? Facing an alley or the side of a warehouse. A panoramic ocean view isn't representative of simplicity."

"The ocean is pure and cleansing. Also, part of Buddhism

is respecting other beings, so I thought it would be a good spiritual practice to have roommates. It's a small house, which means a certain amount of pressure on the relationships."

"We're your religious props?"

He dragged the hoe through the dirt, unearthing more weeds. He knelt and picked them up, one by one, placing them carefully outside the perimeter of the dirt rectangle. It looked as if he was praying, and for a moment, it seemed as if he wanted me to think that.

"Do you have to commute over the hill for work?" I said.

"I'm between jobs."

In less than twenty-four hours, my life had brushed up against one guy who strolled away from his partial ownership of an ocean view home, and another who drove a new BMW and didn't feel the need to generate income. They seemed to care nothing for money, and yet, they had far more than necessary. "If you're not tied to a job," I said, "Why aren't you at a retreat center or something like that?"

"I just told you."

"There are other beings at a retreat center."

"This is a better fit for my needs."

"What are your needs? Besides acquiring annoying roommates to help you seek tranquility."

He didn't smile.

"What are you going to do with all the vegetables you grow?"

"We can eat them."

"Noreen and I are pasta addicts. I suppose chopped tomatoes on top of fettuccini are nice."

Even though his face was turned toward the ground, I saw the quiver of a smile.

"What are you planting?"

"Tomatoes. Zucchini…"

"Everyone plants zucchini."

"It's easy to grow."

"So you're a lazy Buddhist?"

"No. I'm also planning carrots, lettuce, and green beans. You can help."

I stubbed out my cigarette. "I think I'll have another smoke." I scooped out a small hole and dropped the butt into it.

"She doesn't want any smoking."

"She's not here." I went into the house. I pulled a cigarette out of the package. I went into the hallway, headed back toward the front door. I paused, overcome by an urge to look into his room. He was obviously busy on his knees and I was curious. The Buddhist thing piqued my interest. I wanted to see what simplicity looked like. The narrow closet in my room was so full of clothes I couldn't move the hangers along the pole. The closet floor was piled with shoes and purses and my stuff wouldn't fit in my dresser. Maybe if he was stripped down to essentials, I could store some of my overflow in his closet. It was more than that, though. I was curious to see inside his life. I turned quickly and went back to the front porch.

He sat back on his heels and didn't try to hide the fact he was watching me light the cigarette. "Why don't you want to help? Growing things feels good," he said.

"For you."

"Have you ever done it?"

"No." I inhaled and settled back into the cloud of smoke.

"Just because she's not here, and just because she only specified no smoking inside the house, doesn't mean it's okay."

"So why the sudden desire to step out of the frenzy and dig in the garden after buying a Beemer?" I said. "Job burnout? Bad breakup?"

He stood up and brushed loose dirt off the knees of his jeans. "I think burnout is the best description. Life is short." He stared at me as if I'd been the one to speak last and he was waiting for me to finish the thought.

The silence grew.

Three crows flew toward the tree that clutched the side of the cliff. They settled into the upper branches, cawing and nodding their heads as if they were arguing. A car turned down the street and drove past, but neither of us looked in its direction. I took another drag on my cigarette.

"You're a gorgeous woman," he said.

I put the cigarette between my lips, pressing them around it, knowing it reduced my supposed gorgeousness. His comment seemed a rather abrupt departure from burnout and Buddhism. I sucked on the cigarette and blew out a thin stream of smoke, watching him watch me.

"Most women would smile. Or say thank you," he said.

"I'm not most women."

"So I'm beginning to realize."

He hacked at the dirt. The hoe clanged on a large rock.

He picked it up and cradled it in his hand for a moment before tossing it to the side. "I could really use your help."

"It was your idea. And it's *your* religious trip."

He nodded. He raised the hoe over his head and lowered it fast, sinking the blade in the soil. He moved backwards slowly, raising the hoe and gouging it into the earth with each step. It was beginning to make me think of a madman, slamming an axe into someone's head, the soil like soft brain matter, broken apart into something fresh and new. I closed my eyes and took another drag on my cigarette.

"I think your beauty will enhance my spiritual practice."

"How so?"

"Increase the intensity of my awareness of attachment and aversion."

"So I *am* your religious prop."

His hoe clanged on another rock. He removed it with the same gentle care as the previous one. Watching him was addictive. He made lifting and carrying rocks look like the most pleasurable experience in the world. He gave the impression there was something to the Buddhism thing. Although he'd said he was a newbie at it, so maybe it was just him, and the sleek muscles in his forearms. "I didn't know Buddhists had to be celibate," I said.

He grinned. "They don't."

I really wished I'd brought the entire pack of cigarettes out with me, because I could tell I was going to want another.

The silence swelled around us. The crows had stopped their chatter. I glanced toward the tree to see whether they were still there, but couldn't see them from where I sat.

The silence ate at the inside of my head, stirring up all kinds of thoughts about how good looking he was and how just because there'd been a few bad experiences with roommates didn't mean the pattern was destined to continue. Talking about celibacy had spun the conversation in another direction and most guys would interpret that as an open door to start with the innuendo, or an outright suggestion. He said nothing.

The crows started up again. A few more flapped to the tree and joined them, equally raucous.

I raised my voice slightly. "How long until you need to look for another job?"

"As long as I want."

"You have an endless supply of cash?"

"I have enough."

"Because you're all spiritual and don't need a lot? Except for your Beemer payment?"

"Something like that."

I put out my cigarette. I stood and shoved my hands in my pockets and stepped onto one of the flagstones that formed a ragged path from the driveway to the front door. I turned and looked up at the tree. The crows were still there. They were watching us. Maybe they knew what all the hoeing was about and realized that they were going to be given a smorgasbord of veggies soon. Although I wasn't sure crows ate veggies. I think they mostly eat dead things.

"Where are you going?" Jared said.

"Nowhere. Just checking out the crows."

He tossed the hoe to the side, sat down, and returned to

pulling out weeds. I was tempted to help him, just because it looked like too much work for an afternoon, but the temptation for another cigarette was more intense. I wanted to keep talking, but I didn't want him to think it meant anything.

7

The agreement — mostly Noreen's idea, greeted by shrugs from Jared and me — was that each of us would cook one meal a week, and rotate grocery shopping responsibilities every five days. If one of our lists wasn't ready for the shopper on the scheduled day, that person was SOL.

It was my day to shop. It was also my turn to cook. After several nights of Jared's spaghetti and meatballs, and Noreen's angel hair pasta with tomatoes, artichoke hearts, and jalapeños, a night without pasta was called for. Passion needs to be mixed up once in a while.

The cooking and shopping arrangements were a little too cozy. Everything was getting too cozy — food prep, mealtime, martinis with Noreen. It seemed as if Noreen wanted to create a fantasy family. For my contribution, I planned to make a dinner that announced — *I'm not your BFF. I'm doing what was asked to carry my weight in our fourteen hundred square foot house where it's impossible to avoid one another.*

When he was home, it was especially hard to avoid tripping over Jared coming and going in our shared bathroom. In order to keep myself to myself, I'd bought a white plastic caddy to drag my shampoo and body wash and other stuff back and forth, storing it on the floor of my closet, which forced more shoes and boots out into the room. I was drowning in clothes and shoes and purses. It had been that way for all of my adult life, and my pre-adult life, from the time I first had a job and could buy clothes that my mother deemed unnecessary. I love clothes. I love changing clothes and love that I can become a completely different person through a change of clothes and the style of my hair. I could put on a different outfit three times a day, and I often do — a neon pink or green crop top and black, skin-hugging capri pants for running, silky pants and a pleated jacket with a white shirt for work, and skinny jeans with a baggy sweater over a camisole in the evening. I suppose it's not unusual for a woman to wear three outfits in a day, but I do even more on weekends, sometimes changing clothes four times before dinner. It's a hobby. I like being surprised when I walk past a mirror and see something different that what had been reflected the last time I passed by.

Barbecue would have been an easy dinner choice, but that suggested *party*. Meatloaf was too homey and nurturing. I mentally ran through a few more ideas, but they all conveyed a message I didn't want to send. I finally settled on grilled cheese sandwiches with chicken noodle soup made from a box. It indicated a lack of effort, impersonal and unoriginal.

The store was a large, anonymous supermarket. It felt good to walk down the aisle without glancing over my shoulder, watching for someone watching me, trying to maneuver a cart at a high speed, trying to get lost in a crowd. A grocery store shouldn't be a terrifying experience, but there was a time when it had been. The simplest things can turn into nightmares when you're trying to figure out an escape route. I pushed those thoughts away, smiled lovingly at the symmetrical aisles and the organized shelves of food. So much food, so many choices, restocked the moment there's an empty space — reflecting life itself where one creature dies and another moves into its place, the tide of humanity closing over the spot as if it were never there.

I wheeled the cart to the back of the store and grabbed a large block of cheddar cheese. I tossed in butter and four tubs of yogurt — Noreen's addition to the list. Jared hadn't given me a list, which had the effect of making me think non-stop about him as I wandered through the store, grabbing bread, fruit for Noreen's yogurt, granola for Noreen's yogurt, sliced turkey and a bag of greens for Noreen's lunchtime salads.

Jared didn't eat breakfast at the house. Possibly, he didn't eat breakfast at all. He made a cup of tea which he took to the back deck every morning. He stared out at the ocean, sipped his tea, and didn't move except for his hand lifting the mug to his mouth every two minutes. I suspected he was doing some sort of tea-sipping meditation. The raising and lowering of the mug looked so much like clockwork, I timed it. Sure enough, the stopwatch on my phone hit 120 seconds every time the mug went up toward his mouth.

I had no idea what he did during the day while I was at work. Wherever he spent his time, maybe they fed him, or he ate nothing but a piece of fruit, fitting with his striving for a simple lifestyle. He'd eaten Noreen's pasta dish and his own spaghetti, but other than that, there was no evidence of him eating at all. Maybe he was waiting for the produce from his epic vegetable garden. I couldn't stop obsessing over his eating habits. I was annoyed with myself, and annoyed with him because it seemed like he wanted me to think about his food, by failing to give me a list.

An hour before dinner I took out a stick of butter to let it soften.

As I was spreading butter across a slice of bread for the grilled cheese, Noreen came into the kitchen. She watched my hand gliding like the hand of a painter. "What are you making?"

"Grilled cheese sandwiches and chicken noodle soup."

"Jared is vegetarian."

"He made spaghetti."

"It was fake meat. He didn't tell you?"

"Fake meat?"

"Made from soy or something."

"Well the soup is fake chicken noodle. There's no actual chicken, just broth."

"I don't know if he can eat that." She carved off a slice of cheddar cheese and popped it in her mouth.

"Then he can eat a sandwich."

"That's not very nice."

"Nice is irrelevant. I didn't know he was vegetarian."

"It was on his form."

I couldn't imagine why she thought I would know that. Maybe she thought she'd told me, but I hoped she wasn't feeling free to pass around information she'd lifted off the forms. Even if mine was light on truth, I didn't want it repeated. It was a violation.

"It's not very dinner-like," she said. "Sandwiches."

"Sandwiches with soup are filling. And good. And sort of healthy."

"But it's sandwiches."

"So?"

"I just thought you'd put forth a little more effort." She sliced another piece of cheese.

"Stop eating the cheese."

"I ate one slice." She put the cheese in her mouth. She smiled. "Okay, two."

I picked up the cheese knife and started slicing thin strips for the sandwiches. She moved closer, her hands drifting aimlessly as if she were planning to snatch another piece. As her hand approached the cutting board, I moved the knife so it was poised above her finger.

"Watch the knife," she said. "You almost nicked my finger."

"Why don't I finish making dinner and I'll let you know when it's ready."

"I thought you wanted company."

"Why would you think that?"

"Meal preparation should be a community effort."

I disagreed, silently. "Music would be nice."

She went into the living room and started scrolling through her phone.

I set the oven to preheat and sprayed vegetable oil on a cookie sheet. I began building the sandwiches — a slice of bread with the butter side down, eight thin slices of cheese layered over each other, another slice of bread with the butter facing up. Water was boiling for the soup. I tore open two packets at once and dumped the powder and bits of dried noodle into the pot, stirred, and turned down the heat.

Noreen was still scrolling through her phone. Before she could decide on something, the sound of a mandolin came from Jared's room. He walked into the living area, carrying his own player wedged into a small speaker stand, a half smile on his lips. "This okay for dinner music?"

"It's beautiful," Noreen said.

"Dinner music?" I said.

They both stared at me. The timer buzzed. I pulled out the cookie sheet and flipped the sandwiches. While the opposite sides were browning, I lined up plates and bowls on the counter.

I raised my voice over the mandolin. "Jared, Noreen said you're vegetarian. Is chicken noodle soup that has never met a chicken except for the flavoring in the broth okay?"

He came into the kitchen. He stood close. Very close. The heat of his presence was displacing the heat coming from the oven. "Actually, I'm vegan."

"Told you." Noreen spoke in a stage whisper.

"You said vegetarian." I opened the oven and pulled out the sandwiches.

"Same thing," she said.

"It's not. Vegan means no animal products," Jared said.

"Is that a Buddhist thing?" I said.

"Are you Buddhist?" Noreen came into the kitchen area.

Now the heat was too much — his body, the open oven, Noreen's burning crush.

"It's a health thing," he said. "And yes, I'm investigating Buddhism."

"Oh. But...why would you think that fat dude with the silly grin is on the same level as Jesus?"

"Buddhism's not a religion," Jared said. "It's a philosophy."

"Still, Jesus..."

"Tea is fine. I had a big lunch." Jared took the kettle off the stove, filled it, and set it on the burner beside the soup pot, turning the gas to high.

"It's not right for you to have to sit here and watch us eat," Noreen said. "I'll make you something."

He shook his head. "I don't want anything."

"You need to eat," she said.

"Actually, I don't. None of us need to eat as much as we think we do."

She laughed and pulled out her chair. "Are you calling us gluttons?"

"Not at all. I'm speaking generally. It's what I think, for me. It has nothing to do with you, unless it speaks to you."

"Well you said none of us," Noreen said. She pouted. "I don't mind making something. Even yogurt and nuts..."

"Animal product," Jared said.

"Oh, right."

She and I started eating our sandwiches. Jared remained by the stove, waiting for the kettle to boil. He pulled a teabag out of a container he kept in the cupboard, unwrapped it, and put it into a mug.

When the kettle whistled, Noreen slapped her half-nibbled sandwich on her plate. She shoved out her chair and carried her soup bowl to the sink. She poured the soup down the drain. She turned. "I cannot sit here and eat in front of this kind-hearted man who provided angelic music and is now going to starve with nothing but a cup of tea."

"It's okay," Jared said.

"I didn't know he was a vegan," I said. "There are plenty of apples in the fridge. There's leftover fake meat spaghetti." The drama was irritating. I didn't appreciate her using me in her doomed plan to attract Jared's interest. She thought she was fooling him. She thought he'd be touched by her concern, but the tight press of his lips said otherwise.

"Did Noreen tell you about her poor little dog?" I said.

"Alexandra! That was a confidence." She glared at me.

"We should all just chill out," Jared said. "You eat the delicious food Alexandra prepared..."

"Out of a box," Noreen said. "There's no heart in it."

"...food that half the world would be thrilled to have on their plates. I'll drink my tea and have a small fast for the night, and we won't break confidences. We'll just welcome the night."

I rolled my eyes, but he was dipping his bag in and out of the mug and didn't see me. Noreen did.

8

The next morning the sun came up in a cloudless sky. My weather app told me it was fifty-nine degrees at six a.m., so I wore a navy blue sports bra and navy blue nylon shorts, preparing my body to feel like it was seventy-two once I got moving. The route I took for my four-mile run wound through narrow streets lined with beach cottages backed up to villa wannabes built with excess Silicon Valley cash. I avoided the path that ran along the edge of the beach. Most runners and dog walkers love that path, including Noreen, but I stayed far away from it. I didn't want even a glimpse of the water.

Never in a hundred years would anyone from my old life imagine that I'd chosen to re-boot my life near the ocean. If my family, former housemates, a few of my friends and previous co-workers knew anything at all about me, they knew I was terrified of the ocean and would never go anywhere near it. Certainly not a house poised to slip down the side of the cliff and crash on slick boulders during an epic storm. The location of this house was perfect for me, as long as I didn't step out on that deck or wander down to the beach.

I ran down a long street that curved to the bottom of the

cliff and jogged past the slightly sagging cafes and bars. The water I was trying to avoid was right there in my peripheral vision. I turned my head and made it disappear. My earphones blocked the crash of waves. It's terrible to fear something so deeply, letting your life reshape itself around the fear. It works its way through all your cells and turns you into its prisoner, taking hold of even small decisions and forcing you onto a particular path. Being controlled by something is worse than fear, so I try to force myself into proximity from time to time. Someday, I'll face it head on.

I ran back up the incline for my final push.

When I reached the front yard of the bungalow, my upper back and legs were slick with sweat. My face was relatively dry because I constantly swiped my hand across it while I ran. I hate letting my face get wet. It might be tied to my feelings about water in general. Even when I shower, my head is turned at an awkward angle so water doesn't spray in my eyes and across my lips, trying to make its way up my nose. I wash my face with a damp cloth, never splashing water on it like most people do.

I put my left leg on the porch railing, keeping my leg straight and extended up slightly to stretch my calves and hamstrings. I stood for several minutes, relishing the pull of my muscles, the loosening of my joints, as well as the tiny bird hopping about in a tree a few feet from the porch. The position of my leg made me feel yoga-like. I wondered whether Jared could see me from his bedroom window.

I turned to look.

His drapes were open. He was already gone for the day. I

twisted to give my torso a good stretch. From that angle, I saw Noreen standing in his room, looking out the window. She backed away.

A moment later, the front door opened.

"What are you doing?" Noreen said.

"Stretching." I lowered my left leg and raised my right, resting my heel on the railing.

"I meant why were you looking in Jared's room?"

I shrugged.

"He's not here."

"I figured that."

"Why were you looking?"

"I was stretching. Propping my leg up reminded me of a yoga pose, and since he does yoga, he came to mind. It was involuntary."

"Involuntary?"

"Yes. My body reacted to thinking about him."

"I know what involuntary means."

I leaned forward slightly to increase the stretch in my hamstring. I lowered my leg, clasped my hands and raised my arms overhead.

"Are you hitting on him?" she said.

"No. I told you my views on that."

"You're not his landlord, so it's not the same. You might be flirting."

"I'm not hitting on him." I stepped around her and went into the house.

She followed me inside, closed the door, and leaned against it. She crossed her arms. "I hope you aren't, because I called him first."

I pulled the elastic out of my ponytail and shook my hair.

"I had dibs on him."

I laughed. "He's not the last piece of chocolate cake." I sat on the floor, untied my shoes, and pried them off. I studied my feet, making note of the small hole in the heel of one of my socks. I yanked off my socks and stuffed them in my shoes.

"You should air those out."

"I will, just being efficient for taking them to my room."

The smell of my sweat filled my nostrils. I pushed myself to my feet. "I need a shower."

"No argument here." She laughed. "So we're clear on that, right?"

What was clear, was that Jared wasn't interested. He was consumed by his spiritual practices and, for all Noreen knew, he had a girlfriend at his yoga class or in his meditative walking group. She stared me down as if dictating that I stay away guaranteed his attraction to her.

"I'm clear that I'm not interested in a relationship," I said.

"That's good to hear, because it seems like you are."

"I said I'm not. Let's stop talking about it." I turned and went into my bedroom. I dropped my shoes on the floor, and pulled out the socks to make sure the shoes got a proper airing. I left the socks on the floor, gathered my clothes for work and picked up my toiletries caddie.

The bathroom was still filled with steam. It must have been only a short time since Jared left. That, and he hadn't opened the window in the shower stall. The mirrored door to the medicine cabinet hung open. The only thing on the shelves was a tube of Jared's toothpaste, his toothbrush, and a stick of deodorant. I put my caddie on the counter and placed my hangers on the hook behind the door. I stepped into the shower and opened the narrow window. As I stepped back out, I gripped the edge of the shower door, careful that my sweaty feet didn't slide across the wet porcelain. I closed the medicine cabinet door. The mirror had a huge oval of condensation in the center. I rubbed it with the side of my hand. It stayed. I grabbed a tissue and rubbed it harder.

It wasn't condensation after all. The finish was worn off — it looked as if it had been scraped repeatedly with a wire brush.

I opened the door and stepped into the hallway. "Noreen?"

"I'm in the kitchen," she called. "How many cups of coffee do you want?"

"One." I walked to the arched opening into the great room. "What happened to the bathroom mirror?"

The faucet shut off. Her flip-flops slapped the tile as she crossed the room. "Jared trashed it." She spoke in a whisper.

"Why are you whispering?"

"I don't want to upset him."

"He's not here."

"Right." She spoke in a normal tone. "Well, he scratched it up."

"Why?"

"It's some Buddhist thing."

"I've never heard of that. And it's not his house."

"It's not a problem."

"When is he going to replace it?"

"He doesn't want a mirror."

"I need a mirror."

"Can you work around it?"

"No."

"It interferes with his practice."

"Oh, come on. First, that's crazy. Second, it's not his decision."

"Don't make him feel bad about about it."

"I need a mirror," I said.

"I'll get something for your bedroom."

"I don't want to blow dry my hair in my bedroom."

"It'll be fine. He was very serious about it. Please don't say anything."

"Why not?"

"Because he was embarrassed. Seeing himself in the mirror tempts his vanity. He felt he had to do it, and he was embarrassed that he struggles with vanity. You can see why, can't you?"

"Whatever. I need a mirror. This is what I'm talking about, regarding mixing sex and money."

"Don't call it sex. I don't just want *sex* with him, I care about him. And it's not the same at all. It's my choice. I don't think it's necessary to have a mirror in that bathroom."

"I do."

"You'll manage."

"I need a mirror."

"It'll work out, you'll see."

"If you don't talk to him, I will."

"Don't create problems or I'll have to ask you to find another place to live."

I stared at her for a moment.

"Oh, another thing," she said. "I did not appreciate you telling him about Terry. You shouldn't have mentioned that."

"Is it a secret?"

"It's private," she said. "I feel betrayed, to be honest."

"Sorry. I didn't know it was a secret."

"It's not a *secret*, but it's personal."

"Got it."

"Please don't break my confidence again."

I folded my arms. "Noreen. I didn't know it was a confidence. In fact, neither did I know Jared was vegan. You act like I can read your mind."

"You should have sensed it," she said.

"That he's vegan?"

"No, that Terry's death was traumatic for me. The most painful thing I've ever experienced."

I nodded. She was a lucky woman if her dog dying, despite the horrific circumstances, was the worst thing that ever happened to her.

"Promise."

"I won't mention Terry again."

"No, promise you won't betray my confidence."

"Maybe don't tell me any more secrets…confidences. That would make it clean."

"I consider you a friend."

I smiled. "Well if you decide to tell me more, give me

some context."

She nodded. Tears washed across her pale gray eyes. She dragged her fingers through her hair, scooping it away from her forehead. She lowered her chin and glared at me.

After several seconds, it seemed she had nothing more to say. I turned and went into the bathroom. I shut the door, hard. I locked it and bent my knees slightly so I could see my face in the undamaged lower left corner of the mirror.

And this was *exactly* what I'd meant about money and sex. She wouldn't let me get away with that kind of bullshit. He was already using her and she was already changing the rules because of her imagined relationship with him.

Did this mean Jared would now destroy the rearview mirror in his Beemer, since it might tempt his vanity? I didn't think so.

Despite his vagueness about when he might need to return to the workforce, and his diet and his refusal to look in a mirror while remaining the proud owner of a late model BMW, he was an okay roommate. He was quiet. He made no demands. He was a nice guy, as far as I could tell. The mirror thing was a little crazy. More than a little crazy. But if I held my two roommates side by side in my mind, Noreen caused much greater concern. She didn't laugh when it seemed appropriate and the story of her ex's stake in the house and the sad, sad end of their dog's life made my spidey sense crawl. The more it circled in my mind, the more I was convinced I'd been given a sanitized version of their relationship.

It crossed my mind that maybe I should look for another

place to live. But I couldn't. Not yet. Finances were extremely tight since I'd just started in my job. Noreen had asked for a very small deposit — only two hundred dollars — that wouldn't cut it anywhere else.

Finding the right people to share a house with is difficult, and Jared was cool. He kept to himself. Buddhism would be an interesting subject to learn more about. So Noreen was a little weird, it could be worse. Far worse. I just needed to alter my schedule a bit to keep clear of her, and work on extracting myself from that apparent bond I'd tried to establish around running, pasta, and martinis.

The next time I had a martini, it would be in a bar. With a co-worker.

Despite her command not to embarrass Jared by asking about the mirror, I planned to ask. It made no sense that he'd be embarrassed. It was *his* Buddhist practice. He had no problem talking about using us to help him on his path. Besides, there was something about her that invited betrayal. She got so *upset* about minor things, it was rather entertaining to watch.

9

The balcony where Randy and Lisa and I fantasized about killing Dianne was quite large. There was a barbecue grill in one corner near the wall of the building. In the center was a teak table with four extremely comfortable chairs, the wood bent and fitted and sanded to a silken finish to hold the human body without pressing unkindly against any bones or joints. On the opposite side was a matching teak chaise lounge.

Randy always took the chaise lounge and Lisa and I sat at the table. We kept the outside lights turned off just in case Dianne came home. We wanted to be able to see her cross the courtyard toward our building without her seeing us. Of course sometimes we laughed so loud, she would have noticed us from the opposite end of the complex. Or she would have smelled the dope, unless another neighbor was lighting up at the same time. But the result was, we couldn't always see Randy's face.

After our nervous laughter at his initial suggestion faded into the night, Lisa pushed the candle that sat on a plate in the center of our table toward the edge, hoping to shine light on his face. "That's not funny," she said.

"Don't be such a prude."

"There's nothing prudish about not wanting to think about committing murder."

He mocked her tone of voice — "We won't get in *trouble*."

"Why don't we talk about something intelligent?" Lisa said.

"Why do you have to be so superior?" Randy said. "Not everything has to be an advanced seminar."

She didn't respond.

Finally, he laughed. "It's a game, dumb ass. Not for real."

"She's not that bad. This is a cool apartment." Lisa took the joint from me and studied it as if she wasn't sure what it was. She handed it to Randy without taking a hit.

"We can think of ways to make her suffer before she dies. So she'll know she's being punished."

"That's cruel," Lisa said.

"*She's* cruel," he said. "You don't even have a bed of your own! It's insane."

"I'll live," Lisa said.

"She's taking cash right out of our pockets."

"We're not going to pretend to kill her," Lisa said.

"We're not? Who put you in charge?" He inhaled smoke and held it longer than usual. He exhaled slowly. "You go first, Alexandra. You get it. How would you do it? Think about what we'd have — a fantastic apartment..."

"It's twisted," Lisa said.

"You can leave any time," he said.

But Lisa stayed...

"No way to afford the rent on our own," I said.

"Her mother would still pay half," Randy said. "We'd text her from Dianne's phone with inane updates about school. About the new, classy boyfriend." He handed the joint to me. While I took a puff, he said, "Come on. Tell us how, Alex."

"I would put one of her four feather pillows with 1000-thread count cotton cases over her face. I think first I'd get her drunk, explain what a bitch she was, but she wouldn't know what was coming. Then, she'd pass out. It wouldn't require as much effort to keep the pillow in place."

Randy laughed. "You sound like you've given this some thought."

"You're sick," Lisa said. "You're as bad as him."

But she still didn't get up and go inside. She just glared at me as if I'd betrayed a female pact of some kind.

Randy looked at her. "You never thought about killing anyone?"

"No."

"Not ever?"

"I said no."

"What about that guy in high school who posted that nasty poem on your Facebook page?"

Lisa took a sip of white wine. She put the glass down awkwardly, splashing wine on the back of her hand. She stabbed her fingertip at my arm. "Why did you tell him that?"

"I didn't know it was a secret."

"It wasn't meant for public consumption. It was my story, my thing. Not something to whisper about when you two are having sex."

"I'm sorry. It just came up. We were talking about how irritating it is that people can put shit on a Facebook wall and if the person doesn't check in for a few hours, if they don't get a chance to hide it, everyone sees it. Like there's no control over your own life, your own property in cyberspace."

"Oh." Her eyes glistened in the light of the candle flame.

"Didn't you want to kill that guy?" Randy said.

"That's just a...when people say they want to kill someone, they don't mean it. They don't *plan* it. I didn't actually think about how I would *do* it. That's the sick part."

"Isn't it sick when people kill your reputation, or your bank account by extorting money? Money they don't need, by the way? How is that different?" Randy said.

"It's completely different," Lisa said. "It's...it's like you're making it real. Instead of just wishing something, you're putting energy into it."

"We're just bullshitting," I said. "It's a game."

"That's right, a game." Randy got off the chaise lounge and came to the table. He pushed the candle back to the center and pulled out a chair. "You can go inside. More pot for Alex and me." He laughed.

"Okay, fine. But it makes me queasy. And it's just a game. And you can never tell anyone. Not *ever*. And you don't have a good track record with that, Alexandra."

"I said I didn't know it was a secret."

"You should have figured it out. This, this *game* is top secret. Agreed?"

She was turning it into something threatening by trying to swear us to secrecy. It was just talk. She made it sound like something more, as if she was afraid this was the first step toward actually doing it. That night, we each came up with one method for murder. My method was the least violent. There were so many benefits. It was the easiest, the quietest, the cleanest. Randy cracked up when I said that. He couldn't stop laughing, so Lisa was forced to go next. She said she'd push Dianne off the balcony.

"Boring," Randy said. "Obvious. And we're only on the second floor. She wouldn't die."

"It's a game," Lisa said. "I don't care if it's obvious. So okay, I'd do shots with her until she passed out and then push her into the pool."

Randy said he would shoot her. We pointed out he didn't own a gun and he wrote that off to more fixation on details rather than the spirit of the game. He wanted to shoot her because he wanted to see her fancy bed — a bed that was apparently too good for him to sleep in — soaked with blood. He went on a long time about the blood. It was overly hostile, but we were very wasted by then.

In the morning, the memory of it sounded like nonsense in my head.

Then this one night… We'd been playing for a while, and had covered a lot of different methods. It had become somewhat detailed and maybe a little too real. We wanted to keep our interest up, so we gave flamboyant explanations of how we could fool her into thinking everything was okay, how we'd set the trap.

Randy stood up and blew out the candle. He told us to move our chairs so we were both facing the balcony railing.

He stood behind us, the lights out in the apartment as well, so all we could see were curtained lights of other apartments, fuzzy and glowing, and the garden lights lining the paths in the courtyard, and of course, the underwater light in the swimming pool.

He spoke in a quiet voice that was almost a monotone. "Let's go back to Lisa's first idea — water is so beautiful," he said. "It's where we come from, it's almost the entire makeup of our bodies. It's required for life. We can live without food for a while, but not water. We need water to grow our food. We need it to keep clean. We need it for everything. Water is life."

He paused. He put both his hands on my head and held it there, making sure my face was turned in the direction of the swimming pool.

"Water is seductive. The human race gravitates toward waterfalls and lakes, rivers and oceans. The symbol of money is a luscious swimming pool. The best vacations take place on ocean liners and islands and beaches. We all want the water. We're obsessed with it."

This felt like a detour away from the game, and it was disturbing in some way I couldn't explain. Maybe because there was no light and he stood where we couldn't see him. Maybe because he was still holding my head so I felt he could crush it between his hands.

"Water," he said. "One part hydrogen and two parts oxygen. That's all. We die without it, and if we can't swim, or if we're unconscious, if a boat capsizes, we die within it."

I shivered. Lisa put her hand on my arm. Her fingers were

icy cold.

"The best way to kill Dianne is letting her drown. Then, it's not murder. It's water being itself, remaining true to its nature, taking life."

I started to turn. He tightened his grip.

Lisa turned, "But…"

"Shh. Shh. Don't turn around." His voice was a whisper.

"I would give Dianne her favorite sleeping pill. She does love to sleep. Napping all the time, have you noticed? Shh. Shh. Don't answer. I know you have. Sleeping until noon, sometimes one o'clock on the weekends. She sleeps the sleep of the dead, as they say."

"I'd go to the coffee bar and get her a double latte. She likes those. I'd dump the powder from her Ambien into the coffee and bring it to her in bed."

"She won't let you in her room," I said.

"Shh. Shh." He pressed down on the top of my head. The weight was solid and comforting. "Once she'd fallen asleep, I'd dress her in her favorite lingerie. The cream colored satin with the black lace. On top of that, I'd put casual, normal clothes, so it looked as if she just wanted to lounge by the pool. I'd carry her down the stairs and…"

"What if someone saw you?" I said.

"No one is here during the day. They're working so they can afford this place."

"You never know."

"Okay, okay. I'd wrap her in a quilt and pile clothes on top so it looked like I was going to do laundry. I'd go to the edge of the pool and…"

"Someone would see you. This won't work at all," I said.

"Then how should I do it? If drowning is the preferred method?"

I tried to turn, but the pressure on my head increased. "Don't look at me. Speak to the water."

His voice was mesmerizing.

The darkness made me feel as if I was dreaming as I spoke. "You should give her the coffee by the side of the pool. You could even get into the pool and sit on the steps like you're talking. Then when she passed out, no one would really notice. Or put her on a raft, both of you on rafts."

"Oh, Alexandra," he said. "You're so clever and so wicked and so right."

I smiled, pleased with myself in spite of the horror behind what I'd said. It was a game. But he needed to follow the laws of physics and human behavior, otherwise the game wasn't challenging.

"But how would I dress her in the lingerie I'd chosen?"

"You have to forget the lingerie. She has lots of nice bikinis. Compromise."

"Okay. Sure."

We were quiet for several long minutes.

Finally, Randy said, "I guess that was mostly your turn, not mine."

I shrugged. "It was Lisa's idea, we just embellished it. We're teammates. Cooperative play. We all win together. Like the Pandemic game."

He moved his hand off my head and rubbed my shoulders, pressing his fingers into tight muscles until they screamed with pain, but it felt so good because the knots dissolved under his fingertips.

10

Aptos

My job at CoastalCreative Software was easy. All I had to do was make sure other people got shit done. My laptop contained countless tiny blue folders full of complex spreadsheets that tracked the most minute details for the public announcement of every new product the company released. If something had to happen before a product was unveiled to the world, it was on my list — photographs of the packaging, talking points for the press release and industry analyst briefings, product documentation, sales training materials, slides proving CoastalCreative's stuff was better than what competitors had to offer, customer slides, technical customer slides…For a brand new product line, the list was easily three-hundred-fifty items. Each task had an owner's name attached, along with supporting sub tasks.

I didn't actually have to make sure people got stuff done. I just had to run meetings where I asked for updates on their status relative to the due dates, note it on my spreadsheet, multi-layered with pivot table capabilities, and assign them a color indicating how at risk they were for failure. Non-delivery was the official, politically correct term, but I called it failure. Red meant you were in deep shit, yellow meant you were probably lying about how far behind you were, and green meant you would hit the deadline, or, you were a pathological liar and hadn't even started. There were columns to track when material was scheduled for review and feedback by peers, management, and executives. The executive reviews often meant all day meetings followed by a complete re-do because the top dog changed his mind about the marketing strategy or the sales focus.

It was all very complex, for a to-do list.

I was a corporate tattletale. Management often called me into meetings so I could brief them on the numbers of reds and yellows. I ratted out the liars and failures, rather, the risks and potential non-deliveries. It's not that people didn't get their work done. They were all smart, hard driving, career-advancing overachievers, but they didn't like someone watching over their shoulders, checking on their work, treating them like pre-schoolers. And most of the time, there was just too much work to realistically get it all done. Especially with the re-do's.

I'd been at CoastalCreative for a month now, and already every guy and the token handful of women in the executive suite knew who I was. Executives like tattletales. The higher someone climbs up the ladder, the more they're excluded from the gossip stream and they like someone who will tell them what's going on. Most people stand in front of executives and lie because they think executives will be impressed with their accomplishments. But in smaller meetings, execs like the tattletales. They want to know the truth. They need to know the truth.

Some would consider it impressive that I'd achieved this position without a college degree. At the age of twenty-five, I'd started out answering phones in customer support at a software company. Customer support roles don't always require a degree, and when they heard my voice, which is nothing short of melodic, or so I've been told, any nits regarding *college degree preferred* were abandoned. My can-do attitude impressed those above me and eventually I had a chance to become a project manager.

The job suits me. To be honest, I take perverse pleasure in watching people squirm.

I spent a lot of time *going* to college, I just didn't get a degree. My parents understood I needed to find myself, get my head screwed on straight after some rocky years in my teens, so they let me wander aimlessly for years. I took what interested me — ceramics, biology, yoga, astronomy, history, sculpture, literature, modern dance. Randy and I had a lot in common with our grazing approach to college. Maybe that's one of the things that drew us to one another. I skipped as many of the dull, required supporting courses as I could.

After seven years, my father said, *enough*. I left college with a smattering of knowledge in a lot of areas and not a lot that I could put on a resume.

My manager at CoastalCreative was a woman named Tess Turner. She was a loud, aggressive woman, considered a bitch by most men and quite a few women, but very successful in her career. At thirty-four she was already a senior vice president. I was a bit low on the totem pole to be reporting to a senior VP, but she wanted to keep her eye on that spreadsheet. She wanted instant, round-the-clock access to my thoughts about the status of the spreadsheet, the secrets not immediately obvious in the simple color code. She wanted to make sure everyone knew the spreadsheet had bite, even if I personally wasn't at a level or in any kind of position to impact their salaries or promotions or bonus opportunities. She also wanted hallway gossip, another hugely important source of information denied to executives.

Tess and I met for coffee every Monday at seven-thirty a.m.

Defying a corporate culture where the CEO wore jeans, throwing on a sport coat for customer meetings, Tess dressed like she worked on Wall Street — high heels, nylon stockings, nicely cut suits with skirts or slacks, both of which enhanced her long legs. She had short black hair and eyes that were made up as if she were a streetwalker.

Tess seemed pleased by my effort to mirror her appearance, on a budget, of course. I'm good at that — mirroring others' style to make them feel comfortable. It works with clothing, speech patterns, even food choices. Martinis and pasta, for example. It makes people feel close to you. They know they can trust you because you feel safe and familiar to them.

As always, I ordered a double shot, non-fat latte, just like Tess. It made for a very animated conversation, as 300 milligrams of caffeine worked its way through our brains.

The quirky behavior of my roommates fascinated Tess. She'd laughed at Noreen's emphasis on her sweetness and nodded agreeably over Jared's devotion to Buddhism. She rolled her eyes when I told her Noreen had set her sights on Jared.

This morning, she asked for an update.

"Things have gotten a little weird." I sipped my latte through the tiny hole in the lid.

"Weird, how?"

"Noreen acts as if she and Jared are in a relationship."

"Maybe they are."

I shook my head. "Definitely not."

"Maybe wishful thinking, or thinking if she believes it to be true, it will be."

"It's more sinister than that."

"Oooh." She laughed. "So much drama."

"It's hard to describe." I pried off the lid and blew on my latte, which does nothing, but feels like I'm putting forth effort to make it drinkable.

"No, tell me. I'm not laughing at you." She sipped her coffee. She broke off a small piece of croissant and put it in her mouth. She swallowed without chewing. Croissant dough melts on your tongue, but it still looked uncomfortable.

"It's a sense I get, not anything definite she's said. She goes into his room when he's not there."

"That's not cool."

"He probably doesn't care that much, but it's not right."

She nodded.

"The other night she was pounding on his door and he never answered."

"So?"

"He's not interested. But she's very aggressive about telling me to stay away from him. As if he belongs to her."

Tess broke her croissant in half. She took a sip of latte.

"And there was something really weird, disturbing." I described the damaged mirror and Noreen's lack of concern over it, her effort to get me to change my habits rather than confronting Jared, rather than replacing it.

"You need to look for a new place." Tess broke off another piece of croissant. She put it in her mouth and chewed, slowly, as if she were drawing ideas out of the pastry, advice to help me escape the seemingly demented people I'd ended up living with.

"That's not an option."

"It's always an option. They sound unstable. It's not healthy."

I hadn't even told her about the dog. Not that the dog was entirely Noreen's fault. "I don't think she's unstable, she's just..." I sipped my drink.

"It wouldn't hurt to look for a new place, so you have the wheels in motion if she does something more bizarre."

I swallowed the rest of my latte and took a few deeper than normal breaths. I lowered my eyelids slightly.

"What's the matter?" Tess said.

"I can't afford to move again." I made my voice meek, tinged with a note that Tess might interpret as shame.

She licked the corner of her lip and glanced away from me. She put both her hands around her coffee cup and picked it up as if she intended to drink, but she didn't. "Maybe I can do something about that."

"I'm not asking for…"

She held up her hand. "I know that. But you've become hugely valuable to the company. To me. I'm going to look into getting you an out-of-cycle pay increase."

"I don't want to put you in an awkward spot, telling you my sob story."

She shook her head. "Don't worry about it." She pushed out her chair.

As she turned to lift the strap of her bag off the back of the chair, I smiled. People feel so good when they know they have more power than you, when they know they can use that power to help you.

11

Meditation now occupied four hours out of every day, and Jared needed every nano second. As a newbie to the practice, he'd been assured many times that rescuing one's mind from distraction, endless rumination, and mindless chatter was a life-long pursuit. It was normal to have thoughts repeat mercilessly, the fervent demands for attention growing until it seemed as if unwanted memories and imaginings and plans and desires were hurling themselves against the flesh of his brain like screaming infants. He took a breath, and saw Alexandra's face. He let the breath out, and heard Alexandra laugh. He took another breath, and imagined the texture of her hair, let the breath out, and saw her unwavering gaze. It was exhausting.

The classes at the Zen center helped, slightly. Performing yoga poses in a room full of other grunting, sweating, straining bodies helped. His muscles and joints had a way of drawing attention to themselves as he stood in the extended triangle or wobbled in the tree pose. Especially the tree pose, balancing on his left foot while the right foot pressed against the inner side of his left thigh and he tried to keep his arms raised over his head, palms together.

His devotion to pursuing answers to the bigger questions

of life hadn't diminished, but the desire had been smothered by Alexandra Mallory and it was now gasping for life. At the same time, he saw the humor in his situation. He'd found both heaven and hell inside the sagging bungalow.

Every fiber of his being longed for Alexandra. He wanted to know the entire scope of her mind and he wanted her in his bed so badly his ribs ached. His lungs seemed to scrape against the bone with every breath. It was difficult to comprehend that the most enthralling woman imaginable was sleeping and listening to music and taking off her clothes on the other side of the two-foot deep closets that formed the common wall. At night, he thought he could smell the lotion she spread across her skin. Taking a shower after she'd stood under the same flow of water was a religious experience in itself. She was right there in the room next to his. She used the same utensils and dishes when she ate, sat on the same couch, looked out through the same windows, yet she held herself apart. She didn't offer a smile to encourage a conversation outside her bedroom door. She rarely went into the great room, suggesting she was available to talk over a glass of wine. He heard the front door close when she went running every morning before the sun came up. He'd thought about buying a pair of running shoes, but she was gone for so long, he was sure he wouldn't be able to keep pace for all that time. He hadn't run more than a half mile since college.

Then there was hell.

Noreen, with her gray, staring eyes that seemed to want to attach themselves like leeches to his body, had done everything but crawl into his bed to announce her interest.

She flashed her boobs in his face, and asked him endless questions about his family, his career plans, his dreams, his car, his yoga practice, how he spent the hours of his day. She made sandwiches with mashed avocado and shredded carrots and sprouts. They were good, but he didn't need a mother packing his lunch. He'd refused the breakfasts she fixed, which brought tears to her eyes. The woman was seriously unstable. How had *sweet* and *responsible* turned into cloyingly *subservient* and *repulsive* in just a few short weeks?

The need simmering in Noreen's eyes would drive him to find another place to live, but he wasn't going to walk out of Alexandra's life. Noreen could force-feed him runny eggs every morning, constantly forgetting they weren't part of a vegan diet, and he wouldn't budge from the room that shared a wall with Alexandra's.

He opened his bedroom door carefully. Both the other bedroom doors were closed. The house was silent, although with the tile floor, it was often hard to know when someone was moving about. He stood for a few minutes, listening for the sound of a kitchen cabinet door closing, or a coffee mug touching the table. Pressing his lips tightly together, he took a deep breath through his nostrils. There was no odor of coffee or food, just cool, early morning air.

He stepped into the hallway, pulled his door closed, and walked into the great room. Pale light came through the glass panes on the front door. The blinds that covered the large windows and the doors out to the back deck were closed. The kitchen was dark, the counters wiped clean. He released his breath, not realizing he'd been holding it. He wanted a cup of tea, but the piercing scream of the kettle would summon Noreen, even if she was asleep. He took a teabag out of the cabinet, an apple out of the bowl on the counter, and hurried back to his room. He dressed without showering and went outside.

The BMW roared to life. As he put it in gear, he couldn't stop his head from turning to look at the front door. He'd known she would be there. The tip of Noreen's nose was pressed against the glass. She stared out at him. Even though it wasn't physically possible from that distance, he felt he could see the tears swimming across her eyes, the skin of her cheeks pulled taut as her mouth turned down in a look of unbearable sadness.

12

Mountain View, California

Before I got the job at CoastalCreative, I was living in Silicon Valley, sharing a condo with a woman I'd met at the gym. The condo complex was enormous — four eight-story buildings situated beside El Camino Real with a narrow strip of drought-resistant shrubs and ground covered with river rock between us and a six-lane road. El Camino is a constant parking lot because the Silicon Valley section of the state-long highway passes through ten or twelve suburban cities. The entire forty-plus miles is lined with apartment buildings and condo complexes, restaurants and fast food places, shops, service stations, and strip malls. Cars are constantly turning in and out of the river of traffic.

My building had thirty-two units. They were basically apartments, dubbed condos because people desperate to live in Silicon Valley were willing to put more than half a million dollars down on some walls and flooring to call their own, paying a homeowners' association fee on top of that.

I was a renter. Always a renter, with roommates who take responsibility for the lease or mortgage. It's easier to come and go when your name isn't on the mortgage or the electric bill. Someday I'll have a place of my own, but I'm waiting for the day I can buy desirable property. Plenty of property, with a secluded, custom-built home. That day is a few years down the road, but there's no doubt it will arrive before I hit my fortieth birthday. Small steps.

I took a training class at a previous job where they taught us the power of a Japanese practice called Kaizen. It's all about small steps, incremental growth. Instead of looking for a five hundred dollar a month raise, you should consider something smaller, hardly noticeable, make do with the current housing freak show and continue proving your value, feeding the company's desire to retain you at all costs, and wait for the next raise, and the one after that.

In Kaizen theory, you start by doing three abdominal crunches a day, instead of diving into twenty-five or thirty, quickly giving up because you can't stand up straight for a week and it hurts to get out of bed in the morning. Small steps rather than the preferred American method of two huge steps forward and a stumble back. While I was taking the class, I sometimes walked around the condo with very tiny steps to cement it in my mind that small steps are more effective. I'm very American at the core, I want it all immediately. But Kaizen is powerful and tricks the mind into building a smooth, solid path forward.

The condo I shared with Maria Anders was on the fourth floor. I'd met Maria at the gym and we hit it off immediately. She ran on the treadmill when it was raining or cold and windy, and so did I. She wasn't fond of vodka martinis, but she loved Chardonnay, and it's also a favorite of mine. As if the stars were aligned above me, her roommate had moved out two weeks after Maria and I met each other. She was in immediate need of someone to supplement her soul-crushing mortgage. Desperation works well for me — there's less concern about digging into the background of a potential roommate. I moved in. We got along great. We each did our own thing. The only togetherness at home was a Sunday afternoon glass of Chardonnay on the balcony, when both of us were available at the same time. Our meet-ups in the gym continued, and when the weather was nice, we ran along nearby suburban streets with quaint homes built in the 1930s and 40s.

The residents of our building were chill kind of people. Most of them I hardly knew more than to say *hi* to when we passed in the parking garage. There were three other units on the same floor as Maria's. Charlie Denton, a decent looking guy who was studying for the California bar exam lived next door. Across the hall was Sylvia, a single mom with two kids — Josh and Janine. The others on our floor — two guys — didn't give out their names, preferring to pass with friendly but aloof smiles and nods. They never hung out by the pool or in the community barbecue area.

Charlie attached himself to me right away. He always seemed to be emerging from the parking garage just as I arrived home from work. I didn't have a car. I took the train, walking four blocks home, even in bad weather. I didn't mind, it allowed me to avoid that horrendous traffic going up and down El Camino Real. Most days, the train moved faster.

The first time Charlie and I said more than *hi, how ya' doing* with a comment or two on the weather conditions or sports news, was beside the pool. The water was silky turquoise and undisturbed by children or furious lap swimmers. It was the Saturday afternoon before Easter so I suppose all the kids were at egg hunts. I was lying on a pink towel wearing my second favorite black bikini. It has two narrow strands that connect the front and back sections of the bottom. The top mirrors the pants with two coils of fabric connecting the bra in the center front. The top is smaller than some. It displays my breasts quite nicely but without them falling out, which just looks sloppy. I was listening to Tchaikovsky. My eyes were closed, although that wasn't obvious with my sunglasses on. Suddenly, an ear bud was yanked out. The tinny sound that emits from an earbud when it's close but not in your ear spoiled the music. I opened my eyes, pressed pause, and sat up.

Charlie stood there grinning. "You should be in the water, not zoning out to hip-hop."

"I don't listen to *hip-hop*."

He dragged a chaise lounge closer to my towel and sat down. He wore black board shorts with a single red stripe down each side. The hair on his muscular legs was so thick his legs reminded me of a bear's legs. "You look like a hip-hop kind of girl."

"What are the characteristics of a hip-hop *girl*...or boy?"

He grinned. "Out there."

I thought about letting him see my eyes, but there was a lot of glare and I didn't want to take off my glasses just to stare at him until he realized he'd said something offensive. Not that he'd recognize his offense if I didn't spell it out.

Besides, his eyes also hid behind dark glasses and it was best to keep the playing field level.

"Want to go for a swim?" he said.

"No. I'm enjoying the sun."

"You're sweaty."

"Thank you."

"I wasn't..."

I gave him a delicately welcoming smile.

He laughed.

He settled back in the chair and told me about the bar exam and how hard it was to prep for. It was a full time job. He was working *at least eight hours a day*, sometimes ten or eleven. "It's the hardest exam there is."

"The hardest bar exam?"

"No harder than any other test."

"How do you know that?"

"It's a fact."

He continued on about his study efforts. "It's hard to concentrate because of all the noise coming from the zoo next door."

"What noise?"

"Sylvia. Her kids. Other kids. Constant racket. She's in violation of the condo guidelines. She has a friend living there. Did you know that? The friend has a baby and another little kid. All day long the TV is blasting kiddie shows with inane music."

"Close your window."

"I can still hear it."

"Noise cancelling headphones."

"Why should I have to change my environment when they're breaking the law?"

"They aren't breaking the *law*." I liked Sylvia. Her kids were cute, like little puppies and who doesn't like puppies? And Sylvia made the most amazing brownies. Nearly once a week she brought over a plate of brownies, or chocolate chip cookies. Here was a woman who worked *at least eight hours a day*, Mr. Lawyer Wannabe, as an administrative assistant. Sometimes ten or eleven, and took great care of her kids. Her husband had waited until after he fathered two children to decide he didn't want to be a dad after all. She managed to juggle a job she was trying to turn into a career, two small kids, *and* made amazing brownies. So what if she had a friend move in to help with childcare and rent?

"You can't have more than four people in a one-bedroom unit. She signed an agreement to that effect."

I tried to picture where they all slept. It sounded claustrophobic. "Well, she's a single mother. It's hard to get by."

"Tough. Then they should move somewhere cheaper."

"It's not so easy to find housing around here."

"Where's her husband?"

"What business is it of yours?"

"It's my business when I can't study because her brats are rotting their brains in front of the TV."

I said nothing. I never heard any noise from Sylvia's place. I didn't like his attitude. And I was not in favor of her moving away with that brownie recipe.

Eventually, I got tired of listening to him criticize Sylvia, and it was getting hot, stretched out in full sun surrounded by glaring white concrete. The sweat was thicker now, enough that it shimmered on my belly. We went for a swim and fooled around a bit, chasing each other under water and grabbing at bare skin. Once he got off the topic of single mothers, he was okay to talk to. It was interesting hearing about his favorite class in law school — a criminal defense clinic.

I didn't care for his view of Sylvia, but I really liked his muscular back and narrow waist and hips curving into a butt I couldn't take my eyes off. It would be interesting to see whether my body or my brain won this round.

13

Aptos

On Sunday, I had the house to myself. Noreen had gone to visit her parents — again, which seemed excessive parental contact. It crossed my mind that they were helping her plot how to snare Jared, thrilled that she'd met a man who wasn't Brian. Or maybe she hadn't reconciled with her parents at all and she was doing something else entirely. I never assume someone is telling me the truth, it's too easy not to.

Jared was off doing something to save the planet.

They would both be home after dinner. They were very emphatic about that — *after* dinner. The pseudo family dinners had grown strained, but no one wanted to admit the shared meals were forced and burdensome. We had nothing in common. Noreen had gotten herself a job in an elderly care facility and there's not much to be said about that over dinner. Jared was often engaged in the practice of silence at mealtime. I couldn't discuss my job since they thought I was spending my days ringing up sales in a department store, and I certainly wasn't going to tell stories from my past. We were a bunch of misfits. Maybe we belonged together after all.

That morning I'd gone for a ten mile run and my muscles

were feeling pleasantly utilized. After a shower, I put on jeans and a white tank top over a lace-trimmed navy blue silk bra. I left my hair to dry naturally rather than standing in front of the round mirror Noreen had hung over my dresser. It was about six inches too low, forcing me to hold a partial plié in order to see the top of my head. I was certain she'd hung it too low on purpose.

I opened all the windows and doors in my room and the great room. It was a spectacular day — all blue sky and sweet-smelling air, classic rock music drifting out the open window of a house two doors down. They were playing it too loud in a neighborly way, so that everyone could enjoy it without being blasted out of their own thoughts. If you didn't like classic rock, you'd have a different reaction, but most people do like it. That's why it's classic.

I went outside and opened the gate to the side yard. I walked around the patch of dirt. As far as I could tell, despite all the effort every weekend, there were still a fair number of rather large rocks, and the turned over soil revealed thousands of smaller stones. Since Noreen had a garden there before we'd moved in, it made no sense that the area was in such poor shape. Maybe that's why the garden had been short-lived — she hadn't prepped it before planting.

Either Jared was overwhelmed with all the work, or his interests had moved on. Those awkward dinners made him less inclined to want to eat at home, so I suppose there was no need for a vegetable garden.

It's a contradiction to open all the windows and doors, inviting fresh air into the house, then return to the bedroom for a pack of cigarettes and a lighter, but that's what I did.

I dragged a turquoise Adirondack chair out of the garage, put it in front of the open gate leading to the dirt patch, and lit a cigarette. I closed my eyes and turned my face to the sky. The sun was warm, but there was enough of a breeze to keep me from feeling as if I was baking my lips into crispy strips of meat. The breezy warmth offered false security. The sun is eating away at your epidermis even when it's veiled by fog or its heat wafts away on a strong wind. Still, it's easy to forget, and you want to forget, on a gorgeous Sunday afternoon when your roommates are far away and won't be intruding on your peace of mind until *after* dinner.

When the first cigarette was gone, I went inside and poured a glass of Pinot Grigio.

I returned to my chair lit another cigarette, took a quick puff and a sip of wine, and settled back.

The glass of wine was half finished when a pewter Boxster with the roof down pulled onto the gravel strip in front of the house. A thin guy with dirty blonde hair, shaved up slightly on the back and sides, hanging over his sunglasses in the front, climbed out of the car. He wore a pale green t-shirt, army green cargo shorts, and black canvas shoes without socks. There was something about his slender build and hair color that gave the impression he could be Noreen's twin. He looked about the same age, possibly a bit younger.

He pulled a phone out of his pocket, tapped it a few times, and dropped it back inside without looking to make sure his aim was correct. Impressive.

He stared at the house, started up the path, then appeared

to notice me for the first time. He waved and headed toward the front door.

I sat forward in my chair. "Can I help you?"

He made an abrupt left turn and crossed the pale, crisp lawn to where I was sitting. "Where's Noreen?"

"Can I tell her who's calling?"

He lifted his sunglasses, tilted his head, and studied me, his gaze sweeping quickly from the top of my head where my hair was piled in a floppy knot to my bare toes, noting the glass of wine and the cigarette. "Is she home?"

"No."

"When will she be back?"

Despite his abrupt manner and his obvious cataloging of everything about me, he seemed easy-going. Not someone I should worry about. No alarms went off. "After dinner."

"What time is that?"

I took a drag on my cigarette and turned my head to blow out the smoke. "Not sure. Before dark, probably."

"And who are you, pretty lady?"

I blushed. And he noticed.

It was totally stupid. His comment was stupid and my reaction was stupid. He wasn't even that good looking. Nice enough, but not like…Jared, for example. This guy was a little on the skinny side. He was tall and he had a nice smile, a little uncertain, like Noreen's. There was nothing remarkable about him. Except maybe the Boxster. He didn't seem like a Boxster type, not that I can define what that type is. His question was so old-fashioned, slightly aggressive, and it made me feel like a giggly fourteen-year-old. I don't think there's a woman alive who doesn't react if a man says she's pretty. You despise yourself for reacting, but it happens. Unless the guy is a total creep, and even then you react — with disgust and a modicum of anger. This guy was not a creep at all. "I asked you first."

"No you didn't."

"When you wanted to know where Noreen is."

"Oh. *Who should I say is calling?* You sounded like the butler." He laughed.

"Are you her brother?"

"She hasn't spoken to her brother since she was a kid."

"Are you her ex?"

"I wasn't aware she had an ex." He studied me as if he hoped to receive more information without asking.

The wine glass was slippery in my hand. I clenched my fingers, hoping for a firmer grip, although that's difficult with a sweaty glass and warm fingers. I inched my fingers lower so they were wrapped around the smaller part instead of stretched out trying to keep the sides from making a move through my fingers. I took a drag on my cigarette.

"Can I bum one?" he said.

I held the cigarette between my teeth, picked up the pack off the ground, and handed it to him. The lighter was inside the box.

He pulled one out, stuck it in his mouth, and lit it.

"Where can I sit?"

"Did I invite you to sit?"

"Is this your house?" he said.

"No."

"Then why do I need an invitation?"

"Well I live here, even though it's not technically mine."

"Whose is it, technically?"

"You're asking a lot of questions without identifying yourself."

"What difference would it make? I know Noreen, and my name wouldn't mean anything to you."

"How do you know?" He was giving me a warm, glowing feeling, and it wasn't just from the *pretty lady* comment. I'm not a lady. A lady is someone from another era. Modern, self-sufficient women don't view themselves as ladies. But still...

Why was I thinking about that?

I took a puff on my cigarette and a sip of wine. It was his turn to talk. I was sure he wasn't going to reveal his name. It seemed as if I should be worried about that, my spidey sense should be vibrating all over the place, but it wasn't. He felt safe. He seemed decent. It's funny how you can pick up on those things, except, sometimes you're wrong.

"Great beach day," he said. "How come you're sitting by a pile of dirt staring at the street?"

"I like it here."

He nodded. "Lived here long?"

"TMI for a guy who remains nameless."

"I haven't heard your name either."

"I asked first."

"That again?"

"Yep." As I lifted my hand to tap the growing stem of ash on the end of my cigarette, the column of ash broke away and landed on my leg. I put the cigarette between my lips and moved the wine glass to my other hand so I could clean up the mess.

He reached over and brushed the ashes off my jeans. It happened quickly. The gesture was tender, so intimate, I stopped breathing for a moment. The warmth of his fingers went through the denim and sent a shiver up the inside of my leg, making its way to my throat before I could start breathing again. I swallowed. I started to speak, to tell him I could brush away my own damn ashes, but my voice came out in an awkward cough.

"You okay?" he said.

I nodded and took a healthy sip of wine. It made me cough more. I took another sip and a drag on my cigarette and then I was fine. Except for the lingering shiver. "Are you planning to sit here until Noreen gets home?" I said.

"Maybe."

"It'll be after dinner."

"You said that. Am I bothering you?"

He was definitely bothering me, in a different way than he assumed. I didn't like that I was drawn to him, because I intended to steer a wide path around anyone connected to Noreen. The wise choice was to shut down the conversation, pick up my glass and smokes and go into the house. But I didn't want to. I could sit there all afternoon, not knowing his name, smoking, talking in lazy circles. I thought about offering him a glass of wine. "You're not bothering me," I said.

"But you had to think about it."

"Not really. I don't understand why your name is top secret."

"Isn't it more fun this way? Two strangers enjoying a smoke and the sun?"

I shrugged. I sipped my wine. He looked hungrily at the wine, but I was definitely not going to offer him a glass. The problem was, mine was almost empty and I wanted more.

14

After the Boxster-guy left, the wind kicked up. As the sun went down, the wind grew stronger. Shortly after, a knocking sound began to echo through the house, made louder by the tile floor. I went to the front door, wondering if Boxster-guy had returned. No one was there. I walked to the doors leading to the back deck. The cliff-hugging tree was batting its branches against the deck railing.

It annoyed me that I was still thinking about that guy, expecting him, longing for him badly enough that my mind tricked itself into thinking a tree branch was his hand on the door.

We'd smoked my entire pack of cigarettes and talked about nonsense. I'd managed to resist the temptation to offer him a glass of wine, which meant I hadn't been able to refill mine. He said he'd be back but didn't specify whether it would be that evening or another day. He declined to leave a message for Noreen. As soon as his car turned the corner at the end of the street, I wished I'd offered the wine.

I wasn't sure whether I should tell Noreen about her visitor. If I mentioned the car, would she know who it belonged to? Even if the car was new and she wasn't aware of it, I'd be able to describe him well enough. Besides, how many guys came by to see her? I couldn't shake the feeling he seemed like her twin. It was eery how much they looked alike, yet not. Even their mannerisms struck a similar note. She'd mentioned her estranged brother, but hadn't noted he was a twin. In my experience, most twins are so consumed with the wonder of being a twin they tell you right away, trying to impress you with their place in the world — taking up twice as much space as everyone else.

Jared must have gone straight to his room the minute he arrived home. The only reason I knew he was in there was I'd heard him flush the toilet and then his bedroom door opened and closed.

About ten minutes after that, there was a knock on my door.

I was sitting on my bed drinking the rest of the Pinot Grig and watching *The Following* on my tablet. I'd found the show in Noreen's streaming account. I'd asked her twice how much I owed for access, but she insisted it was a free perk because we were friends. The show was quite addictive. At the start of each episode, I told myself it was the last, and then I'd read the teaser for the next one. I'd think about the rough, cynical sexiness of Kevin Bacon and hit play. Not to mention the serial killer that gave the show its name. He was a gory, horror show of a person, but between his sublime mouth, alluring eyes, and that British accent, it wasn't hard to see how someone like him might acquire quite a following.

I got up and opened the door. Noreen yawned and stretched, making a big production of how tired she was, and said she was going to sleep.

After she went into her room and closed the door, I carried my wine through the great room to the French doors that opened onto the deck. The tree was swaying and bending over the house like a huge, shadowy figure trying to look inside. I took a sip of wine and went into the kitchen. I got out the vodka and vermouth and a shot glass. I poured the alcohol and ice into the shaker. I wrapped the shaker in a towel to muffle the noise and moved it back and forth gently, hoping to avoid drawing Noreen out to the kitchen for a drink and a chat. No matter how tired she was, I didn't think she could resist a martini.

The house was dark and silent.

I took the almost empty wine glass and the martini to the great room and sat on the couch. It felt good to stretch out. My room was nice, but it was small, and sometimes it's critical to feel empty space around you, to move without obstacles, to stretch out your legs instead of trying to maintain a comfortable position sitting in bed with pillows propped against the headboard. Watching a movie while sitting in my small armchair wasn't always appealing, but I get twitchy and jumpy when I sit too long in bed.

I leaned back, propped my feet on the table, closed my eyes, and finished the wine, letting it wash through the inside of my head.

The martini was a perfect biting cold and the alcohol unwound all the twitching muscles in my legs. I pointed my toes, barely visible in the darkness. The branch began knocking again. Even though I knew it was the branch, the impulse to check the front door kept returning. My body remembered his fingers brushing away the ashes. I took another sip of the martini.

A door opened. I held my breath and supported my glass with two hands so I didn't spill on my lap.

Bare feet tapped the tile floor in the hallway.

I moved my glass close to my lips and tipped it to let the liquid slide into my mouth.

There was another sound of flesh on tile.

From where I was seated, I had a view of Jared's door. Noreen stepped across the hall from her room and stood in front of his. Her long, streaked hair glistened in the semi-darkness. She wore a thong and a silky, clingy camisole. It was impossible to tell their color in the dim light filtering into the hallway from the open door of her room — maybe cream or pale yellow. I wanted to grab her hair and smack her face. Why was she so completely lacking any radar toward the opposite sex? Was this what came of a girl shoved into adult life before she was fully raised? Although, lots of girls slip away from the parental influence before they're fully grown, and they don't enter the world without any shred of pride.

She put her hand on the door, palm flat, her fingers spread. Did she think he was going to feel her vibe, sense the heat coming from her skin and open the door?

I sipped my drink and waited.

She stood with her hand on the door for several minutes, mustering up her courage, or hoping he might receive a supernatural revelation that she was waiting.

Finally, she tapped one finger on the door.

Nothing.

She knocked gently.

Nothing.

She knocked harder. Then, she started knocking faster and didn't stop. The noise drowned out the tree branch, it filled the house and started to feel as if it was pounding inside my head. Her wrist didn't appear to grow tired as the steady beat continued. It went on for two minutes, maybe more. My drink was half gone when Jared shouted — *What do you want?* Funny, he didn't shout *who is it?*

"It's Noreen."

I suppressed a giggle — a result of sipping the martini too fast, right on top of a glass of wine.

"I'm trying to sleep." His voice was still loud, as if he hoped to scare her away with sheer volume.

"I have something for you."

Now, I did giggle. Thankfully she didn't hear me as he continued to speak at an extreme volume, talking over my laughter.

"Not interested," he said.

"How do you know?"

"I know."

"Jared, I'd really like to come into your room. I won't keep you awake more than an hour or so. I…"

"Please leave me alone."

She leaned against the door. "You don't know what you're missing."

He didn't respond.

"You really don't."

"Okay. Good night," he said.

"Jared, please, it'll only take two seconds to open the door."

"You said an hour."

"Well two seconds to see what I have for you. The hour is up to you."

My face grew warm on her behalf. I plucked an olive out of my drink and sucked it quietly.

"I said good night," he shouted.

Her body seemed to turn to liquid and she slid slowly to the floor. She didn't move until I'd eaten all three olives and there were only a few sips left in the bottom of my glass.

She stood up, turned, and squinted. "What are you doing?"

I held up my glass.

"Were you there the whole time?"

"What whole time?" I was mildly buzzed, more interested in being silly than tactful, eager to wind her up.

"Don't play dumb. The whole time I was standing here."

"Unfortunately, yes."

"What does that mean?" She walked into the great room and turned on the table lamp. She put her hands on her hips and glared at me like I was a child caught spilling juice on the coffee table.

I sat up and abandoned my mocking tone. "You're humiliating yourself."

"What business is it of yours? And I'm not."

"He's not interested."

"You have no idea what you're talking about." She took a step closer. "What is that?" She pointed at the table, but I couldn't make out what she was looking at.

I sat up straighter and peered at the surface. There weren't any water marks from my glasses that I could see.

"The wine glass," she said. "Were you having drinks with him?" She moved closer and grabbed the glass triumphantly, as if holding it proved I was doing something behind her back.

I laughed.

"Don't laugh at me." She threw the wine glass right at my head.

I flung myself on my side, knocking the martini glass on the edge of the table. Both glasses shattered. I was afraid to move, not sure whether there was a blanket of glass fragments covering my body.

"Turn on the other light," I said.

"Why?"

"There's glass everywhere. What the hell is wrong with you?"

"You were having drinks with him. Otherwise why would there be two glasses?"

"How could I be having drinks with him? He's in his bedroom! Turn on the light."

"Don't be a crybaby."

"I'm not being a crybaby. There's glass all over the place and I need to see so I can sit up without getting my skin sliced open. And you need to get a dustpan and broom."

A moment later, the room was filled with light. Noreen's face was red, color spreading across her forehead, up past her hairline, making it seem as if the red of her scalp was glowing through her hair. I reached for a pillow and used it to brush glass off my legs. I sat up carefully. "Will you get some shoes and sweep this up."

"Don't tell me what to do. This is my house."

"I can't move."

"First tell me when you were having drinks with him. Before I went to his door, obviously."

"I didn't have drinks with him."

"I can see two glasses."

"I finished my wine and made a martini, you moron."

Her eyes grew teary and she turned and left the room. I sat motionless, afraid of slicing my foot or hand if I moved in any direction. She returned a moment later with a pair of flip-flops which were inadequate for the mess. She was wearing a long t-shirt over her *seduce Jared* outfit.

She murmured to herself as she swept glass into a dustpan. When it was safe to move, I went into my room, closed the door, and locked it.

15

Los Angeles

When Randy and Lisa and I played the game of how to murder Dianne, we were sitting in the darkness. We didn't look each other in the eye as Lisa worried over it...every single time. She would eventually get into it, but she had to start with the worry, as if that was part of the game itself, like shuffling cards before a hand of poker. She worried we were bad people, that we were indulging in wicked thoughts that would damage our humanity.

"That's what's wrong with men! You have to extract revenge for everything. You have to turn the slightest inconvenience into an excuse for violence. It's sickening. The human race will never evolve until men stop behaving like beasts."

"It's a game," Randy said. "It's a *game*."

He and I knew that life itself is a game. There are winners and losers. It's not fair. It's brutally unfair. Life is blatantly incomprehensibly *un*-fair. Why are some people born into famine, under oppressive or brutal regimes? Why are some women born into cultures where they're stoned to death if they dare to have sex, while other women are born into an environment that grooms them for an exclusive, protective college that provides a stellar education and a lifetime of supportive social connections? A college where everyone cheers them on when they go to Miami for Spring break and run around without the tops to their bathing suits? And that's just one microscopic, irrational example. *Life. Is. Not. Fair.* Wonderful children get cancer and die, others are slaughtered by drunk drivers, and kids who are thugs in the making, future prison inmates, skate with perfect health and seeming immunity to death. How do you live with that? Yet, we do.

After verbalizing her worries, Lisa would get a second drink or take another toke on our joint, and shift to silent worry. Strangely, her guilt and her violent antagonism toward Randy never prevented her from coming up with murderous ideas of her own.

There aren't that many ways to kill someone and the game should have run its course after a few weeks, but we found twists and embellishments to keep things going. The murder weapon and type of death were altered, the settings, the participants, the events and conversation leading up to the crime.

A few weeks after we started playing, Mr. Perfect — Tom Normandy — moved into Dianne's bedroom. That's when the trouble escalated.

The first thing to happen was that Lisa got tossed out of Dianne's bedroom. Randy and I were told to make room for her in ours. It wasn't that we didn't have the space. It was the injustice, and the lack of respect, and the total disregard for Lisa, treating her like a sack of discarded clothes for the

Salvation Army truck. But Dianne had all the cards. Or one card, the ace — her rich, clueless mother. We had no cards.

Tom Normandy was perfect on the outside only. He was everything Mrs. W desired for Dianne — pretty and glamorous. But he was dumb as shit. A nice package with nothing inside.

It started on a Saturday morning when Lisa was making waffles. Randy and I were at the table drinking coffee. Dianne was still in her room, presumably sleeping. Tom came striding out of Dianne's bedroom, naked. Lisa blushed and asked him to put on sweats before he ate breakfast with us.

"Got a problem with the human body?" Tom said.

"I don't want to eat breakfast with your cock waving in my face," Lisa said.

Tom laughed. "But it's so handsome."

Lisa turned to the stove.

Tom marched across the kitchen, bent his knees, and rested his chin on her shoulder. "Aw, don't be a prude."

"I'm not. Please get off me."

"Maybe you've never seen one before?"

"Of course I have."

"I don't believe that." He straightened. He took her shoulders and turned her to face him. He put his hand on top of her head and bent it forward so she was staring down at his groin.

She twisted to the side. "I'm trying to cook. Let go of me." Instead of sounding angry, her voice trembled. It was quieter than normal and Tom recognized that fact.

"Go easy," Randy said.

"Come on, Lisa. This is your chance. An ugly girl like you has never seen a guy like me. You and your sad little breasts and your over-sized ass. No wonder all you care about is studying, trying to be so smart. It's all you have." He tapped her nose. "A nose like Cyrano deBergerac, sniffing out misbehaving men."

Randy shoved out his chair, stood up, and walked around the table. "You're going too far."

Tom smiled. "The truth hurts."

Lisa was crying. Her nose, which was large, but had a lot of character, was bright red, glossy with mucous collecting inside of it.

"You are an ugly little girl, any way you look at it," Tom said. "Go ahead and have a good cry. You deserve it. If you ever get a guy at all, he'll be a short, fat, ugly dude. And you two will pop out short, fat, ugly kids and the cycle will go on forever! But you need to cool it with the brainy shit. No guy wants a smart ass girl. Leave the lawyering and the politics to men." He strutted around the room, throwing his head back, chortling.

I pushed back my chair, rushed at him, and smacked his face. Tom put his hand on his cheek. "Hey, you want to wind up with no place to stay?"

"Shut the fuck up," I said.

I went to the stove. Lisa's cheeks were covered with tears and her lips trembled violently. I put my arm around her, but said nothing. There's really no comfort when cruel observations are hurled at someone. She owned a mirror.

She pushed me away. The spoon fell on the floor,

splattering waffle batter on my legs. She picked up the bowl, walked to the living room, and poured the batter on the carpet.

"Clean that up," Tom said.

Lisa slopped her feet through the batter and continued across the living room, leaving gooey beige footprints on the blue carpet.

"Get back here," Tom said. "Clean up this shit."

Lisa headed toward the hallway.

In three strides, Tom crossed the kitchen and was well into the living room. Lisa hurried around the coffee table, but she misjudged. Her shin banged the corner. She shrieked and lost her balance. She managed to keep herself from falling, but now Tom was on top of her. He grabbed her hair and twisted it until she screamed. Shoving his face close to hers, he stuck out his tongue and waggled it, brushing her lips. She turned her head, her face contorted.

He took her wrists, and gripped both in one of his large hands. He twisted so he was looking over his shoulder at Randy and me. "You two get out of here."

"No way," I said. I was on my knees, scooping gloppy puddles of batter with fistfuls of paper towels.

"And leave that. She needs to clean it up."

I kept scooping.

"I want you both out of here. This girl needs to be taught a lesson."

Randy edged his way toward Tom.

"Get back," Tom said.

I got up, walked to Dianne's bedroom, and pounded my

fist on the door. Dianne's phlegmy, half-sleeping voice called out, "What?"

I opened the door. "We have a problem with your classy boyfriend."

Dianne shouted at me to get out of her room and stop bothering her.

Randy shoved Tom into the armchair, extremely careful to avoid contact with the lower half of Tom's body. "I said, you're going too far."

Lisa stood up. "No. It's okay. What he said is true. I'm not blind." She laughed harshly. "Let's not turn this into something violent."

"Why are you naked?"

I turned at the sound of Dianne's voice. She stood in her bedroom doorway. She went back into the room and returned with a pair of jeans. She walked over to Tom. "What's going on, Babe?"

Tom stood up, took the jeans, and yanked them on. "Tenant problems."

"We're not your fucking tenants," Randy said.

Tom pushed his hair off his face, weaving his fingers through it, making him look a bit like a woman, fluffing up her hair, her last check in the mirror before returning to the dance floor of a club. "Poor pathetic valedictorian got her feelings hurt 'cuz I told the truth about her chances in the romance arena."

"Not what happened," I said.

Dianne held up her index finger, keeping her attention on Tom. With her other hand, she yanked on the waistband of her boxer-style pajama pants that were inching down the sides of her hips. She laughed. "My mother accused me of picking an ugly girl to share my apartment so I'd look better in comparison."

Tom walked over and put his arm around her waist. He glanced at me, closed his eyes, and pulled her up close. "You're drop dead no matter who you're standing next to." He folded his mouth over hers, their lips swallowed up by each other, her neck stretched back, turning white with the strain, her tendons working hard to give him a deep kiss while trying to close the height distance between them.

While they tongued each other's throats, I went to the couch and held out my hand to Lisa. She let me pull her up.

As if he could feel Lisa's movement behind him, Tom yanked his arm away from Dianne's waist and pulled his face off hers. He lunged at me. He did some kind of move on my arm that made me cry out like an animal with her foot caught in the teeth of a trap. I collapsed on the couch. Tom grabbed Lisa's upper arm, propelled her toward the door, scooped his keys out of the bowl on the narrow shelf beside the door, and went out. Lisa didn't pull away or try to resist, tripping and stumbling alongside him as if he had every right in the world to drag her out of her home.

"Stop him," I said.

Dianne looked at me. Her face was flushed, her eyes watering as if the depth of the kiss had moved her to tears. "Calm down."

"What's wrong with him?"

"He's very sensitive."

"Bullshit. Where's he taking her?" I said.

Dianne shrugged.

"Well text him. Or go find them. Do something."

"Let them settle it."

"He treated her like a piece of shit. She was trying to make breakfast and he started waving his cock in her face."

Dianne laughed. "Really?"

I grabbed my keys out of the bowl and threw open the door. My feet were bare and I was wearing running shorts and a tank top. It was cool outside, but not enough to make me go back for a sweatshirt. I ran down the stairs and across the small garden in front of our apartment. The grass was wet, forcing me into a slide as if I'd run onto a frozen pond. I glided to the edge and kept running. When I reached the carport, Tom's car was gone. There was a puddle of vomit near the parking space he used. I turned away.

16

Aptos

About fifteen minutes after I locked myself in my room to escape Noreen's despair over her failure to gain entrance to Jared's bed, I heard her door open and close. The wind had died to a soft breeze and the branch was no longer knocking.

I brushed my hair, peeked in the too-low mirror, and rubbed brown pencil around the edges of my eyelashes to make my eyes deeper and darker. Gripping eyes, I've been told. Bewitching.

I yanked off my tank top and jeans, put on a ballet-type black skirt and an off the shoulder black top. I bent over and ran my fingers through my hair, then straightened and flipped it back so it fanned out across my shoulders and fell over my collarbone in front. I pushed my bangs to the side.

Carefully turning the doorknob, holding it tightly so it didn't click, I opened the door a few inches. The tiny hallway where all of our rooms ran into each other was dark. I stepped out and closed my door, releasing the knob without making a sound.

The danger of mixing business and sex obviously didn't apply to me. I was just another renter living five or six steps away from a very good looking guy. At the same time, opening his door was potential housing suicide. This was nothing like the tangled roommate relationships I'd had with Randy and Dianne, although I didn't pause to think how it was different. Maybe it wasn't that different. If Noreen found out, I was dead. But there was something about white wine, followed quickly by a martini, alongside the frustration of sitting in the sun with a guy I was drawn to and doing nothing about it all afternoon, not to mention his very seductive way of getting my attention by keeping his identity a mystery, that had my body amped up. When I decide I want something, I'm not very good at remaining patient.

I brushed my fingertips on Jared's door and whispered, "It's Alexandra."

Speaking was a risk. For all I knew, Noreen was pressed up against her door, believing with all her mad reasoning that I'd had drinks with him, waiting for me to show my true colors. It was equally possible she was curled up under her covers, crying and plotting her next move.

Jared opened his door and I stepped inside.

The lamp beside his bed was on, but it had a rather low wattage bulb which reflected off his orange and green bedspread, giving the room a warm glow. His dresser top was stripped bare of knickknacks. There was a small rug near the far corner of the room. In the center of the rug was a round, thick meditation pillow. In the opposite corner he had a narrow shoulder-high bookshelf filled to capacity, and on top of the case was an unlit dark green candle. There was indeed no mirror in the room. I thought about asking what was up with his vandalism in the bathroom, but there was time for that later. I wanted his body, not an explanation of his bizarre attempt to defang his vanity.

I pulled off my shirt and he did the same.

He put his arms around my waist and pulled me to him, every inch of our skin touching. I tried to remember how long it had been since I'd had sex. I couldn't pinpoint the last time, meaning it had been far too long. He kissed me, long and deep. It felt as if his tongue reached to the center of me, stirring up a warm puddle that swam between my hips and legs. We kissed until I thought the ache inside was going to split me in two.

Finally, he took my breasts in his hands, stroking them and rubbing my nipples, proving the earlier ache had been nothing.

After that, we went fast. I yanked off my skirt and thong while he stripped off his jeans. Then, he lifted me in his arms and placed me on the bed. If this was what Buddhism did to a guy, made him treat a woman as if he was presenting her as an offering, it might be a philosophy worth looking into.

When he moved on top of me and put himself inside, I stopped thinking. I came twice, maybe more. It all ran together in a series of swelling, crashing waves as I tried not to make a sound loud enough to hit Noreen's vigilant ears.

Exhausted and limp, we slipped under the covers. I propped myself up on my elbow. I absolutely could not fall asleep in his arms. I'm a sound sleeper and the likely outcome would be falling unconscious and sleeping until after Noreen was awake.

We put our faces close to each other, noses touching.

"You didn't seem surprised to see me," I whispered.

He brushed his lips against mine as if he was speaking into my mouth. "I knew it was only a matter of time."

"You did not," I said.

"I hoped."

"That's entirely different."

"I felt a connection."

"Funny, that's what Noreen thinks about you."

"Can you get her to back off?" he said.

"Already tried and failed."

He closed his eyes and flopped his head down on the pillow. Then he moved to make room for me to share. I shook my head and remained propped up.

"Lie down," he said, pulling gently on my neck.

"If I fall asleep, I might not wake up."

"Ever?"

I laughed, slightly above a whisper. He put his hand over my mouth. We looked at each other with laughter in our eyes.

I sat up. "I need to go back to my room."

"Aww." He put his hand on the back of my neck again and rubbed gently. He moved his fingers through my hair, slowly so they wouldn't get caught in the tangles. "You are so beautiful."

I smiled. "Thank you. So are you."

He smiled and blushed slightly.

I slid out from under the covers.

"Please don't," he said.

"I have to. She'll kill me if she finds me in here."

"We should kill *her*." He winked.

I shivered. "That's not very Buddhist. You almost sound serious."

"Of course I'm not, but she's driving me insane."

"I thought that was the point of your practice."

"It's certainly testing me. But if it doesn't stop, I need to find a new place to live. I feel like a prisoner in my room, or that I can never come home."

"There must be a way to get the message through to her," I said. "Although like I said, I've tried several times and it seems she can't even hear me."

"Thanks for going to bat for me," he said.

"No problem. But it's not working."

"So we kill her. Take the house for us."

I laughed. "When I was in college, we had a roommate that was gouging us on rent. We were stuck there because there was nothing available mid-year."

"The rent here is fair," he said.

"I know, but the point is, we ended up playing a game, two of my roommates and me, where we thought up ways to kill her. Just as a game, when we were getting stoned."

"Sounds fun." He sat up. He sounded like he thought it might be more sick than fun. His mouth in the golden lamplight had taken on a shape of uncertainty. "I was kidding, you know."

Part of me wanted to mess with his head and play up our *how-can-we-kill-Dianne* game, but I didn't want him to dismiss me as a sicko. I wanted an open door to return to his room when I felt the need. Many men are happy with that type of arrangement — a drop in partner for sex — but I wondered now whether Jared was formed from a different mold. The fact that he wanted me to stay and sleep suggested he thought we were going to transform into a couple. Nothing was further from reality.

I crawled around on the floor picking up my clothes. "I can't find my thong."

"Then you'll have to stay."

I laughed softly. "Not happening. I have plenty more." I pulled on my skirt and let my loose top fall over my head and arms. Everything was hanging slightly crooked from my body, but I only had a few steps back to privacy.

As I bent over to kiss him, he put his arms around my back and forced my knees to bend, pulling my upper body on top of his. "Stay."

"Do you want her to kill us?"

"No one is killing anyone," he whispered. "This will show her she's on a futile mission."

"What do you mean?"

"When she sees we're together, she'll accept reality."

"We aren't together. Not in that way," I said.

"After what just happened between us? After blowing every nerve ending in my body? That was like a spiritual awakening."

If he thought this was the best sex ever, he'd had a somewhat limited experience. It was good, I felt very fine. He'd turned my body into putty, but I'd been pure desire, the deprivation of weeks, months without relief. An afternoon basking in the sun under the gaze of a nameless man.

Buddhism had taken a back seat. He looked at me, his eyes full of a different kind of need, a little scared, maybe. Of course, who really knows what's in anyone's eyes. We imagine we're seeing things, seeing what we want to see, or hope to see. When really, they're just eyes. They aren't saying a word.

He sat up. "What are you thinking?"

"Nothing, except I need to get back to my room."

"She's asleep. Relax. And who cares if she sees you?"

"I do. I'm not in a position to move again quite so soon."

"You can always find another place to live."

Maybe in his world. "Please let go of my hair," I said.

He released his hands from my hair. "I want you."

"Another time."

"When? Or I can come to your room. Or we can meet somewhere…"

I did want him again. I also wanted the guy who talked to me for hours without telling me who he was. "I really need to go." I stood up. I'd meant to kiss him, but bending back down again would prolong it. A quick clean good-bye is the best.

17

Tess asked whether I wanted to meet for drinks. She seemed to be searching for a connection beyond boss and employee, despite the land mines in a personal relationship with a subordinate. The situation wasn't unlike Noreen and Jared, confusing a close business relationship with friendship, turning it into a hybrid where each aspect might stop functioning as it should. I suppose it's lonely at the top, but it can be lonely in other places too — at the bottom and in the middle. All of life is lonely. You're born alone, with no idea what's waiting as you make your way into the unknown. You never remember, except in your dreams, what terrors confronted you in the first years of your life when there was no way to communicate except by screaming your head off. No one knew what you wanted to say with those screams — they simply guessed, made assumptions about physical needs, never considered what fears or desires you might want to express. Those terrors are lost forever in the back corners of our psyches. In the end, you die alone. Even if people surround the bed and hold your hand, you take that last breath and cross over to wherever you're going all by yourself.

We agreed to meet at a place called Henry's at seven-thirty. I liked the symmetry of it — seven-thirty on Mondays for coffee, seven-thirty on a Friday night for drinks. Henry's was my suggestion. I arrived before Tess and sat watching the door, situated at what had become my favorite table after drinking there two other times. The table I liked was on the side of the room, the last in a string of small booths for two. Between the row of booths and the bar was a lounge area furnished with comfortable chairs and sofas. The opposite side of the room had floor to ceiling windows, and was lined with tall tables and stools to show off the patrons' legs to passersby.

With Tess's usual ownership of any room she entered — looked *at*, more than looking *for* — I wasn't aware my location had registered on her radar when she stepped through the doorway. Her clothes were Friday casual, for Tess — skinny jeans, buttery navy blue leather pumps with three-inch heels, a short cream colored jacket that skimmed her hip bones, and a cotton shirt with a stiff collar the identical blue of her jeans. Without appearing to search faces for mine, she crossed the room and slid into the seat across from me. A server appeared immediately — one of the reasons Henry's had so quickly become my preferred bar.

We ordered martinis. I asked for an extra olive, Tess did not. She's obsessive about calories — every single one counts. Twenty-five calories in a pimento-stuffed olive, two or three olives per martini, it adds up, if you're fond of martinis.

Until the drinks came, we talked about the upcoming product announcement. We continued talking about work after the drinks came. We discussed the new format for quarterly business reviews, the tedium of meetings during which a handful of people felt compelled to state the obvious simply to ensure their voices were heard and they were noted as active participants. Cautious, in case a competitor was drinking at a nearby table, we lowered our voices when we discussed the three-quarter sales forecast.

As the alcohol loosened our brains, we started dishing on co-workers. I'd eaten all my olives and was ready for a second drink by the time we exhausted the recent acts of stupidity and career suicide.

Tess moved her glass in a circular motion on the table, suddenly twitchy, looking away from my gaze. "Do you ever think about a different kind of life?" She turned her head and caught our server's eye. She raised two fingers.

"Like what?"

"Something without the regimen. The sameness. I love the adrenaline rush, the pressure, the challenge of getting customers to say *yes*, but still...it's the same, quarter in and quarter out. Lately, I think about doing something wildly different. Traveling around with nothing but a backpack..."

I absolutely could not picture Tess with a backpack, much less flopping down on the floor of a hostel with a bunch of other wanderers.

"Do you ever think about that? Living so that every day is a complete surprise? Living without expectations and having to make yourself into a virtual robot to succeed?"

Our drinks arrived. Tess ordered a side of deep fried artichoke hearts.

When the server left, Tess shrugged. "Or another kind of

life altogether, one with the VP husband and the two cherubs?"

"Who needs that? *You're* the VP." I raised my glass.

She smiled, but it looked forced, or sad. "You never think about doing something crazy? Unconventional?"

"I guess my life is already unconventional."

"Not really." She sipped her drink.

The insult was sharp in my throat. "I had sex with Jared," I said.

She smiled. "I saw that coming fifty miles away."

"Did you? Interesting, because I didn't." That was a lie, but I was annoyed that she considered me predictable. "Things happened, and there we were. Might not be the best for my housing stability, but still…"

"You did it anyway. You're quite the risk taker." She sipped her drink. "*Things happened*, indeed." She laughed softly.

"You took a lot of risks to get where you are so fast."

"Not that kind of risk." She rubbed her nose as if she had a furious itch. She sipped her drink, then rubbed her nose again. "Sometimes I close my eyes and see myself riding a conveyor belt into old age, my clothes no longer looking so awesome, trying too hard because now I'm a scrawny middle-aged woman instead of a slim up-and-coming woman. My hair color obviously fabricated by a salon, the gloss fading along with my estrogen. Soon, my makeup is too heavy on my skin, and…I don't know." She took a long swallow of her drink.

This was not the woman I'd thought I was working for. Was she having some sort of mid-life crisis? She wasn't mid life, but maybe she was an over-achiever in that arena just like she was with her career and fitness accomplishments.

"Maybe I'm depleted because I worked all last weekend," she said. "Maybe I need a vacation."

"You should try one of those wilderness trips where you test your mettle. That would silence all those questioning voices fantasizing about living out of a backpack."

"Unless it's the baby gene ticking, ready to blow," she said.

"Do you want a kid?"

"I never thought I did. But I've had these weird dreams, and you start to think, what if motherhood really is as awesome as they say it is."

"That's a huge risk. No way to verify. And it's not the same for everyone." I sucked an olive off the stick and chewed fast. "For some people, maybe it's awesome, but there are a lot of things that can make it a nightmare. And you're stuck with a kid for life. They take over your house, your job, your sex life, your social life, your brain. They own you. It's like you're swallowed alive."

"That's cynical."

"Just realistic. It's what I've observed. I didn't grow up in the most idyllic circumstances. And now, I have enough trouble taking care of myself without signing up to manage someone else's life for eighteen years. Or more."

"You sound almost...bitter."

"If you want to talk about having babies, I'm the wrong person to ask. Why don't you talk to Eileen? Or Stacy?"

She rolled her eyes.

"Okay. Fair enough," I said.

Eileen and Stacy seemed to believe they were the first women on the planet to give birth, as if their little bundles of flesh came wrapped in skin made of eighteen karat gold. Running into one of them in the coffee shop required superhuman tongue-biting and gag control.

"So why did you sleep with Jared?"

"I told you he's hot."

"You also said you wouldn't go near your roommate. And double that when your other roommate is trying to nail him."

I shrugged.

"Are you two in a relationship now?"

I shook my head. "I just needed to blow off steam. But I think he's assuming we are, so that's a bit of a problem I'll have to deal with."

She smiled. "What if you need to blow off steam again?"

"I'm sure I will. But I don't want to be hanging out together all the time, trying to sneak around behind Noreen's back."

"Maybe you two should get a place together."

"No."

"Why not?"

"I don't want anything like that. I don't want to have to cook for some guy and wash his jeans and prop up his ego."

She laughed. "You are so cold."

"Maybe. Sometimes. I guess I am."

"You say what I'm thinking but would never say."

I knew that. That's why I said those things. Some people are born with a musical ear or a good head for math. Like I said, I was born with the ability to mirror other people back to themselves. It's why people like me. They don't realize they're just falling in love with themselves. Narcissus — enraptured by his reflection in a pond rather than the woman who loved him. It's fun, it makes me feel like I have a purpose, like I fit into the world and provide something people need. It's why Jared was taken with me and why Noreen felt we were best friends. It's the reason Tess had so much respect for me in my job, and now treats me like her closest friend. Maybe I am her closest friend.

"I feel like I'm missing something — the cherubs and the type of husband who takes care of me. I never thought I wanted those things, not really, but I can't stop thinking I might be missing something important. I feel like I *should* want it. Do you know what I mean?"

I nodded. "Absolutely." I picked up a piece of lightly battered artichoke heart, dipped it in the aioli, and took a bite. I could eat those things all night.

"I need a change, that's what I'm saying. And naturally I think that a major aspect of life is drifting out of reach, headed for the rapids, and maybe I should pursue that before it's too late. I got the platinum education, the cherry-on-top job, the scramble to the highest rung of the ladder. Well, almost the highest. I have the satisfaction of helping a company be successful. But it's the same damn thing week in and week out, year in and year out, and one day, I'm going to wake up old. You hear stories of people who live in one location for a year or two, then they go somewhere totally different — I mean totally — Thailand to Germany to Brazil, maybe. Alaska, LA, New York city. They try all kinds of different jobs — one year you're a bartender, the next year work on a co-op farm."

"It sounds very glamorous when you're not doing it. Starting over all the time would get old after a while too. It can be stressful."

"How do you know?"

"I have a good imagination."

"Maybe you don't do it forever," she said.

"You're burned out. When was the last time you took more than a weekend off?"

She lifted her drink to her lips, then returned it to the table. "I guess…three years ago?"

"Are you seeing anyone? Is he antsy for kids?"

"No. That's probably why I haven't had a vacation. No one to share it with me. I haven't been with anyone for almost a year now."

"That's why the wilderness escape is what you need. It would get you out of your head. Find out what you're made of. Rebuild your confidence and feeling of power. You can do horseback camping trips, rainforest treks, rafting. Or take a mule to the bottom of the grand canyon."

"You're way too excited about this." She laughed, but she sounded nervous.

"The fear is what makes it life-changing."

"Are you trying to get me killed?"

"You said you wanted something different. It's a good way to experiment without walking away from your job and everything you've worked for."

She sipped her martini. "So you don't think it's the

biological clock?"

"I really don't know."

She looked at me as if she were trying to see inside my head. Good luck with that.

After a few minutes, she narrowed her eyes. She picked up her glass and took a sip of her drink. "You know, I keep feeling as if I've seen you before."

"I don't think so."

"How would you know? I don't mean that I met you, but I saw your photograph."

I shrugged. There was a little wiggle in the pit of my stomach, but I ate an olive to make it settle down. I had nothing to worry about. Even if she remembered where she'd seen me, I was pretty sure she wasn't one of those *justice-must-be-done* types. Seemed more like an *I-mind-my-own-business* type, unless pushed into it. Of course, that's assuming she'd seen the photos posted online somewhere, and I had no indication they had been. Most likely it was the doppelgänger feeling everyone gets occasionally. It's amazing the subtle qualities that make people *think* someone looks familiar — the sensation has nothing to do with actual physical appearance. It's more of a sixth sense, a gesture or choice of words that strikes a chord from your past. And really, the person you're looking at has no physical resemblance to the person you're thinking of.

"Maybe a vacation. I'll give it some thought." She sat up straighter and tugged the sides of her jacket together as if she could settle her indecision by straightening her clothes. She sipped her drink and was quiet for several seconds that drifted casually at first, then turning into a minute or more. A minute is nothing until you find yourself wondering what's passing through another person's mind, trying to decide if you should move the conversation forward or shove it in another direction.

She licked her lips. "But I'm not really sure a vacation will fix things." She glanced toward the bar and continued talking without looking at me. "I lost my temper with a pissed off customer. I was trying to explain how the extended service contract works. They had a fundamental misunderstanding, but they kept interrupting and talking over me. Steve Montgomery was in the meeting with me, and he really let me have it afterwards. I know he's telling everyone about it, and I know the men are all nodding and mumbling about emotional, irrational women who can't handle angry customers." Her eyes were glassy and she continued to avoid looking at me.

"They'll move on. They always do."

"But they'll remember."

I didn't disagree. She was too smart for patronizing bullshit. They would remember. The question was, could she overcome it?

She turned her face toward me and smiled. "It's not like it's the first time I've had to rip off the *overly emotional female* label. I'll figure it out."

"You will," I said.

We lifted our glasses and tapped the edges. We took, slow, luxurious swallows of cold vodka.

"Well, enough about me. Back to your roommate triangle."

"There's nothing to get back to."

"It's a little dangerous — doing what you did, under your circumstances."

"It'll work itself out."

"What if he tells Noreen you hooked up?"

"I don't think he'd do that."

"You're rather trusting, for someone so cynical." She gave me a ghoulish smile, almost as if she hoped my trust was misplaced. "And someone who was so worried about her lack of housing options."

"If it happens, I'll figure out an alternative. There was no choice. When I want something, I go after it without a lot of analysis."

She stared at me as if she was suddenly a little afraid of me. Maybe I'd said too much. Maybe she'd mirrored myself right back at me, and I'd started feeling all friendly and said too much. Like I said, martinis make me chatty, although usually it takes more than two.

Tess and I had the same issue — failure to control our impulses. But her lack of control, if it damaged her reputation, would bleed into my life. I needed a boss who would fight to the death for me — the confident woman who promised to look into getting me a salary increase long before it was time for annual reviews and the usual three percent. I hoped that woman returned soon.

18

The house was silent when Jared's bare feet touched the cold tile floor at three-fifty a.m. He lit the candle on his bookcase, settled himself on his meditation cushion, wearing nothing but boxer shorts, and spent the next twenty minutes pretending to meditate. His concentration had deteriorated even further, he couldn't inhale without smelling Alexandra's skin. He couldn't close his eyes without seeing her naked body. The only time thoughts of her settled to a simmer was when his stomach wove itself into knots over Noreen.

When he'd suggested to Alexandra that having roommates would help his Buddhist practice, he'd been telling the absolute truth, at the time. She'd seemed simultaneously offended and amused. Now, he couldn't imagine a worse situation than the one he faced. He should talk to the class leader at the meditation center, but he was terrified he'd be advised to find a new place to live. Most of the guides were firmly rooted in the idea that meditation practice required the support of an insulated circle of like-minded seekers. Two woman who knocked on a man's door at night craving sex were not seeking to live on a higher plane of existence.

He uncrossed his legs, stood up, and blew on the candle

flame. It wavered but didn't go out. He blew harder. It leaned to the side, then sprang back up. He felt like spitting on it. He let out a huge puff of air and succeeded in extinguishing the flame while spraying liquid wax across the top of the bookcase.

He put on the clothes he'd laid on the chair the night before so he didn't have to risk waking Noreen by rummaging around in drawers and the closet. He'd taken to showering and shaving at night as well. He would hold his bladder until he got to the coffee shop where he would order tea and catch up with the world on his tablet until the sun rose.

The door creaked as he opened it. He looked into the hallway. All the doors were closed. He went into the great room. The air smelled of something sweet. A single light under the hood of the stove burned in the kitchen. Food sizzled in a pan.

Noreen stepped out of the dark corner by the refrigerator. "You're an early riser," she said.

"I am."

"I made breakfast for you. It's not good to be out doing whatever it is you do all day without sustenance."

Who used the word sustenance? He felt as if he were standing in the kitchen of a homestead in the nineteenth century. "I'm not..."

"Don't tell me you're not hungry. It's called break-*fast*. You're supposed to break the fast of the night. It's not healthy to skip the first meal of the day and expect to function on a few cups of tea."

"I don't eat breakfast. I never have. It's not that unusual. I think breakfast was a custom that developed when people performed hard physical labor all day."

"Yoga requires a lot of exertion."

"Please don't assume you know what I need. And please stop cooking meals that I don't want."

"It smells so good. How can you resist?" She grinned. "Tofu bacon — I didn't even know such a thing existed. You're teaching me so much." She broadened her grin. "I mixed it with some kwinoah, and…"

"Keenwah."

"What?"

"It's pronounced keenwah, not kwinoah."

"See, teaching me again." She tipped her head to the side and lifted her hair back behind her shoulder with her left hand. "I added shredded carrots. It's not a breakfast food, but I thought the orange looked pretty, and some green onions, and mushrooms and avocado."

It sounded delicious, but he couldn't. He couldn't let her insert herself into his life with niceness. She seemed to think persistence was the key to taking ownership of his heart.

She came around the counter and took hold of his wrist. He pulled his arm away but she tightened her grip until it felt as if thick ropes bound his wrist to hers. "You hurt my feelings when you didn't let me into your room," she said softly. Her eyes were wider than usual, the white visible around the pale gray iris.

"I was trying to sleep."

"I'm crazy about you." She tightened her grip.

He glared at her.

"Why won't you give me a chance?"

The smell of burning food, probably tofu bacon, wafted toward them. The food sizzling in the pan now gave off a dry, crackling sound.

"You better get that pan off the stove."

Her eyes filled with tears. "My breakfast is burned."

He tugged his arm.

Instead of releasing him, she turned and walked to the stove, forcing him to stumble along behind her.

"Please let go of me."

"I want to talk to you."

"So you're going to take me prisoner? You can't force someone to talk to you."

"Or to like you," she whimpered. "You don't even know me and you've decided you don't like me."

"It's not that."

She turned the flame off and lifted the pan onto a cold burner. His left forearm and elbow felt slightly numb. She was cutting off the circulation.

"What is it then?" she said.

"I don't want a relationship right now." It was a mistake to lie. Once Noreen found out that he and Alexandra were together, she might lose it entirely. But telling her the truth wouldn't go well, and he wasn't in the mood. The sun wasn't even up. He'd let things progress with Alexandra and then they could find another place to live. Noreen could figure it out after the fact.

"Is it because I'm not Buddhist?"

He laughed.

"It's hard for me to like a fat bald guy when I have Jesus."

"That's not it at all."

"Then there *is* something!" She cried out as if she'd discovered he was hiding gems inside his meditation cushion. "Why won't you tell me? I'd be willing to try Buddhism. I'm cooking without meat. And animal products."

"I don't need you cooking for me."

"Every man wants a woman to cook for him."

"Where did you get that idea?"

"That's how it is."

"Noreen. Let go of my wrist. I need to get going."

"I would make you so happy. Have you ever been in love? It's more blissful than yoga or any of that other stuff."

"I don't want a relationship right now." He twisted his arm. Her grip tightened. "You're not making me like you, grabbing me, refusing to let go. I'm going to be late."

"How can you be late at five a.m. in the morning?"

He looked away to hide his smirk. "I just am."

The sizzling in the pan had stopped. From the corner of his eye he saw the tofu bacon, black and withered. The mushrooms were equally dark.

"Why don't you want a woman in your life? That's a little weird, don't you think?"

"I'm fine."

"Is there someone already?"

"Maybe."

She let go of his wrist. "Why didn't you tell me?"

"I don't have to explain my life."

"Well you didn't mention it when we were chatting...the

day you came to look at the place."

He shrugged. He rubbed his wrist bone but the movement irritated the skin and made his fingers feel numb again. "Sorry about your breakfast." He took a few steps back.

"Is it her?"

"What?"

"You didn't have a girlfriend when you moved in here. I can tell. I can sense when a guy is available. And now, you act like you do. Is it Alexandra?"

"I don't want to talk to you about this."

"Is it?" She moved closer. She folded her arms and jutted out her chin. She didn't blink. Her lips were pinched, working hard to prevent the contorted features that came with crying.

He blinked several times. "I want you to leave me alone. Stop cooking for me and stop asking personal questions. If you don't, I'll have to look for another place." He immediately regretted saying it. Until things solidified with Alexandra, he couldn't possibly look for another place. If he left Noreen's bungalow, he might never see Alex again.

19

When Tom took off with Lisa, leaving nothing but the contents of her stomach in a rank puddle, I stood in the carport for several minutes. I thought about getting in my car, but had no idea where he might have gone. Our living situation was tense enough and now he'd escalated it into something potentially violent. It was baffling that he'd suddenly turned on her after mostly ignoring her. The vomit stank of Lisa's terror.

I walked back to the apartment. Randy was slumped on the couch and Dianne's bedroom door was closed. The lake of batter on the carpet was forming a skin.

"Where are they?" Randy said.

I shrugged. "His car's gone." I slumped beside him and propped my feet against the edge of the coffee table.

Randy draped his arm over my shoulders and pulled me close.

He put his hand on my ear, stroking the lobe.

"She threw up in the carport," I said.

"That's not cool."

We sat there, staring at the wall, not talking.

No matter how unjust the financial arrangement, I didn't want our shared housing to blow up in my face. It was clear who wouldn't escape the shrapnel — all three of us would be homeless. Part of me was furious with Lisa. If she hadn't let Tom see how he'd gotten under her skin, he might have stopped his assault on her dignity. It's not that it was her fault, far from it, but guys like that are encouraged when they see weakness or fear. It spurs their need to ensure their victims see how powerful they are. Their enflamed egos won't let them back down. If they do, everyone will understand they're just as afraid — afraid of the beast living inside of them.

About fifteen minutes later, Dianne came out of her bedroom wearing a black bikini, carrying a beach towel and sunscreen. "Where's Tom?"

Randy lifted his arm off my shoulders. "He took off with Lisa."

She looked at the slop on the carpet. "Who's going to clean this up?"

We stared at her.

"Well it certainly won't be me," she said.

We continued staring at her.

"What did she do to get him all riled up?" Dianne said.

"She didn't do anything," I said. "He's a bully."

"He is not. He's very gentle. A little sensitive, if you want to know the truth. Did she hurt his feelings?"

"How much are you gouging him for?" Randy said.

"It's not gouging and it's none of your business." Dianne dropped her towel on the floor and kicked it out of her way. She put her foot on the edge of the dining table and squirted a long, white ribbon of sunscreen up her shinbone, across her kneecap, and along her thigh. She placed the tube on the table and began rubbing the sunscreen into her skin. The scent of coconut filled the room, a thick, cloying odor that mingled with waffle batter and made the room smell like a candy shop filled with rotting treats.

I dragged my feet off the coffee table and stood up. "Where do you think he took her? She was so scared she puked in the carport."

"That's gross," Dianne said.

"Did he text you?"

Dianne held up her hands, displaying the white cream smeared across her palms. "I can't be checking text messages, dummy."

"Aren't you going to do anything?" I said.

She wiped her hands across her ribs to remove excess lotion and picked up the tube, running a ribbon up her other leg. "What do you expect me to do?"

"He basically kidnapped her."

"Basically?"

Even if Dianne didn't care about Lisa getting bullied, why didn't she care that her boyfriend had gone off somewhere with another woman?

"Why is he doing this?" I said.

"How should I know."

"And you don't care?"

"It sounds like she upset him."

"Exactly the opposite," I said.

"That's your perspective, which we all know is distorted."

"What does that mean?"

She waved her hand in Randy's direction. "Him."

"What?" I walked around the table.

"You had sex with him to try to hurt me," Dianne said. "That's sick."

"No I didn't."

She gave me a look that was supposed to imply she could see through my lies. "Lisa was disrespectful of me. Both of you are. I should have kicked you out ages ago."

"But our money is so sweet."

"I'm just too soft-hearted. I don't want to see people without a place to live."

Behind me, Randy snorted with laughter.

"So you knew he was going to take her somewhere? What's he doing?" I said.

"I really have no idea." Dianne picked up her towel. She left the open tube of sunscreen on the table, grabbed her bag, and went to the door. "I'm going to nap in the sun. All the noise woke me up too early and I'm sleepy." She went out, slamming the door behind her.

I turned and stared at Randy.

He stood up and came around the table. He put his hands on my hips and let his fingers creep under my shirt. He slid his hands up my ribs and over my breasts. He massaged them gently. "Should we try to find Lisa?" he said, not sounding at all like he wanted to look for her.

"I don't know where to start."

We started kissing while he continued holding onto my breasts. My thoughts that I should help Lisa, that I was somehow responsible for her, slipped to the back of my mind and then disappeared altogether. After a while, we went into the bedroom and made love despite our unwashed bodies. We fell asleep and when we woke up an hour later, I was starving. Randy's back was facing me. I kissed his spine and ran my finger down the knobs, which gave me a sudden and obvious craving for ribs. I wriggled up and kissed his neck. "I'm hungry."

He grunted and moved slightly. I wasn't sure if it was a dream grunt or he was answering my question. I tapped his shoulder. "I'm *very* hungry. Should we make something or do you want to grab burgers?"

He turned on his back. "Burgers."

I got up and pulled on my jeans and tank top. I slid into a pair of leather flip-flops, bent over and ran my fingers through my hair, then raised my upper body quickly, flipping my hair over my shoulders and down my back.

"I love it when you do that," he said. He yawned.

I picked up my purse. "Hungry. I'm really hungry." I pulled out my phone. "It's twelve-fifteen."

"I wonder if Tom's back," he said. He got up and dressed, grabbed his wallet, and opened the bedroom door. The apartment was silent. We were greeted with the fighting smells of sunscreen and waffle batter. He wrinkled his nose. He walked to the sliding glass door, opened it, and stepped out onto the balcony. A moment later he came back inside. "Dianne's still out there sunning herself."

"Let's go eat before I pass out."

In the carport, the vomit had attracted several flies. It

looked as if someone had stepped in it. I shuddered and steered a wide path around it.

We ate burgers and drank beer at a place with an outdoor patio. We didn't return to the apartment until close to dinner time. The vomit was still there, hard and dry. Likewise, the waffle batter and the opened tube of sunscreen. The apartment was empty and Dianne wasn't by the pool.

It seemed as if we should do something, but neither of us could figure out what that might be. We took a shower and crawled into bed, made love, and fell asleep.

I dreamt I was looking for Lisa, but the faces of all the women I saw were blurred and I couldn't tell which one was her, if any of them were.

20

Aptos

Jared stayed out until after midnight, practicing yoga in one of the smaller rooms at the Meditation Center and then sitting on his matt, back against the wall, reading an article about global warming. It was ridiculous to be paying for a room but having no place to go — hanging out in coffee shops and the public library and the Meditation Center all day and into the evening. He couldn't even sit on the beach because he was overcome with an irrational fear that Noreen would look over the deck railing, see him, and run down to join him.

This wasn't what he'd planned when he chose this place. It had seemed idyllic, perched on the cliff — a spectacular view, secluded from surrounding homes. It had been weeks since he sat on the deck and gazed mindlessly at the ocean or closed his eyes and listened to the blend of song birds and shore birds, their cries carrying on the breeze. The vegetable garden remained a bed of infertile dirt overrun with rocks. He wanted the pleasure of working in the earth, eating things he'd grown himself, but he wasn't allowed to eat in his own home. Noreen dictated what meals were served, and her effort to modify recipes to suit him didn't matter, she was still in charge.

The house was dark. Both women were in their rooms. He went into his room and closed and locked the door. He turned on the light. Dark flecks of wax dotted the top of his bookcase. He hoped it wouldn't leave discolored spots on the wood when he scraped it off.

The meditation cushion was where he'd left it near the edge of the small rug. His bed was made, slightly rumpled, also as he'd left it, but something felt off — a smell, maybe. He took a deep breath. It had been nearly two weeks since he'd done laundry. Dirty clothes sitting in the basket, the door closed all day, never anyone around to open the window and let in fresh air. He needed to get to that tomorrow. He'd spend the morning at a laundromat rather than risk an encounter with Noreen and an offer to wash and fold his clothes.

The smell seemed more potent, more foul than unwashed clothes. He yanked the blankets off the bed. They looked clean enough and no additional odor wafted up from the sheets. He opened the closet door. The laundry basket sat on one side, everything else was in order. He went to the window, turned the lock, and pushed the window up. The wood frame refused to slide further than a third of the way. It was enough for a cool, damp smelling breeze. Better, but the odor was still there.

He knelt on the floor and looked under the bed. A small lump sat halfway back from the edge of the frame. He pushed the comforter onto the bed so he could get a better look. It was still too dark. He reached into his pocket and pulled out his phone. He turned on the flashlight and directed the beam under the bed.

Tiny eyes stared at him. There was a dead animal — a rat? It was tangled in a piece of pink fabric. Alexandra's missing thong. He'd forgotten it was there. He backed away and stood up. He went to the closet and pulled a shirt off a wire hanger. He untwisted the neck of the hanger and straightened it. He knelt on the floor, his phone beside him. The beam pointed at the ceiling but cast enough light under the bed for him to see. He grabbed the poor dead thing with the hook and pulled it toward him. It was a smallish dark gray rat. He shuddered.

In the kitchen he found a box of plastic bags. He yanked one out and returned to his room. He used the hanger to nudge the corpse into the bag, taking the thong with it, and sealed the edge, pressing to make sure the plastic strip secured along the entire length.

Outside, he buried it in the garbage can beneath several lumpy plastic trash bags so Noreen wouldn't see the pink thong wrapped around the dead animal.

After he'd cleaned beneath the bed with disinfectant, he climbed into it fully clothed, exhausted. He closed his eyes. The room still felt different. Had a rodent changed the atmosphere so dramatically that he was left feeling someone had entered and distorted his space? The staring eyes of the rat, filmy with days of death, flickered through his mind. Was it possible Noreen had been in his room? Had she left the corpse for him to find? He wasn't sure why he thought such a thing, but the more he pictured the rat, the more he felt it hadn't just dropped dead on Alexandra's thong. He turned on his side and tried to quiet his thoughts but it took a long time for sleep to consume his mind.

21

Unlike any other unattached guy on the entire planet, Jared had informed me he wasn't *into* one night stands. He believed we were now in a relationship and we needed to be *up front* with Noreen. I wasn't telling Noreen anything, and I had to figure out how to paint a realistic picture for him.

So far, we'd had three conversations on the topic. The first two were teasing, joking around, with an undercurrent of *what is wrong with you?* coming from Jared. Next, he asked me out to dinner and I declined. He asked me out for coffee. I declined. He came up behind me when I was brushing my teeth, the bathroom door not fully closed. He put his mouth close to my ear so I could feel his breath inside my head. When I shivered, he invited me to go away overnight. I spit out toothpaste, and declined.

The third and most recent conversation had scared me a little. I got out of my car, hit the remote to lock it, and started toward the side door of my office building.

"Alexandra!"

The volume of someone shouting at full force traveled across the parking lot. I turned. Jared was striding across the pavement, weaving between cars, breaking into a jog when he reached unoccupied spaces. The sun was coming up over the top of the building and it hit directly at his eyes. He squinted and slowed his pace. So much for keeping my work life fenced off from my roommates.

He stopped a few feet in front of me. "You keep acting like you're too busy to get together." His expression was sad, hungry for affection, a puppy wanting a ball toss and an ear rub. Those large brown eyes didn't help.

I put one hand on each of his shoulders. "Jared. Pay attention. I don't want a relationship. I told you that. Several times."

"Are you breaking up with me?"

"There's nothing to break up."

"We had mystical sex."

"Yes, we did. That's all."

"There's so much chemistry between us."

I nodded.

"So what's the problem? Are you really that scared of Noreen?"

I shook my head.

"I can see why you would be. That thing with the mirror was a little freaky."

"What thing with the mirror?"

"Scratching it up like that." He shuddered.

"She said you did it."

He put his hand over his brow and squinted, but the sun was no longer hitting his face. It was a squint of confusion. "Why?"

"She said you couldn't look in mirrors. Some Buddhist, excess vanity thing."

"There's no Buddhist *thing* about mirrors."

"She said you were concerned about your temptation to vanity."

He laughed. "I guess she thought we wouldn't talk to each other," he said.

Of course she thought that. She'd threatened me with eviction if I even glanced at him. It never crossed her delusional brain that I might ignore her instructions. Why on earth would she destroy her own mirror? I tried to remember what she'd said about it. The story about Jared's Buddhist beliefs slipped off her tongue with a tasty blend of pity and reverence. Maybe she was just messing with my head, trying to make Jared out to be leaning toward the freaky side, so I'd have extra incentive to stay away from him, or maybe she thought she'd keep me out of the bathroom as much as possible, confined to my room so there was less chance of Jared and I speaking to each other at all.

I grabbed his arm and dragged him around the side of the building into a small garden. It's not the nicest garden, since cars are parked six feet away, but there are a few benches and a short gravel path lined with agapanthus. I sat down. He sat beside me. I glanced at my phone. Seven-forty-five. I had plenty of time, although I wasn't excited about a co-worker observing me having a personal conversation at work.

"Did you ask her what happened to it?" I said.

"No."

"Why not?"

He put his hand on my leg. It felt nice, but I shoved it off.

"Hey."

"I'm at work."

"Not yet," he said.

"It's a proprietary move."

"It didn't mean anything."

It meant everything. It meant he thought we were a team and should tackle the Noreen problem together. It meant he felt he could touch me whenever he pleased. It meant he didn't care that I was at work, that I already looked vulnerable, exposing a piece, no matter how small, of my personal life to my co-workers. It meant he didn't care at all about my career and what kind of reputation I'd built up with my colleagues. It meant he wasn't afraid of me. Touching me like that meant he thought my body belonged to him. A proprietary touch suggests a man knows what you're thinking, that you're in the mood for physical contact, that you need comfort, and a man should never assume he knows what a woman is thinking. Especially me. "You saw a trashed mirror and didn't think to ask her about it?"

"I try to avoid getting into conversations with her. And to be honest, it scared me a little. There was something angry about it."

"You should ask her. Now that you know. Just to see what she says, if she puts it on me."

"I'm not interested in having a conversation with her." He moved closer. "Why are you pushing me away? It doesn't matter why she does anything."

I stood up. I adjusted my skirt so the seams were more perfectly aligned with the sides of my hips. I told him I was late for work. When I reminded him again that I wasn't interested in a relationship, he called out the sad, puppy eyes and asked if there was some other guy in my life. I said no and I wanted to keep it that way. He stroked my lower arm, squeezing it gently. He informed me that everyone needs a mate, it's how the human psyche is structured. I stared and wondered why he thought he knew anything about my psyche, as if we all have the same wires running through our brains. He whimpered that I'd slipped inside of him and taken over his heart, changed its rhythm. I suggested it sounded like an addiction and he should meditate his way out of it.

After a long silence, during which I checked the time again — seven-fifty-five — he nodded and agreed that meditation was always a good suggestion. He moved closer. I smelled his shampoo and saw the hairs of his beard sprouting on his jaw and cheeks, tiny dark needles, threatening to puncture the palm of my hand if I touched them. A piece of crust left over from sleep clung to one of the bottom lashes on his right eye. I wanted to pluck it away, but it would be interpreted as an intimate gesture. He needed to leave. I needed to get to work, not stand in the parking lot with an increasing flow of people, turning their heads as they tried not to look at us. A few slowed their pace in an effort to catch a few words so they could have insight into the drama, a little sip of blood, drawn from someone's heartache to make them feel better as they started the day.

"I guess I can't make you like me," he said.

"I like you."

He glowed, like the dog who's delivered the ball back to his master and received a rub on the head, slobbering with joy that he's been able to please.

"Even more, I like doing what I want when I want. I like not having attachments."

"That's very unusual," he said.

"It is." It looked as if he wasn't going to leave without a virtual shove. "It's time for me to get to work." I grabbed my purse off the bench and walked to the door. I held my pass card in front of the reader. The light turned green and the door clanked as it unlocked. Those doors sound like they're opening an airlock into a vault. The sound is designed to make it clear to the badge-less — they aren't one of the elect.

I didn't look back. Rather than letting the door close on its own, I pulled it into place behind me. It's not that I thought he was inching toward stalker territory, that he'd try to slip in while the compressor was easing the thick, dual pane glass and aluminum back into place, but maybe my animal instinct thought differently. I ached to turn around and check whether he was headed toward his car, but if he was still there, he'd believe I cared about what he was doing. I did not.

Good sex doesn't mean two people should join their lives at every point — eating together, spending weekends watching movies or going to clubs or hanging out, skin grafting together until it's not clear where one person ends and the other person starts. A shivery orgasm or two doesn't mean you should start sharing your families and secrets and money and the history of your lives. After a while, you can't breathe, as if someone is swallowing you and you no longer know which thoughts are your own and which belong to another.

Even though I left him standing in that sad little garden at the edge of the parking lot, he'd managed to attach himself to my thoughts. All I could see when I looked at my computer screen was the scratched bathroom mirror. Thinking about Noreen's ridiculous Buddhist vanity story, I couldn't understand why I'd fallen for it. If you don't want to look in a mirror, don't look. Why had I believed that a guy who was relatively calm and sure of himself, would make a violent assault on someone else's property?

I stood up and went to the window. Half the parking lot was visible from my office. Beyond that was a building leased by another company, and a tiny sliver of the Santa Cruz mountains. Jared's white BMW wasn't immediately obvious, and there was no sign of him anywhere in the lot. It was possible he'd already left while I was walking down the hall and up the stairs to the third floor. Maybe he hadn't lingered at all, accepting the finality of the secured door. But for some reason, I had the feeling he was still out there.

Usually when a woman feels stalked, the guy is a creep, someone who gives off the vibe of terrible self esteem buried below a garbage heap of rage. But that wasn't the case with Jared. He was good looking — I guess that's been mentioned. More than once. He had money, and he wasn't needy or clinging in a pathetic way, the kind of neediness that makes you feel ashamed for the other person. He seemed to be genuinely infatuated with me. It was the sex, of course.

There's no greater aphrodisiac for a man than a woman who wants sex as badly as he does, and doesn't surround it with all kinds of romantic requirements, relationship rules, and ultimatums that *we need to talk*.

It wasn't a new problem.

But now he knew where I worked. He was out there, possibly saying inappropriate things to my co-workers. Worse, he might be asking to be let into the building, creating a story with those creamy brown eyes that would make most women and a number of men cave to his sweetness.

The company can post signs on all the walls and doors, send weekly emails, and require employees to take online security training, but human beings want to trust each other. They don't want to think someone is manipulating them. No one wants to think a young, gorgeous guy is out to steal their laptop or cell phone, or worse, cut their throat. If I closed my eyes, I could see Jared's smile with his perfectly aligned teeth. I could see the sparkle that swims to the surface of those dark brown pools, and the almost imperceptible tilt of his head giving an impression of boyish innocence. Half the women in the building would gladly hold the door open and invite him inside.

There was still no sign of him crossing the parking lot.

I felt something behind me and whirled around. My office was empty, the door half open as it had been when I'd entered. There was no one in the hallway. I walked around the desk and closed the door. There was no lock.

I sat down and spun my chair to face the window, taunting the unlocked door and the sensation that someone was watching me. It was a sunny day. The building was filling with people. Even if Jared was inside, so what? And it wasn't as if he wanted to hurt me. He just wanted me seated across from him at the dinner table every damn day of the week.

22

Mountain View

A week or so after I hung out by the pool with Charlie
Denton, he took me out for a juicy, bloody steak dinner that
left me with a dopamine high. The next day we hung out by
the pool again, and then went back to his condo where he
mixed two martinis. After downing the martinis, we had sex.
Not great sex, but nice. Diversionary. Lying in bed after, he
wanted me to quiz him to help with his bar exam prep, but I
declined. His personality was like sex — diversionary.

We met at the pool again on the Fourth of July. The pool
was mobbed. Charlie brought a six pack of beer, which wasn't
allowed in the pool area, but was acceptable in the grassy
picnic spot adjacent to the pool where there were a few tables
and several large magnolia trees providing thick shade. I
brought a bag of tortilla chips and homemade salsa from the
Mexican place two blocks away. We spread our towels on low
lawn chairs. I was wearing a pink bathing suit that looked
really good next to my nicely developing tan. We sat and
watched all the craziness in the water. We didn't talk much,
just munched chips and drank the icy beer, which was quite
pleasant.

After his third beer, Charlie stood up and pulled his phone out of his pocket. He tapped it and turned it sideways, pointing it at me.

"Don't take my picture," I said.

He laughed.

I sat forward. "I mean it. Don't."

"You're gorgeous. You should be photographed on a daily basis."

"I don't want my picture taken. Put it away. Now."

"Don't be so shy. You look hot. There's no reason to feel insecure." He tapped the screen twice.

I stood up. "I'm not insecure. I don't want my picture taken." I took off my glasses so he could see the hardness in my eyes.

He laughed, moved in close, and tapped the phone several times, taking a series of close-ups before I lunged at him and tried to grab the phone. He held it above his head.

"You're not gonna get my phone."

I moved away. I sat down, picked up my beer, and took a long, slow swallow. I would absolutely get that phone, but I wasn't going to make a game out of it.

He smiled and dropped the phone in his pocket. He sat beside me, leaned over, and bit my earlobe. He put his lips close to my ear. "I won."

I smiled and took another sip of beer. I always win, but he didn't need to know that. He wouldn't believe it anyway.

For the rest of the summer, we mostly hung out by the pool, went out to dinner, and had lots of sex that didn't improve much. I was stuck with him until I could find an opportunity to get that phone. I looked for an opening, but he kept it in his pocket except when we were in bed, and he never fell asleep while I was there. It wasn't urgent, but eventually I had to have it. When you're mostly living under the radar, it's not a good idea if photographs are floating all over the internet, living on smart phones, taking on lives of their own in the cloud. It was bad enough I had to have a photograph taken for my key card at work, and the driver's license I only used in bars.

It might seem contradictory to wear showy swimsuits and give a lot of attention to keeping my body strong and sleek, to pay high-end salon prices for my hair and nails, then get angry when a man tries to take a photograph. But the photograph wasn't the only irritation, or even the most critical problem. The unforgivable aspect of his impromptu photography session was his utter disregard for my wishes. I'd clearly said, *don't take my picture*, and he took my picture. He didn't even hear me. Rather, he heard me and decided what I wanted was unimportant. Would he do the same if I said I didn't want sex? And then he went further, inventing his own explanation for my desires. Insecure my ass. I haven't had an insecure moment in my life. It's a colossal waste of time. What is there to be insecure about? Insecurity means doubting your place in the world, it means measuring yourself against others and coming up lacking. It means believing someone else is somehow better or more important than your own self. Why on earth would anyone think that way? You are what you are.

There was no way he was keeping those photographs of

me. Nothing would stop me from getting his phone. If I couldn't guess his password — he seemed a likely candidate for 1234 — the phone would have to be destroyed. He had no right to possess anything of me that I didn't expressly give him.

As the summer wore on, I learned Charlie didn't have a lot of variety in his conversational topics — the bar exam and complaining about Sylvia were his primary interests. Splashing around in the pool with him was fun, but I was getting tired of hearing about minutiae in California law, and even more tired of his view of Sylvia's supposed *illegal* behavior.

As I was leaving his condo early on a Sunday evening in August, he said, "I'm reporting her to the homeowner's association. She and her crowd of kids will be evicted."

"You can't evict someone from their own home."

"She doesn't own it. She's renting."

I shivered. What kind of man picks on a woman over a bit of excess noise that could be easily blotted out by headphones? And Fall was coming, they wouldn't have the sliding glass door open all the time. Her kids would be in school.

"Don't be a bully."

"I'm not."

"Her husband left her with two kids. She gets up before dawn five days a week and feeds and dresses her kids and herself. She commutes forty minutes and busts her ass all day. So what if she has someone there to help her so she doesn't have to drive the kids to daycare, or rush away from work and jeopardize her job if they get sick? It's hard raising kids, a heroic effort doing it all by yourself. She's mom and dad, she cooks, cleans, does the laundry, pays the bills..."

He shrugged. "Not my problem."

I thought about her brownies and her cute kids. If they could tolerate five people and an infant in a one-bedroom apartment, they deserved respect for making it all work. "You can't report her. She'll have nowhere to go."

"Next meeting. In September."

"You're a jerk," I said.

He laughed. "That's what everyone says about attorneys."

"You're not an attorney."

"Soon."

I said good-bye and went back to my place. I made a martini and lit a cigarette. I sat on the balcony and watched the sun fade across the brown foothills. The sounds of kids shrieking and splashing in the pool filled the air. They sounded like wild animals. I wouldn't let Charlie report Sylvia to the homeowners association. He wanted to send two women into what would likely be transient housing, dismantling six lives because he was too self-righteous to put on a pair of headphones.

23

Aptos

Jared wasn't home, Noreen had been in her room all evening, and the hall light shone dully on the scratched surface of the bathroom mirror, driving me mad with curiosity every time I glanced at it.

I mixed two martinis and placed them on the coffee table. I lit two of Noreen's noxious candles, plugged in my phone, and brought up a new age playlist. I went down the hall and knocked on her door.

"Jared?" Her voice was soft and hopeful.

I clenched my fists and took a deep breath. "It's Alexandra."

"What do you want?"

"I made martinis."

There was silence on the other side of the door. A moment later she opened it. I was hit in the face by the thick, pungent odor of nail polish. "Martinis? That's a nice surprise." She held her hands stretched out, shaking them gently to dry the pale pink polish.

"*Girls'* night?" I smiled and made my eyes wide, my gaze vulnerable, as if I couldn't wait to sit beside her, sharing secrets and getting tipsy.

"How sweet. I've missed our friendly dinners."

I frowned gently and looked down at my feet. She could read my saddened expression as being equally regretful, without any need to add words to the lie. I looked back up at her. "They're nice and chilled, we shouldn't let them sit."

"Let me change." She was wearing pink sweat pants and a pink and blue flowered bathing suit top. She flapped her hands and looked anxiously at the glossy polish.

"You'll wreck your nails." I didn't see why she needed to change her clothes. It wasn't a party, just a drink in the living room.

"It's cold out there."

"The drink will warm you."

"Not really. Can you put a quilt over my shoulders after I sit down? And can you bring my phone?"

"Sure."

She followed me to the living room and settled on the couch. She pulled her lower legs onto the cushion, crossing them at the ankles. I tugged a small white and green quilt off the back of the couch, laid it across her shoulders, stuck the phone beside her leg, and handed the drink to her.

I sat beside her, picked up my glass, and took a sip.

"Aren't we going to toast?"

"What for?"

"The renewal of our friendship."

"Okay." I took another sip to downplay the phony toast, then touched my glass to the edge of hers.

"Sometimes, you're not very nice," she said.

"That's true."

"You should try harder."

I took a few more sips of my drink. She stared at me over the top of her glass, waiting for me to   promise I'd get to work on altering my personality. The quilt slid off her shoulder and the bathing suit strap followed it.

"Oh, can you fix me?"

"Come on, Noreen. I'm not your personal assistant."

"You're the one who made drinks without checking whether it was a convenient time for me."

I pulled the quilt over her shoulder. As I moved away, her drink splashed on the back of her hand. Fortunately, none got on her sticky nails or she probably would have asked me to touch up the polish.

"My strap. It's bugging me."

"Enjoy your drink and you'll forget about all your little discomforts."

Her phone chimed. She glanced at the screen and took several rapid sips of her drink. She moved her leg to cover the phone. It chimed a second time.

"Do you need to answer that?"

She shook her head. Her expression was somber, her eyes slightly glassy.

"Are you okay?"

She stared at the gently swaying candle flames.

"Who's texting you?"

"It's…" She lifted the glass to her mouth and drank some more. "It's my brother."

"You look upset."

"We haven't spoken in a long time. That's all. Never

mind." She turned toward me and smiled. Her stretched lips looked parched despite the recent contact with vodka and vermouth.

I put my glass on the table. "So...I wanted to ask you — why did you tell me Jared destroyed the bathroom mirror?"

"Because he..."

"He didn't do it."

"He's lying."

I don't know what I expected, but it wasn't that. "I don't think he is." I stood up and carried my drink across the room. I stood by the candle and lifted the glass close to my face, breathing in the cleansing aroma of alcohol to blot out the sweet gardenia scent wafting from the candles.

"How would you know?"

There wasn't any way to know. There's no way to ever know with absolute certainty who is telling the truth, a partial truth, or an outright lie. We all have our own truths. We filter the truthful things we say through wishful thinking and faulty memory and ego and manipulation. In fact, it could be argued there is no such thing as pure truth. Still, there was no reason for him to lie about it. At the same time, there was no sensible reason for her to destroy a piece of her home. The only indisputable truth was that the mirror was so badly scratched it was unusable.

"I asked you not to talk to him about it," she said.

"That's ridiculous."

"Your loyalty is deficient."

"I wasn't aware I owed you loyalty along with the rent."

"I thought we'd be friends. We live together. Our

bedroom doors are ten feet from each other. We eat the same food and breathe the same air. We should be taking care of each other."

Maybe we were all using each other. Jared was using us to enhance his spiritual practice, I was using them as a stopgap until I could find a more suitable home. And Noreen was using us to create a makeshift family. Her original family fractured abruptly, and the only love affair she'd ever experienced had been sheered off even more suddenly. Noreen was a lost lamb, wandering around looking for her flock. But she picked the wrong person. Two wrong people. Jared wanted to stay further away from her than I did. For all her list of shared housing rules, she hadn't mentioned that she wanted our companionship and loyalty and access to our souls. I shivered and the candle flickered in response to the ripple of disgust that ran through my body. "I know you destroyed the mirror. I don't understand why you'd make up a lame story like that."

"Why do you believe him and not me?"

It was a good question. Was it his puppy brown eyes? Did I believe him because he was male and our whole culture is geared toward expecting men to be guileless and women cunning and manipulative and false? It's commonly believed that most men don't have hidden agendas and secrets. Most men will tell you *what you see is what you get. I'm a simple guy with simple needs.* Of course there are the big headline scandals erupting out of men who keep dangerous secrets, but not the average guy. The guys who grab headlines are sociopaths and megalomaniacs who think they can have whatever they want.

Did I believe Jared because he was good looking? Did I not believe Noreen because she was a touch homely and her expression was a permanent blend of fear and need? And part of me wondered why I cared. All I wanted was a new mirror, it didn't really matter who trashed it or why.

I lose patience when I'm expected to accept blatant lies. If you're going to lie, at least be clever about it. Clearly she was the liar because if she were telling the truth, and she had any shred of normality, she would have made Jared pay for the mirror. If she worried that confronting him and demanding payment might dampen his desire for her, she would have replaced it herself. She would not have hung a useless, too low mirror in my bedroom. No one styles their hair or puts on makeup in the bedroom. Maybe they did in the last century, when women had huge vanity tables with mirrors, and they perched on delicate chairs with puffy pink cushions and frothy skirts to cover the chair legs, admiring themselves as they powdered and painted. But not now.

I returned to the couch. "Why are you going out of your way to make Jared look absurd instead of simply telling me why you trashed it? And replacing it?"

"If I could trust you, if I felt you were a true friend, I might tell you. But you're one of those women who bonds with men instead of being loyal to your girlfriends. I know your type. You think nothing of betraying my friendship by telling my secrets to him."

I stretched out my legs and put my feet on the coffee table. I leaned my head back and closed my eyes. After a few minutes of silence, feeling her eyes on my face, expecting something from me that I couldn't discern, I moved my legs and sat forward. I finished my martini in one swallow. "If you want something to be a secret, you have to tell me. And I really no longer care why you destroyed the mirror. But I rented a room with access to a functioning bathroom. I want it replaced." I stood up and carried the empty glass to the kitchen. I left it on the counter and started toward the hallway.

"Wait."

I stopped. I crossed my arms and leaned against the corner of the wall.

"Can I trust you to keep my feelings just between us?"

"Yes."

She looked so pleased, I wondered if she really believed it was that simple. Tell someone your thought is a secret and extract the words you want to hear and all is good. It's incomprehensible to me how foolishly trusting people can be.

"You really don't know, do you," she said.

I raised my eyebrows slightly.

"You have no idea why I would do that?"

I waited.

She picked up her glass and stared into it. Without moving her gaze away from the dancing liquid, she started talking in a low voice. "I see how he looks at you. I'm perfectly aware how much prettier you are. It's not fair."

"Men care about more than a pretty face."

"And you think mine is dull."

"It doesn't matter what I think."

"So you do think it's dull?"

"You're not bad looking."

She put her glass down and wiped her eyes. "I walk by the bathroom and see you looking in the mirror. You're happy, smiling. You can go without any makeup, or plaster it on. You look great either way. You don't have to try and fail every day to make yourself look better. You never even consider whether guys will be attracted to you, because you know they are."

"You have a distorted perspective. Maybe it's from looking at a damaged mirror."

She didn't laugh.

"I saw you putting on mascara," she said. "Smiling at yourself. I could tell, the way you flicked the brush around, it was just something to do. You didn't need it. You knew you looked good."

"Okay."

She finished her drink and took the olive out of the glass. She popped it in her mouth and held it there for a moment before she chewed. "Anyway. You left for work. I'd been chopping carrots for the stew and I went into the bathroom. The mirror was a little steamy and it seemed like your face was still there, smiling at me, looking superior. I went a little nuts with the knife."

Even though I'd seen the evidence, thinking of the frenzied knife scraping across the mirrored glass was unnerving. I uncrossed my arms. "News flash, Noreen. We aren't competing."

"Yes we are."

I shrugged and walked around the corner. I went into my

room and closed the door. I stuffed earbuds into my ears, and tapped over to my Rachmaninoff play list. I clicked up the volume until I felt the piano inside my head, chords crashing against my skull, drowning out crazy. I kept my eyes open so I didn't form an image of her taking that carving knife to my face.

24

Running in the fog was a pleasure I hadn't experienced before I moved to Aptos. It makes the world feel silent. No one can see anything but a shadow moving through the white. It was rare when fog that low and thick came off the beach and into the streets where I ran, but when it happened, I took a longer than average course — at least seven miles, sometimes ten. The feeling of disappearing into the whiteness was an added exhilaration on top of the run itself, which consumed every part of my body, transporting me to another dimension.

It was mostly the silence I liked.

Fog makes some people anxious. They freak out that the low visibility makes it dangerous to drive, and walking or running is deemed even less safe. Cars reveal themselves to each other with headlights, while a small body, even in reflective clothing, disappears. The whole point is the lack of visibility. It feels like running in an alternate reality. The houses fade into nothing and it's just you and the pavement. Running in the fog is like having the entire world to myself — the streets belong to me, casual observers glancing out their windows are unlikely to see me, and if they do, I'm just a shadow moving past. Fog mutes the sound of my footsteps. My breathing fills my head as if I'm wrapped in a cocoon. It's quite a trip.

In honor of the fog, I didn't wear one of my usual neon outfits. I wore a white sports bra, a thin white hoodie that would be removed the minute I was warmed up, and white running shorts with black and white shoes. I put on the Chopin playlist and strapped my phone to my upper arm. I tied my hair in a ponytail and drank half a glass of water. I don't drink water when I run. A lot of runners do, but I don't like the extra weight, and I don't like the change in pace required to pop open a bottle and swallow water without splashing it all over my face.

I started down Seacliff Drive, past the houses facing the ocean. Each time my foot hit the pavement, the impact shot up through the bones in my leg. It's commonly believed this isn't good for your body longer term because joints deteriorate and injuries start to take over your life. But the body exists to move — to dance, fuck, walk, climb, run. My joints are just fine. I don't always run on concrete sidewalks and I think my body is durable and flexible enough to handle the impact on an occasional basis. Sitting in a chair for hours at a time turns your joints into rusty hinges, eventually immobilizing them. Running on a hard surface can't do any worse.

Fog pressed against my face and drifted in through my nostrils with my long, easy breaths. As I increased my pace, it became something solid, filling my lungs, drifting softly inside of me. I was part of the fog, wrapped up in its damp blanket while it stroked the inside of my body.

About two miles into it, as I crossed the small bridge

leading to the path that a quarter mile later branches off to a road with a hairpin turn, winding up toward the cliffs again, I felt a car twenty or thirty feet behind me. I hadn't heard it approach, but the speed was matching my own. I ran faster. The car mirrored the increase in speed. I slowed. I wasn't going to turn and let the driver know he had power over my sense of tranquility, my thoughts. He already had it, but he didn't know it, tapping the power right back onto my side of the table.

The engine revved and the car pulled ahead of me — a pewter Boxster. Seeing it wasn't surprising. I'd seen him multiple times, cruising by the bungalow, driving up the hill from the beach, parked at the top of the cliff staring out at the ocean with music thumping through closed windows. He was, without much subtlety, watching the house. But his timing was always off. As far as I knew, he never made his forays through the neighborhood when Noreen was the only one home.

I heard the window slide down.

"Hey."

I lifted my hand in a wave and kept running.

"Can you stop for a minute?"

"I'm running."

"I can see that. I wanted to ask you a question."

I stopped abruptly, turned, and put my hands on my hips.

"I went by the house, but there's a white BMW in the driveway. Does Noreen have company?"

"The car owner lives there."

He nodded. "Okay. I really was hoping to catch her alone.

Maybe you could help me with that."

"Why would I do that? I have no idea who you are or what you want."

"A long lost relative. Wanting to surprise her."

It slipped out easily enough, and seemed plausible, but if it was that simple, he would have mentioned it when I first met him, if you can call it a meeting when no names are exchanged. "How would I help you?"

"I could give you my number and you can text me when she's there by herself."

"If I'm not there, I'm not going to know for certain when she's by herself."

He rubbed his forehead, pushing his hair to the side of his face.

"Your behavior could be interpreted as creepy," I said.

"Am I creeping you out?"

"No."

"Then why did you say that?"

"Just telling you how it might look to someone who isn't me."

He laughed. "Do you want to go get coffee with me? We can figure it out, how I can surprise Noreen and not creep anyone out."

"I'm running."

"Not any more."

I began jogging in place. His gaze immediately moved below my face. I changed the jog to a straddle hop from side to side. His eyes remained locked in place and he smiled just a bit.

"If she hasn't seen you in a while," I said, "Why don't you just text or call? Isn't that a surprise enough?"

"I want to see the look on her face."

I nodded, keeping the side to side hop going. "It looks like you're SOL."

He moved his gaze back to my face. "You're a very intriguing person."

I nodded.

"You're agreeing with me?"

I shrugged.

"Why no coffee?"

"You're a complete stranger."

"Yet you sat in your yard and talked to me. And now you're standing here talking. Didn't you mother tell you not to talk to strangers?"

"No."

He smirked. "Now what?"

"Now nothing."

"I think you like talking to me," he said.

I smiled.

"Can you stop jumping around? What do I have to do to get you to have coffee with me?"

"Tell me your name, or tell me how you're related to Noreen, or get out of the car and kiss me."

He steered the car close to the curb, shut off the engine, opened the door, and climbed out.

"So how are you related?"

"I liked the last option best," he said.

Of course he did. I was fond of it myself. It really didn't

matter what his name was. He didn't know mine either. Flirting with someone, relative or not, from Noreen's world was dangerous. But what fun is life without danger? It's important to stir up the animal instinct, stay in the center of life. Danger makes me feel alive, in most cases. Not always. Not water, the most dangerous force of all. Or maybe kissing is the most dangerous force since he was moving toward me and my heart pounded as if I were nearing the end of a sprint after a seven-mile run. Blood pushed against my skin, making the fog steam around me as if my body heat might burn away the thick white clouds before the sun did.

It was a strange situation. Jared was so much better looking. This guy wasn't hot, but he was sexy in a rock star kind of way — thin, with a funky haircut and a bony face and a seductive way of moving. He had longish fingernails and he was dragging the nail of his index finger along my cheek. I shivered.

"You don't worry about kissing a stranger on a public street?" he said.

"No."

He took my chin and turned my face up toward the blank sky. He held it tightly so that I felt his control but it didn't hurt. He left his other arm hanging limply by his side. There was space between us, filled with fog, nothing touching but his fingers on my jaw and now, our lips brushing against each other, the pressure increasing ever so slightly and incredibly slowly. When his tongue slid into my mouth, every one of my organs slid down toward the pavement and I thought for a moment my bones might follow.

We kissed for several long, timeless minutes. Our eyes were closed. The fog smelled clean and seemed to grow warmer as it pressed against our skin and hair, leaving a thin covering of moisture.

He let go of my jaw before he released my lips. He stepped back. I looked at him. His eyes remained closed.

"Well," he said. His eyes were still closed.

"Yes, well," I said.

I bent over and touched my toes, stretching out my legs and back, readying them to continue my run. When I straightened, he was looking at me.

"I'd like to do that again sometime," he said.

I smiled. He held my gaze for a very long time.

I turned and began a loose, easy jog. I rounded the corner and still hadn't heard his car start up. Not knowing his name was to my liking after all. It's like going to a masked ball, flirting with a man whose face is hidden. His mouth moves and takes on greater importance because only the color of his eyes are revealed, not the shape or the creases of skin that indicate expression. The structure of his nose is concealed and there's no way to know if he's handsome or hideously deformed in the parts of his face that are covered. The connection is on another level, cutting past the usual ways of assuring trust. In fact, there is no trust.

Hiding what's normally revealed suggested we could satisfy physical needs rather than social. It suggested there wouldn't be any obligations.

Over the years, I've received a certain amount of criticism for my attitude toward sex. I've been told I'm like a guy, a not-very-nice guy. I've been told I'm undermining feminist advancements, when in truth, I'm the ultimate feminist. I've been called a slut and a ho' and told I'm full of self loathing. I've been accused of *stealing* men who belong to someone else, and of creating an atmosphere that allows guys to skate around commitment. People have said I'm going to end up diseased and alone and unwanted. As if ending up alone is the worst thing that can happen to a woman, seemingly oblivious to the fact that the majority of the human race is alone at the end. You don't get to die drinking tea with your BFFs or watching a sunset with your soul mate.

I don't care if people want to paste a label on my back. Men get to enjoy sex without being called ugly names and told their behavior has a far reaching societal impact. I like the almost sweet taste of rare steak and the rich creamy texture of potato salad. I like Indian food and Chinese food and pasta and Mexican food. I like pizza and chocolate ice cream. I adore the cold silky taste of martinis made with top shelf vodka and the salty alcohol-soaked olives. I like classical music and old movies. I like running until my body is bathed in a sheet of sweat, and training my muscles until they turn to pudding. I like smoking an occasional cigarette or two. I like dancing to music so loud all I can hear is the thud inside my head and my body moves without my conscious direction. I like sex in exactly the same way. Simply because two bodies are drawn to each other doesn't mean they should buy a house and spend the rest of their lives arguing about how to squeeze the toothpaste and whose turn it is to take out the garbage.

It's made my life quite enjoyable but it has caused problems from time to time. Serious problems.

25

Los Angeles

The morning after Tom dragged Lisa out of the apartment, it felt quieter than usual when I woke. The empty space left by a missing human being, I thought. Randy was deep asleep beside me. I crawled out of bed and pulled on leggings and a football jersey I'd *borrowed* from a boyfriend in high school. I still love that thing. It's red with a huge number one and his name across the back — Masters, Dave Masters.

I went around to Randy's side of the bed to open the window. Lisa was curled up on the floor, wearing the same clothes she'd worn the day before. She was lying on top of her sleeping bag with a quilt wrapped around her shoulders and back. Her bare feet looked pale and tender, poking out beneath the dark blue fabric.

I left the window closed and went into the living room.

The puddle of batter was hard as a chunk of concrete. The sunscreen tube was open on the table. I closed it and tapped the end of the tube on the solidified batter to confirm its consistency. I walked to Dianne's bedroom door and knocked. No answer. I knocked again. I put my ear up to the door, as if I might hear the sounds of them sleeping. I couldn't but it didn't mean they weren't in there. I opened the door. The room was empty, the bed made, the drapes closed.

Leaving the door open, just to piss off Dianne, even though she wasn't there for me to enjoy her aggravated state, I went into the kitchen. I pulled on a pair of white rubber gloves, took a metal spatula out of the drawer, and dragged the trashcan into the living room. I chiseled at the batter. It came off in thick, pliable strips. The smell was sickeningly sweet. When everything that could be removed with the spatula was in the trashcan. I pulled off the gloves. I went into the bedroom and got a pack of cigarettes out of my dresser drawer.

For the next thirty minutes, I sat on the balcony and let cigarette smoke scrape the odor of batter from the inside of my skull. I thought about the vomit in the carport and wondered who would clean that up, or if it would harden and dry, eventually scuffed off by shoe heels as people walked over it, no longer recognizing what it was. It would disintegrate into tiny fragments and get swept up with crumbled leaves and pine needles and dust.

When I felt ready to inhale more batter, I went back inside and got a brush with stiff plastic bristles and a bottle of dish detergent. I began scrubbing at the mess to try to return it to a liquid state where I could wipe up more. A carpet cleaner would be required, but I couldn't keep looking at it and smelling it without trying to remove as much as possible.

An hour later, I was having another cigarette when Randy stumbled onto the balcony. His eyes looked like he'd consumed double the number of beers I remembered.

He flopped in the chair beside me. "What's up? When did Lisa get home?"

I shrugged.

"She's a trip."

"What do you mean?"

"I dunno." He stretched his arms over his head. His ribs jutted out. He left his arms raised, clasping his wrists, and yawned deeply. "I'm gonna get cleaned up and head out."

"Where to?"

"Take the bike for a ride."

"Lisa was…"

He shrugged. "Glad she's okay. Don't need to hear the drama."

I held his gaze.

He made a face, drawing his lips into hard lines. Finally, he looked away.

"The weather's perfect for a ride," I said.

He lowered his arms, nodded, and yawned again.

"Don't fall asleep while you're riding."

"Not to worry." He went inside.

The day before, he'd seemed ready to defend Lisa, but now that I thought about it more, there was something false in the way he'd acted. He wasn't a fan. Lisa's prudish views irritated him, the murder game being a good example. He didn't like her rabid feminism and her aggressive dreams for political office. As if it had anything to do with him. At times, she'd made it clear she considered him sub-human, simply because he was male.

After Randy left, I changed into workout clothes and went for a run. Only three miles, but I pushed myself to sprint for nearly a mile of that. I felt loose again, back in control. Cleansed, as I usually do after a run. I came home, showered, and made a ham and provolone cheese sandwich with tomatoes. I was on the balcony drinking a glass of wine when Lisa appeared in the doorway. Her hair was wet and her face shiny clean. She wore jeans and a faded black t-shirt that Randy loathed. In bold, red lettering it shouted — *Angry. Liberal. Feminist. Killjoy.*

"What happened?" I said.

"Can I have some wine?" Her voice was thin and faint.

I put my glass on the table and stood up. "Anything to eat?" I was still hungry, and my mind ambled to potato chips and dip, or popping frozen egg rolls in the microwave.

"I'm not hungry."

In the kitchen, I poured her a glass of wine, dumped a bag of chips into a bowl, and opened a tub of green onion dip. I gently placed the dip container on top of the chips and carried everything to the balcony.

As I handed her the glass, Lisa looked past me into the living room. "Are they here?"

I shook my head.

"I don't want to see them."

"I understand." I put down the food and closed the glass door. I sat beside her and took a sip of wine. "Are you okay?"

She shook her head.

I went back inside and got the wine bottle and chiller. When I was settled again, I held up my glass. She tapped her glass against mine, but didn't say anything. Her face was expressionless.

"Do you feel like talking about it?" I said.

"Give me a minute," she whispered.

"Did you throw up in the carport?"

She nodded and put down her wine. She leaned forward, holding her stomach. After a minute or two, she sat up and took a long swallow of wine. "I know some men are threatened by strong women, but I had no idea."

She was right, to a point. I'm a strong, self-reliant woman and men are often threatened by me, but I also know how to tone it down. I don't need to announce my opinions on a t-shirt. I keep a lot of thoughts to myself. Some might call me passive-aggressive, even a liar. Of course I lie when it's necessary to keep things going my way, to make sure people are drawn to me and accept me as being like them. Lying is a critical skill, but I never lie to myself. A few white lies wouldn't have hurt Lisa. Most people don't want to know the specifics of every single opinion you hold.

"He said women like me need a dose of reality."

"For what?"

"He's tired of me acting so superior, as if I'm smarter than him. He's sick of hearing about my political ambitions. I'm arrogant for carrying a double major and aiming for law school. He thinks I have an *agenda* to emasculate men. Funny. What hit me was that he even knows what emasculate means." She laughed with a bitter sound.

"And he thought shoving his prick in your face was the solution?"

"It's so much worse." She took several sips of wine. She pulled the bottle out of the chiller and added more wine to her glass.

The sun had moved lower in the sky and was shining directly onto the balcony. Even with my sunglasses, it seared my eyes. I turned my chair so it was behind me. Lisa did the same. I scooped some dip onto a potato chip and ate it, followed by three more.

"When we got to his car, he tied a plastic strap around my wrists. He had it all ready to go in the glove box. That's when I threw up. He shoved me in the car and tied a rag around my head to cover my eyes. We drove around in silence for about twenty minutes. When he stopped the car and took the rag off my face, we were parked in front of a pink house with a yard full of weeds and windows that were missing all the screens. Instead, there were bars covering the windows. Flies were swarming around the front porch as if they were waiting for their next meal."

I felt queasy, knowing her story was going to turn ugly. I ate a few chips without dip to settle my stomach. I finished my wine and refilled my glass.

"It was a brothel of some kind. He knows someone involved with it, although it wasn't clear how. I'm pretty sure it's a human trafficking situation. The women looked scared and not very healthy. Their skin had this stiff quality, and a grayish color. They were so young. About ten of them were sitting in the living room. Four were smoking a joint. They weren't wearing anything but thongs and bras."

She paused for a sip of wine. I joined her. I nudged the

chips toward her but she ignored them.

"I…he…" She drank more wine and put down her glass. She leaned forward. "It's so strange. I feel ashamed. I don't want to tell you what happened. But why do I feel ashamed? I didn't do a damn thing. He's a fucking pervert."

I waited.

Without sitting up, her voice even lower than before, she told me.

While the women watched, their eyes glazed with boredom, Tom tore her shirt. He didn't bother to remove the plastic straps from her wrists. He unhooked her bra and slid it down to her wrists. He took off her shoes and pants and made her stand naked at the edge of the living room. Then he walked around her and commented about the shape of her ass — too soft and kind of droopy. Her breasts weren't symmetrical… If she looked like that now, he couldn't imagine what she'd look like in ten years. He poked her breasts and then told her to take a good look at the women in the living room.

He sat down on a couch between two women and put an arm around each one. They giggled and leaned into him. They slid their hands behind the waist of his jeans. He stared at Lisa, half smiling. He said women were put on the earth to please men. She should read her Bible, or any religious book that fit her inclinations, and wake up to the reality of the world. He said it was BS for women to think they could be attorneys or run for office. The whole reason the world is so screwed up now is because of women taking men's jobs away from them, government quotas that force businesses to hire women. She needed to stop spending so much time studying, and put some of that effort into getting her body in shape, making herself more sexy like the girls sitting in that room. Then she might get a man and then she'd have something worthwhile to contribute to the planet.

Lisa paused for a few minutes. Then she told me about him covering her eyes again and driving her around, half undressed, until two or three in the morning, ranting about everything wrong with the world the whole time. Most of his rants were about how men were being marginalized.

We finished the bottle of wine and opened a second one. I listened while she continued talking, circling back to the beginning of the story, relating more details each time.

I ordered a pizza and we ate it in our bedroom in case Tom or Dianne, or both, came home. We drank wine and Lisa talked. After a while she stopped talking. She sat with her back against the wall, sipping wine. She closed her eyes. I stripped the bed, went down to the laundry room, and threw the sheets in the washing machine. When they were dry and fresh smelling, I made the bed. Lisa curled up in the bed Randy and I usually shared. I pulled the blankets over her and turned out the lights. I sat on the floor with my knees bent, thinking. Someone needed to be punished.

26

Aptos

Like most office workers do when they first arrive at their desks in the morning, I was surfing the web. I'd checked my email and nothing screamed for immediate attention, so I skimmed Twitter, scrolling through the massive string of commentary posted since I'd last visited. I looked at what was trending, and then glanced through Tess's feed to see what she was up to. I hadn't found Twitter accounts for Noreen or Jared, but that didn't mean they weren't out there. You have to know exactly what you're looking for, and people who avoid using their legal names are impossible to locate.

I don't tweet often, I don't need that kind of visibility, but I have a profile, more than one, actually. Every few weeks I send out something innocuous about my latte being too hot or the horrible traffic backup, without revealing city or street information. I could be anywhere in the world, stuck in traffic. Everyone can relate, and I usually get a few likes. The feeling of being trapped, unable to move the vehicle forward and unable to leave the vehicle stirs up a universal emotional reaction to being trapped. The updates I send are enough so the Twitter police don't kick me off the platform. I'm not sure if they actually kick people off for not tweeting, but I've heard it's a possibility.

I like to see what the world has to say, not just the experts and people in power and people with faces everyone knows. Twitter gives me the pulse of the world. Or at least a certain part of the world, the part that feels the need to make their thoughts and opinions and breakfast food public. Even if no one is tweeting back and all you hear is an echo of your own voice.

It's an efficient way to get the news. The stories that float to the top reflect what people are saying in the hallways or in bars. Twitter provides an automatic filter for stuff that won't be useful in casual conversations. A person who has a daily intake of Twitter news is considered well-informed, even if that information comes at the cost of a sound-bite view of the world, at the cost of being subjected to unwanted ranting, from the ugly, angry, bigoted, misogynistic, hysterical fringes. Sometimes I wonder if they're not the fringes, if they're actually the core of the human race, but I prefer to think it's the former.

Tess knocked on my door, catching my eye through the glass panel in the center. She was already pressing down on the handle with her other hand, opening the door while she knocked. I dragged my mouse to the corner of the screen and put the computer to sleep.

She closed the door and sat in the chair facing my desk. Normally, I'm sitting in her much larger office in the supplicant chair facing *her* desk. She looked small, even in the somewhat insubstantial metal frame chair with its ultra thin seat cushion and back. The red fabric is supposed to echo the splashes of red in the corporate artwork to make the offices bright, and stir up subliminal energy and enthusiasm in the employees.

Tess chatted about the weather and her morning workout while she looked down at her phone, scrolling through email, or maybe Twitter. After a detailed description of the *asshole* at the gym, using the treadmill next to the one she was running on — his belief that it was okay to conduct a conference call in the gym because he wasn't talking, so he couldn't annoy. Sure enough, he didn't talk, but every forty seconds — she tracked it on the timer on her treadmill — he said, *uh huh.*

"It started to sound like the drumbeat for keeping his pace. *Uh huh. Uh huh. Uh HUH!* I wanted to shoot him."

I studied her face, waiting for more. People are so casual with that statement. It never seems to make them feel guilty and they fail to recognize how extreme it is. Quite a lot of people say it. Even about their lovers, *I could have shot him. I wanted to shoot her. Shoot me now.* If they paused for even half a minute and pictured themselves pulling out a handgun, aiming it at someone who cut in line or took their parking space, pulling the trigger and watching a man or woman stagger and fall, blood spreading across the ground, would they still say — *I wanted to shoot him?* It's a serious threat. Sure there are hotheads who *do* pull guns in those situations, and it's a horrific tragedy, talked about in shocked, shrill voices on the news. Tweeted — #isthiswhatwehavebecome. People should be more cautious about mentioning a desire to shoot someone.

Tess put her phone in her jacket pocket. Using just her thumb and two fingers, she tugged gently on the lapels of her jacket, adjusting the fit. It didn't need adjusting. It fit as if it had been sewn onto her body.

When she was settled, I mimicked the gesture, tugging gently on my perfectly fitted jacket.

She leaned back as much as the minimalist red chair would allow. "I don't think I told you, a guy was in here looking for you the other day."

"What other day? What guy?" I sat up straighter. I smiled, relaxed my shoulders, softening the hard edges of my words with a look of mild disinterest, modifying the demanding, irritated tone that had echoed around them.

"Tuesday. Last week."

The day Jared had hunted me down in the parking lot. I felt my shoulders relax without effort.

"In the building?" I said.

"Yes. I don't know who let him in. I was so relieved when I found out he knew you. But people are just stupid the way they allow anyone to follow them in the door. Why do they think we have a receptionist? And key cards? And security patrols in the parking lot? They just don't think. It's so easy for a con man to talk his way inside with a lame story and a charming smile."

I nodded. It was very easy. Self-effacing smiles and talking about how stupid you are can take you a lot of places in this world. "I didn't see him," I said.

"I told him he couldn't wander around unescorted. He was on your hallway and I asked if he wanted me to show him to your office. He blushed. It was kind of cute."

And that's how he got in. Did she realize it could just as easily have been her, letting someone in without thinking of potential danger, thrown off her instinct by a luscious smile and blood-infused skin?

"I think he was embarrassed to be bothering you at work. He said he'd see you later. I took him back to the lobby. Very good looking guy."

"Jared."

"Suddenly it's all clear." She smiled and twisted her left earring. She let her hand fall back into her lap. "Anyway…"

"I'm glad you mentioned it. He didn't say anything to me," I said.

"He was embarrassed."

"Maybe."

"It was really very cute."

"Okay. I get it. You sound like a teenage girl."

"There's nothing wrong with noticing a cute guy. And that blush."

I wanted to shoot her.

She took out her phone and held her thumb on the button to unlock the screen. She scrolled through her messages. It seemed as if she was waiting for something, but I couldn't figure out what. Maybe she wanted the scoop on my sex life. "Did you decide to book that wilderness vacation?"

"Still thinking about it."

"What's to think about? It defeats the purpose if you debate it forever. The whole point is to take a risk. Weeks of analysis isn't risk."

She nodded.

"Any more fallout from that awkward customer encounter?" I said.

She shrugged. "If there is, it's not taking place where I can hear it, obviously."

"Taking extended time off might clear it from everyone's memory."

"Or cause it to grow out of control," she said. She smiled, rather coyly, I thought. "So why was he looking for you?"

"How should I know."

"I think he's really into you."

"What's the problem? You can't make up your mind about taking a challenging vacation, you can't get the upper hand with Steve, so you're living vicariously through my sex life? Is that your fetish?" It was a terrible thing to say to a boss. Any career advisor or mentor would have said I was crazy, shooting myself in the foot with a question like that. But I had a sense of Tess. Part of the reason she liked me was because I was similar to her in some ways, and I scared her in others. She wasn't going to get offended.

She laughed. "Maybe I am. Give me more details."

"There's nothing to give."

"He has it bad for you. Don't be cruel to him."

"I'm not."

"He seems like a sweet guy."

"He is." Sweetness was becoming a theme.

"What's the problem?"

"You know nothing about him. Just that he's good looking."

"Well, that blush…"

"Stop it with the blushing."

"You don't think it's charming?"

A tweet formed in my mind — *One person's charming is another person's smothering.* It needed work. The sentiment was there but it was a little wordy, or maybe too pedestrian.

Knowing Jared had entered the building when I'd told him to leave moved him awfully close to the line of stalking. It's hard to say where that line is. Often, the line isn't visible until it's crossed. Of course Jared wanted more. There's nothing like withholding something to make a person crave it, even if previously, they didn't. They become obsessed. The wanting takes over their minds like a drug, directing the flow of blood and nerve impulses. We want what we can't have. Some of us are better than others at figuring out how to get it. But even when you have everything you thought you wanted, there's more. Always more.

Tess was a perfect example. She had a single-minded focus on getting to the top, and she was as close as most people get. And young, so the pinnacle was definitely still within reach. But now, she was talking about a husband and babies and a growing sense of boredom and feeling old. Gushing over Jared's blushing cheeks. We weren't close friends sharing our woes, she was my boss. I needed her to get back on her game. I hadn't heard another word about the pay increase. Things were going off course. I needed her to feel I was indispensable to her career and her sense of herself, her position at the company. I was, and she recognized that fact, but she needed to feel it more intensely. She needed to fear losing me. She was acting as if I needed her help with Jared. I did not need help at all. "It's disturbing that he followed me into the building," I said.

"He likes you. A lot."

"It doesn't mean he should sneak into a secure building."

"He didn't sneak in, lighten up."

I looked at her, waiting for her to hear how that sounded. The Security department would be thrilled to know a senior vice president was so cavalier about an unauthorized visitor wandering the halls, going wherever he pleased because he was good looking and he blushed. "I'll ask him tonight what that was all about."

"And then tell me."

I needed her to talk about my raise, but I didn't want to ask. With another five hundred bucks a month, plus enough to cover the government tax on my existence, I could start planning to be out of the bungalow on South Bluff Drive and into something less precarious. Every time I saw Noreen's sad mouth and teary eyes watching me, I was less sure of the place I'd chosen. That's what happens when you rush into a decision. That's what happens when funds are limited. The choices shrink with them. People like to spout the idea that money can't buy happiness, but it can get you damn close. Besides, it all depends on what makes you happy. In my case, I'm very content with spacious rooms, comfortable, stylish furniture, good food, good wine and vodka, great sex, a quiet place to run... "Anything you need from me today?" I said.

She shook her head.

"I assume you saw my charts on how we only have fifty-seven red deliverables for this launch. Last time, before I was working here, there were eighty-four at this point in the schedule."

She nodded.

"I think at the next milestone, I can get that below fifty."

"You are amazing." Her smile looked vacant. She tugged on her jacket and felt the pocket as if she needed to assure herself her phone was still there.

"What's amazing is the power of a well-functioning spreadsheet. It's like all the cells are tiny little whips."

She laughed, but still looked like she wasn't completely engaged. She stood up. "I was going to check into getting you an out-of-cycle increase."

I smiled and ran my fingers through my bangs.

"I haven't done that yet. I will. As soon as I work out a few other things." She turned toward the door, then turned back. "I still think I've seen you somewhere before. The feeling won't go away. Can you think of where we might have crossed paths?"

"No." I held her gaze until she looked away.

"It's your eyebrows. I don't always see them because of your bangs. They're very distinctive. Perfectly shaped. Women would kill for those eyebrows."

"I doubt that." Damn her. She shouldn't be worrying about running across my face once upon a time. What did it matter? And she should not be promising money if she wasn't sure she had the political skill to get it. I needed something to change before I was tempted to sneak into Noreen's room at night and shoot her. Obviously that would solve nothing. Then it would be just Jared and me. Too cozy.

27

It was two-fourteen a.m. Jared stared at the ceiling, even though he couldn't actually see it in the darkness. The skin of his face was warm and pulpy. He'd been flat on his back, the blankets pulled up to his ribs, the pillow curled under his neck, since eleven and still his face was hot with shame.

Why had he followed her into the building? For days, the memory had tormented him. If Alexandra found out, and surely she would — the woman who'd showed him around would mention it — she'd think he was stalking her. It was just so difficult to figure out what was going on with her. He'd never met a woman like Alexandra. She'd come into his room and taken off her clothes without an invitation or any preliminary conversation. Then, she'd touched him in a way that made him feel they were connected beyond their bodies, that she knew something about him he was only dimly aware of himself. She'd slid out of bed and disappeared without lingering even for a kiss.

She refused his invitations to go out and didn't want to discuss any kind of relationship. What kind of woman didn't want a relationship? It was like she was an alien. Weren't women the social sex? Women were the ones who wanted to put down roots and nest and form communities and support groups. They were the ones who wanted to talk. Maybe she was playing some kind of game.

Most of the time now, she remained in her room. During the first few weeks they'd lived in the bungalow, she'd come into the living room several evenings a week for wine or a martini. The three of them had eaten dinner together. It was understandable why she no longer wanted to do that — like him, she was steering a wide path around Noreen. But why wouldn't she talk to him? She'd seemed a little angry when he showed up at work, but he'd thought she refused to talk at the house because Noreen might overhear. Meeting her outside of her office had seemed to make sense. It had been well before the start of the workday. The tiny garden was designed for casual conversation, why had she been so cold?

He closed his eyes to stop them from straining to see through the darkness. His back ached and his muscles longed to reposition themselves, urging him to turn on his side, but he wanted to keep the pressure on his body. He would subdue it. He would use his body as a meditation practice, since clearly he was failing to subdue his mind.

When he sat to meditate, he couldn't begin to silence or even slow the flashing speed of his thoughts. Even the effort to objectively observe his thoughts as they raced by was a complete failure. They flickered so rapidly, he forgot he was supposed to be witnessing and allowing them to just *be*. His stomach clenched and a cramp ran along the bottom of his foot. He had to get off the cushion and stand on one foot to ease it back into its relaxed state.

His eyes opened of their own accord, straining again. He

took a deep breath of cool air. He'd managed to force the window open wider and kept it that way whenever he was in his room, no matter how stiff the wind, hoping to wipe out the lingering smell of the rat. Or did he imagine the smell? A blast of night air was the only way to keep it from crawling back up his nostrils. Once, he'd left the window open during the day, resulting in a strongly worded lecture from Noreen that he'd jeopardized the safety of his roommates. According to her, it was a crime-riddled neighborhood and everything had to be secured at all times. She really didn't even like him keeping the window open when he was sleeping, but he'd mentioned the rat and she backed down.

He hadn't found the nerve to ask whether the rat was her doing. If it wasn't, he'd appear demented. Besides, after her lie regarding the damaged bathroom mirror, he knew she was fully capable of telling all kinds of plausible-sounding stories without a single tremor of her lip to indicate she was fabricating a wild tale, reeling it out of her brain as she talked.

There was a soft tap on his door. He groaned, too loud. He faked a snoring sound.

A moment later, he heard a rustling near the door. He sat up. If he turned on the light, she'd know he was awake. He opened the flashlight app and shone it several feet from the door. A slip of white paper lay on the floor. He carefully moved off the bed and walked soundlessly to the door. He picked up the note and returned to the nightstand. He directed the light to the note.

It's me. —A.

It would have been so much simpler if she'd sent a text

message. For a woman who worked at a technology company, Alexandra was strangely averse to using a smart phone. She'd refused to give him her number. Surely her job required instant communication, but he'd only seen a phone in her hand once. It must have been a company phone. When he'd worked for technology companies he was issued a phone that allowed a certain amount of personal use. Maybe it was a beach community thing. He was used to the buzzing, constantly connected, always communicating world on the other side of the foothills. Life was quieter over here. People were more prone to distancing themselves from digital addiction.

He unlocked the door and opened it slowly. Alexandra slipped into the room and he closed the door. She put her arms around his neck and began kissing him. He slid his mouth off of hers. "Wait." His voice was hoarse. His body shouted at him — *wait? Wait?! What the hell is your problem?*

"I need to know what's going on with us," he said. "What does this mean?"

Even as he spoke, he realized one thing it meant was she didn't think he was a fool for smiling his way into her workplace, wandering the halls, sneaking up on her. He'd seen her sitting behind her desk, the chair turned as she gazed out the window. He'd longed to know what she was looking at, what she was thinking about at that moment. Then a guy had passed by and given Jared a puzzled look. Jared hurried after the woman who'd shown him Alexandra's office and let her lead him out of the building.

"I want you," she said. "That's what it means."

"But how? Are we…"

She slid her hands under the waist of his boxers and pulled them down until the elastic reached the middle of his thighs. They fell the rest of the way on their own. With her mouth on his lower lip, she wriggled out of her white leggings. She nudged him toward the bed, letting go of his lip.

He stumbled with the boxers around his ankles. "Alexandra. Wait."

"No. It's already late."

"Are you kidding me?"

"You know you want me."

Of course he wanted her, but not…

She pulled off her t-shirt and knelt at his feet. She lifted first one foot then the other out of the trap of his boxers. She stood up, took his wrist, and pulled him toward the bed.

Tomorrow, he'd be more confused than ever, but it was crazy to keep resisting. She might leave. He'd worry about it tomorrow. They fell onto the bed.

When he woke, the room was still pitch dark. A light rain tapped the tree outside his window, brushing against the glass like her fingertips on his door. He didn't have to feel around the bed to know she wasn't there. He turned on his side and pulled the blankets over him. He didn't want to know what time it was. The idea of lying on his back, forcing his body to submit to quiet breathing, making it wait for its demands to be met was laughable now. He felt like crying, something he hadn't done since he was a little kid.

She held his mind like a ball of dough in her hands. He wanted her so badly. Was this some kind of trick, withholding herself to drive his craving to a fever pitch, so their relationship would start out on an unequal footing? Or...? He didn't even know what the other possibilities might be.

A darker thought appeared.

Women schemed together all the time. Why hadn't that crossed his mind? The same night Noreen knocked on his door, Alexandra had come in an hour later. Was he a toy in some game of theirs? Alexandra had seemed annoyed when he suggested the two women would be good for his spiritual practice. Maybe they'd devised some form of payback. Maybe Noreen didn't want him at all, or maybe they had concocted some convoluted plan in which they imagined Alexandra could steer him in Noreen's direction. It made no sense. He sat up. There wouldn't be any more sleep. It would be a long day filled with aching, twisted thoughts trying to figure out what they might be up to. Maybe nothing at all. Maybe his focus on crawling through the dark crevices of his mind, spending hours sitting on a tiny cushion with his eyes closed, had stirred up paranoia.

28

Mountain View

Charlie's smart phone was on the kitchen counter. Charlie was in the shower. He'd begged me to join him, but I needed to get close to his phone, not him. I'd managed a faint blush and hinted at my period. He backed off quickly and disappeared.

As water pounded against tile in the bathroom, I tapped the home button and the lock screen appeared. 1234 didn't work. I tried 4321. I tapped in the last four digits of his phone number and the same numbers in reverse order. No luck. I'd underestimated him. I let the screen go dark and thought about his house number and the current year — to commemorate his law school graduation. I tried the year of his birth. Nothing.

It seemed that in his case, I wasn't the hacker I'd hoped.

While I let my mind drift, searching for other significant numbers or dates he might have mentioned, a message floated across the screen.

When are you bringing that bitch down?

I picked up the phone, as if holding it might tell me who *that bitch* was. Me? I didn't think so. As far as I could tell, he was hooked on me. Unless someone else thought his interest in me was a bad idea. I put the phone back on the counter. I tried a repeat of his age — 2828.

Teach that ho she can't get away with being a tease.

It definitely wasn't me. A lot of things can be said about me, but not that.

The message was followed by icons of a woman's lips and a bunch of heads with tiny curls at the top denoting children.

Deleting the photographs of me slipped slightly on my priority list. To be rid of them, the phone would have to go missing, but that would take planning. I hoped he was as negligent as most people are about backing up his data. But now, I was more interested in the woman he was hoping to bring down.

I put the phone on the counter and went into the living room. I sat on the couch and waited for his shower to end. Nearly fifteen minutes passed before the bathroom door opened. A minute later he was in the living room doorway. "Ready?"

I stood up. I'd been ready since I rang his bell at ten to six for our dinner date, expecting him to be showered and dressed.

"You look great," he said.

"Don't forget your phone."

He went to the counter, shoved it in his back pocket, and we left.

We were seated on the open balcony looking down on the courtyard at Nola's in Palo Alto. Charlie was sipping a vodka tonic and I was admiring the seductive liquid in my martini glass, wrapping itself around two glossy olives. A drink without ice diluting the alcohol is so much more satisfying. I let him take a few more sips. When he looked up, I ran my tongue across my upper lip.

His eyes settled onto me and he put down the drink.

"Do you have any enemies?" I said.

He laughed. "That's random. Why?"

"Just making conversation. I was talking to Maria about it."

"How did that come up?"

I lowered one shoulder. He looked down at the neckline of my top.

"She has a friend who seems to attract enemies," I said. "Maria's never had an enemy in her life, as far as she knows, and she wondered how common it was — to have enemies." It was probably true. Maria was a trusting, forgiving person. If we'd had the conversation, that's how it would have gone.

"I never thought about it." He picked up his drink and tipped it, swirling the ice cubes.

The server came and took our orders. When he was gone, I gave Charlie a questioning, friendly look. "It's okay to tell me."

"There's nothing to tell. I never gave it any thought."

"I would think, studying law and all, you would think about things like that."

"Well I haven't."

"No list of who you'll sue first, once you pass the bar?"

"I'm not becoming an attorney to sue people."

"But if you want to, it's convenient not having to hire an attorney."

"I suppose."

"Don't look so worried," I said. "You'll pass. You study all the time, and you're a very smart guy."

He tried not to smile. "I'm not worried."

But he was. I heard it in the faint waver beneath his words.

He sipped his drink and picked up a piece of bread. He took a bite and chewed. "I know you're defensive of her, so don't start arguing with me, but I guess that woman with the illegal roommates is an enemy."

"Silvia?" I sipped my drink.

He swallowed most of his.

"It must be frustrating, trying to study so hard for something *so* important, and having kids' TV shows disrupt you. They can be pretty inane. It's hard to concentrate."

He nodded. "So you're on my side now?"

"Absolutely." I ate one of my olives.

"She's kind of a bitch," he said.

Our meals were delivered. Steak for me, catfish for him. We ordered two more drinks.

I stabbed my piece of beef with my fork and sliced the serrated knife through the meat. The red inside opened up, the color of an uncut ruby. "It's probably a strain on the plumbing and all that, with so many people in one unit. That's not good for the building overall," I said.

"Exactly."

"Do you know her very well?"

He looked down at his plate and shook his head. He said something I couldn't hear.

"What?"

He shook his head again.

I chewed the piece of steak and put down my cutlery. "Did you ask her to keep the noise down, apply gentle pressure, so she knows she's risking her housing?"

He looked up. "I put a lot of pressure on her. Being able to concentrate is critical. I don't want to be one of those guys taking the bar two or three times. It doesn't look good."

"What did she say?"

"It was disgusting. You won't believe it."

"Yes I will."

He leaned forward. "She suggested she'd fuck me, if I kept my mouth shut about it."

The scenario he described might play out with a lot of women, but not Sylvia. The glazed look in his eyes, the barely concealed rage, said that it had been exactly the opposite. He'd been the one to make the proposition. And now...

"She's such a whore."

"Shh. People can hear you."

He shoveled fish into his mouth and took a drink before he finished chewing.

I looked away, my appetite fading as the contents of my stomach rocked gently.

"I'll tell you in the car," he said.

We'd parked in the garage below the historic Spanish building that housed Nola's. Charlie started the car. The Mustang roared to life. He backed out and drove up the tightly curved ramp, turning left onto Ramona Avenue. Once we were on Central Expressway headed back toward

Mountain View, he let loose.

"That bitch thinks she can do whatever she wants. She can move in extra people in flagrant disregard for the rules that make this place livable for everyone. She thinks she's above it all and that we should all feel her burden. We aren't responsible for cutting her slack just because she can't keep her husband. That's not how society works. She's a slut. Those kids have two different fathers and she didn't marry either one of them. It's inhuman to bring children into the world without a family unit. She gets herself pregnant..."

"I don't think you can get *yourself* pregnant."

He grunted. "You know what I mean."

"I do, it just sounds funny."

"Ha ha. Anyway, this is a nice place in an upscale town. We don't need trash like her and her friend, we don't need kids who grow up to be thugs without the firm discipline of a man. The racket from that TV proves she's not raising them properly, parking them in front of idiotic shows all day and half the night. And to come onto me like that..."

"When did this happen?"

He took his hand off the wheel and flapped it at me as if he were brushing away my question, or a fly. "Not important."

"Is that why you need to bring her down?"

He glanced at me then put his attention back on the road. "Exactly."

"How did she come on to you?"

"I don't think I need to describe it. You know how those things go. Thinking I'd be on her side, that I could be bought for a blow job or something. Like I have no integrity. Strutting around in her little skirt and skimpy top."

"Did she actually say something, or you...thought she was implying..."

"She's a tease. She's the definition of a whore."

"What are you going to do?"

"I'm not just reporting her to the association. They have no teeth, and even if they reprimand her, it'll take forever. I got the information for the owner of that condo. I'm reaching out to him, man to man, and suggesting he evict her."

He was precise enough and vague enough that I knew it hadn't been the way he described it at all. He liked her legs and her cute little skirts. And they were little. He thought his outrage over her disturbance of sacrosanct study time would frighten her. He thought a single mom, lonely for a man, worried about keeping a stable home for her kids, would cave with a wink. She told him to get lost and his law school ego was bruised.

"Don't you need legal..."

"I know the law, Alex. You don't need to explain it. I'm checking into what's required before I give him a call."

It was clear he imagined himself pacing in front of a jury box, articulating his point of view and her failure to obey the laws — mostly those in his own, early twentieth-century mind. Instead, he sounded like a misogynistic madman.

I thought of brownies and working all day, coming home to diapers and meals to fix, lunches to pack, dishes to wash, laundry, baths, reading stories, bedtime. I couldn't imagine the entire list. The father of those kids should be there doing half that work. I thought of those kids with their big gray eyes, like kittens — playful, cunning, and fierce. Like me.

29

Aptos

Falling into Jared's bed again had not been the best idea. Confusion erupted out of his mouth in short bursts of unfinished thoughts. But after the Boxster driver's startling, searing, sidewalk kiss sending ripples of warmth to the soles of my feet, my body hummed with wanting.

My body can be a confusing tangle of cells and muscles and nerves, sometimes woefully mis-communicating with my brain. Take smoking. Only someone who has lived in a cave is ignorant about what cigarette smoke does to your body, and the risk of an ugly, early death, or a bloody cough that allows you to live but dogs you every step of the way to your grave. The problem is, it feels so damn good. It's relaxing. It releases your thoughts to float casually over the surface of your brain, no single thought turning into a troublesome nagging sound that won't let go. And no matter how much the American Cancer Society shows pictures of haggard, withered people with cigarettes stuck to their dried lips, they can't beat Hollywood. Smoking is sexy. Everyone knows it's sexy — lips wrapped around a slender tube, smoke gliding out of your mouth in a thin, delicate stream. Yes, it leaves behind tobacco breath and clings to your hair, and even fresh, fruity lotions fail to cover the odor. But standing in front of a nice restaurant or an exotic hotel, smoking a cigarette, gives me a feeling of power and control. No one can touch me.

I was turning Jared's head inside out, messing with his life, but he was too good looking to keep my hands off, and too convenient. In the time it took to breathe in and out, I could slip into his bedroom. It was like having a bowl of potato chips on the table and expecting it to remain full.

The night after we had sex for the second time, I had to get out of the house. He'd be hunting me down, trying to discuss our relationship. Even if we didn't discuss it, staying at home raised the chances of two nights in a row. That would give him the impression that our *connection* was locked into place.

I put on brown leggings topped with a baggy cream colored sweater over a red camisole, and dark brown boots with medium heels and brass zippers down the backs. The bangs I'd had cut to adjust my image toward the sweet end of the spectrum were getting tiresome, but now I needed to keep them thick and long to prevent Tess from fixating on the familiarity and perfection of my eyebrows. It was unlikely I'd see Tess, so I styled them to the side. I lined my eyes with soft, chocolate brown pencil, stroked on a bit of mascara, and left my lips naked. Noreen was right. I don't need makeup, but it's so much fun, and there are so many ways to transform your appearance with colors and shadows and lines.

I flicked off my bedroom light, walked though the great room, and went out to the porch. Jared's car was gone. I could have stayed home after all. I stood for a moment, staring at the darkened house across the street. Once you're wearing the outfit for going to a club or bar, it's hard to reverse direction. Besides, a martini in a bar was more appealing than mixing my own, drinking it in my increasingly claustrophobic bedroom.

Henry's Bar was quiet on a weeknight and I snagged one of the booths. I ordered fried artichoke hearts, an assortment of sausage slices, and a vodka martini.

The first olive was gone and I was halfway through the drink and the artichokes when a man's voice spoke just behind me on the left. "If I order another plate of those, can I share this one with you?"

I turned.

The Boxster guy. What the hell was it about him that captivated me? He was tall, which was accentuated by him standing over me. I like the feeling of a tall guy. Especially when I know he's in my power, weak with wanting me, so there's this weird dynamic of strength from his height advantage over me and the opposing strength from my advantage over him. This guy was thin for my taste, but it was impossible to take my eyes off his assured, fluid movements. The shape of his lips flooded my own with the memory of kissing him.

"Absolutely," I said.

He slid into the seat across from me and put his bottle of Blue Moon on the table. He dipped an artichoke heart in the aioli and popped it into his mouth. "Love these things."

"Me too."

He lifted the beer and tapped the neck on the edge of my

glass. The vodka and vermouth undulated.

"It's an odd coincidence," I said.

"What?"

"Seeing you here. I had the impression you didn't live in the area."

"I don't."

"Are you following me?"

"Maybe." He smiled.

"That's creepy."

He shrugged.

We finished the plate of hearts and he ordered another. I pushed the sausages toward him. "Help yourself."

"I will, thanks." He stabbed a piece of sausage with one of the bamboo spears on the side of the plate and popped it in his mouth without mustard.

"You're very persistent, waiting so long for your surprise attack on Noreen."

"The timing needs to be perfect. I'm a patient guy."

I took a sip of my martini.

"Are you ready for another?"

I ate the olive. "Sure. Vodka. Grey Goose."

He ordered the drinks and more sausages. We gobbled the food and talked about what we liked and didn't like about Santa Cruz and the surrounding beach towns. Oddly, the subject of water — beaches, surfing, boating — didn't come up. We mostly discussed the flood of homeless people, the ready availability of medical marijuana, and the political extremes. Then we moved to the mundane topic of traffic. From there, we talked about our favorite places to eat and the never-ending supply of great, reasonably priced food. He was obviously familiar with the area.

When my glass was nearly empty, he reached across the table and pulled the pink stick holding the last olive out of the glass. He held it close to my mouth and I sucked the olive off the stick.

"I liked kissing you," he said. "I bet you taste great with a vodka-soaked tongue."

"I do, if you like vodka."

"I'm staying at a Motor Inn — the Ocean Breeze. Do you want…"

"I do," I said.

He went to the bar and paid for the food and drinks. On the sidewalk outside, we stood on the edge of the curb and he gave me a long, slow kiss. I got in my car and followed the Boxster to the Ocean Breeze.

Despite the dreamy, lighthearted name, my first thought when I saw the motor inn was of the Bate's Motel. It had the same string of rooms connected by a single porch running the entire length, and the same run down appearance. The sense that the rooms had been unoccupied for a very long time, maybe always, added to the chill circling my spine. It had the same old-fashioned sign with thin red tubes of light forming the name. I climbed slowly out of my car, smiling at how a movie with two memorably unnerving scenes can live inside your head for years, until it starts to feel like part of your own history.

Inside, the room was nothing like the Bate's Motel. It had updated pale gray carpet and a bed with an iron headboard and footboard. The remodeled bathroom featured a sleek pedestal sink and a dual flush toilet. Most importantly, the shower was a stall with a stationary glass panel to keep the water contained — no tub, no opaque shower curtain hiding a freak with a butcher knife.

After he removed my clothes, article by article, and suggested I do the same for him, we made love. Twice. It was not disappointing.

We slept for a while, and at twelve-thirty I got up and gathered my clothes. He didn't object to my leaving. Ending the evening without a discussion of our status was pleasant. I felt light and drained of all aggression and tension. I zipped my boots and stood up. "You know, you could have seen Noreen tonight. Jared was out, and here I am."

He gave me a lazy smile.

"When you saw me inside Henry's..."

"Next time," he said.

"Next time, what?"

"I'm sure you'll go out again. And I'm noticing the owner of the BMW isn't around much lately."

"So you're not in such a hurry to surprise Noreen after all?"

He smiled. "There's a right time for everything."

"If you knew he wasn't around, and you saw me leave..."

"You're more enticing than Noreen."

I smiled. "Thank you." I opened the door.

"Joe," he said. "My name's Joe."

A nice solid name. A low-key counter to my rather flamboyant name.

"Alex," I said. Maybe another time I'd tell him all of it.

30

Back at the house, Jared's BMW was still gone. I parked and went inside. Noreen was sitting on the couch watching Legally Blonde. She gave me a watery smile but said nothing.

I stood there for a moment. Finally, I moved closer to the couch. "What's the progress on the mirror replacement?"

"I put a mirror in your room."

"Not acceptable."

"I thought it was settled?" she said.

"How did you come to that conclusion?"

"Because I told you I had a temper tantrum. I told you I..."

"None of that has to do with replacing it."

"Where were you? You look tipsy. I hope you didn't drive drunk."

"Nothing to worry about, *mom*."

She scowled.

"If you don't replace the mirror, I will. And I'll expect you to reimburse me."

"We'll see."

I started toward the hallway.

"Do you want to watch this with me?"

I shook my head.

"I get nervous when I'm here by myself."

She picked up the remote and paused the movie. "It seems like you and Jared are never here any more."

"We have our own lives."

"But I thought...I don't like being here alone."

"We're renting bedrooms in your house, Noreen. We're not here to be friends or some kind of substitute family."

"That's not what I want."

"I'm going to crash."

"Your hair and makeup says you already had a *nap*. I'll make martinis." She stood up.

"No thanks."

She slumped on the couch and stared at the TV but didn't re-start the movie. I walked into the hallway, went into my room, and closed and locked the door. I sat in the armchair, unzipped my boots, and pulled them off. I dropped them on the floor and imagined Noreen, staring at the wall shared by my bedroom and the great room.

I popped open my laptop and fired up the spreadsheet where I track my expenses and savings. If Tess came through with a decent pay raise, I could be out of this delicately balanced little house in three months. I wondered if I'd make it that long.

31

Mountain View

So many people are indiscriminate with their drug and alcohol use, viewing them as nothing more than a pathway to a good time. Brain altering stimulants are streamlined vehicles for letting go of their rational minds and *pursuing a long, prolonged derangement of the senses* — a line Jim Morrison adapted, aka stole, from the poet Arthur Rimbaud. But it's okay. Many intriguing ways of expressing truth about life have been stolen, and Jim brought the concept into the modern world. I'm sure Rimbaud appreciated his second fifteen minutes in the spotlight.

Rimbaud insisted the systematized *disorganization* of all the senses creates visionary poets. It's not clear whether he supported the chemical or herbal path to *disorganization*, which is a hell of a lot less terrifying than derangement, but he did believe vision came out of disorder. Rimbaud was a cool guy, an avant-garde thinker, considering he lived in the late 1800s. Arthur R — how's that for poetic — proposed that women should have their eternal slavery destroyed, living for themselves and through themselves. He imagined women might become poets. Imagine that. All this would come about through *abominable mankind setting* her free, of course. He believed *man*kind would wake up and do just that. He didn't quite recognize that women had considerable more free will than he allowed them. Still, he deserves kudos even though his vision is not how it played out. Mankind did not set women free. Women took their freedom into their own hands. We still do take freedom into our own hands. It's a wrestling match that's lasted thousands of years. At least he recognized something wasn't right.

Smoking weed leaves you dreamy and relaxed, the shared escape tightens the bonds of friendship. Doing shots and sipping wine softens the brain, removes the excess clutter of life, and brings you into the moment. We're all seeking to be *In The Moment*. As long as you don't go too far. Two or three glasses of wine are nice, ten puts you on the bathroom floor, which is a *Moment* I prefer to avoid.

While people smoke on patios and meet their friends in bars, they rarely stop to think about what easy targets they become for a killer. They think, most of the time, about not getting behind the wheel of a car. They think about not making utter fools of themselves. Most women think quite a bit about making sure they don't end up a victim of rape after four martinis or shots with the guys.

But they don't think about murder.

Alcohol and pot are perfect murder weapons for a woman. Or at least part of her toolkit. Vodka and whiskey and cannabis take away the natural disadvantage of a smaller form, and upper body strength that's not a match for even a medium-sized man. I've been lifting weights since I was fifteen years old. I can curl twenty-five pounds and I can bench press one-hundred-thirty-five pounds. I'm toned and lean, but still lithe. My strength is startling to people when they encounter it for the first, or last, time.

Whether a woman is using a knife or a rope, water or a pillow or a plastic bag — drugs and alcohol are a huge help. It's like having an accessory to the crime. A murder partner. Guns are so loud and messy, and like most women, I prefer to work quietly and as neatly as possible.

Once I came to realize the world would be better off without Charlie Denton, that Sylvia and her kids would be able to continue eking out their existence without some asshole going out of his way to cut the fragile strings holding them aloft, I also knew immediately that a bit of pot and an evening of vodka shots were essential to getting the upper hand with him. The trickiest part would be figuring out how to do shots and smoke dope while keeping my own senses arranged.

Taking possession of Charlie's phone was an added benefit. But you don't kill someone over an unwanted photograph.

The world didn't need another attorney, a man who believed women existed solely for his pleasure, a man who blamed a woman for a man's failure. A man who labeled a woman a whore because she didn't yield to his crude offer. His views were obscene and dangerous.

He was a man who wanted to destroy six lives for the sheer satisfaction of being right. Instead of plugging his ears, he wanted to silence all of them.

This was a man who needed to be prevented from sowing his seed and raising yet another generation of misogynists.

32

Tess was in my office. Again. Gushing about Jared. Again.

Since I'd started working for her, she'd begun to remind me of a butterfly defying the laws of nature — a silky black and golden orange creature lighting on whatever object pricked her desire, now turning and crawling back into the husk of her cocoon, pulling it around her and allowing her body to deteriorate into a worm again.

I'd done everything I could to reflect her narcissistic face back to her, and she'd turned into something else entirely. She no longer elicited my respect and admiration. I couldn't remake myself into something quivering and needy. I could try to mirror some of those traits, or say things that suggested I had similar fears, but I wasn't sure it would come off as genuine.

"Maybe you should introduce him to me," Tess said. She crossed her legs and ran her fingers gently over her kneecap.

"He's having sex with me."

"You said he's not happy with that situation." She stood up. "I'm antsy. Do you want to go to the gym with me? We can take a long lunch and do some weight lifting."

"You don't have any meetings?"

She shrugged.

I couldn't have this. The moment I'd walked into my interview with Tess, I'd known she was a good candidate to be my protector at CoastalCreative. I'd been certain she could give me job security, to defend me if I ever made a mistake. She was there to sing my praises to her peers, to deliver pay increases and good performance reviews. There had been too many job changes in my life, and if I was going to make any forward steps toward long-term financial security, the kind of money that allows a mind to free itself from ever thinking of money. I needed someone on my team.

In the past, my managers and bosses had been men. It's easy to recruit a man to be on your side. A night or two of inappropriate sex with a subordinate and they were steadfastly watching out for my interests. But I'd believed a woman would be more passionate in a different way. A woman would go further to ensure a solid career because the strength of sisterhood, the feeling that my success was her success, was alluring. The bond that's not unlike the bond of shared military bootcamp, lasting a lifetime, the result of fighting for your place in what's still, let's be honest, a man's world. Business and politics and money are dominated by men. Nearly two decades into the twenty-first century, that's still the case. The only change is that male domination has now become a subterranean thread, running through Wall Street and Capitol Hill and Silicon Valley — superficial respect and equality instead of blatant shunning.

When I met Tess, the final interrogator for my application

to CoastalCreative, she'd presented a stunning package of accomplishments. She was fully in command of every step of her career, not to mention every ounce of fat and muscle in her body, every choice in her life. She'd mapped out a career path before she exited the MBA program at Stanford — complete with weekly and monthly goals, each step forward a seductively polished stone. Even as a young senior vice president, which would satisfy many women, she'd suggested she wanted more. She needed me as much as I needed her. She needed a confidante whom she could trust absolutely. She needed a project manager that was zealous and treated every single mundane task like a mission with life threatening consequences. She needed a colleague who would be loyal to the death.

I thought I had a perfect setup. I thought a woman's support would embody all that passion and loyalty, that it would be more long lasting than a man's. Permanent. I thought removing sex from the equation was brilliant on my part. Loyalty and a higher vision of the need for women to have each other's backs would go far deeper and become much stronger than support born out of a simple fear of scandal.

I couldn't understand why she'd changed. Unless she'd always been needy and insecure and obsessed with finding a man and she'd kept it hidden until we became close. It was hard to know.

I wheeled my chair away from the desk. "Sure. I'll go to the gym with you."

"I have extra workout clothes you can borrow."

"No need," I said. "I keep running clothes in my trunk."

Six minutes later I pulled out of the parking lot, following Tess's white Mercedes to her gym. The car gleamed in the late morning light. It looked like a powerful, rare white tiger. That was the car I would have someday, although I might want the small SUV model. I slid my hands down the side of the steering wheel and shifted in my seat, imagining the feel of premium leather and the purr of an engine that functioned so well the parts seemed to be cast from platinum.

The lobby of Tess's gym overflowed with clusters of tropical plants. There was an eclectic mix of wicker and leather furniture. Baskets of bottled water and body lotion were nestled between love seats and chairs. A few low tables had fresh flowers in Steuben vases. The receptionist acted as if Tess was her best friend.

We changed into spandex capri pants and sports bras and went into the cardio room with its liberally spaced elliptical machines and treadmills. The treadmills faced a garden with a pond and a small waterfall. In the middle of the day, there were only three other women using the twenty or so machines. Tess and I climbed on side-by-side treadmills, set the incline and speed, and started walking. Tess checked her phone while she walked, obviously quite used to the rhythm of walking or running on an artificial surface that moved with her. Four minutes into it I wished I was outside, running on a path or a sidewalk, creating my own pace. Treadmills are for rainy weather, that's all.

After a few more finger-flying taps at her phone, she slipped it into the back pocket of her workout pants, stabbed her finger at the controls, and began running faster. I did the same. We looked out the window and didn't talk, which I appreciated.

We ran for nearly forty minutes. When I heard Tess's machine shift to a slower speed, I lowered mine as well. The machines ground to a halt. We stepped off and wiped down the handles. We both grabbed a second bottle of water from the basket near the door and went into the weight room. It was empty. Tess sat on the end of the bench press and stretched her arms overhead. "I wanted to tell you something." She lowered her arms and ran her fingers through her hair, pushing it back in thick, sweaty black tufts.

I bent forward and touched my toes, angling first one toe and then the other off the floor to give an extra stretch to my calf muscles. "Uh huh." I pushed my upper body gently lower until my palms were flat on the floor.

"No go on the pay increase," she said.

The clank of weight bricks on the benchpress almost drowned out the last word. Almost.

I straightened and looked at her. "That's a surprise."

"It shouldn't be. I told you an out-of-cycle increase had to be negotiated."

"You sounded confident you could manage it, though."

"It doesn't mean we don't recognize your value." She lay on her back and grabbed the handles of the machine, ready to lift.

"I have no doubt you see my value, that's why I'm surprised."

"I was able to get you a spot bonus. Fifteen hundred

dollars. For the analysis you did on how metrics have improved since you came on board."

Fifteen hundred dollars was nice, very nice, but it was the ongoing infusion of cash that meant something. I closed my eyes and saw the beige tile floor and the gently sloping deck of my current home. I thought about the scraped up mirror and Noreen's breathless requests that we hang out together. I thought about Jared and his exquisite smile and the proximity of his bed to mine. But every night he was in there longing for me with a desire that sucked the oxygen from my room. So much for his Buddhist exercise in letting go of desire and attachment. He wanted too much.

It seemed as if he lay in his room, waiting for me. I could feel him breathing, hear him breathing, the whole house pulsed with his long, deep breaths. My bedroom wall grew warm from the heat of his breath, unhindered by the closets lining our shared wall. I could hardly sleep with the sound of his breathing, the knowledge of his open eyes, fixed at the back of his door, staring at the doorknob, waiting for it to turn. Every night I found myself creeping into the kitchen at eleven or twelve and mixing a martini, taking it back to my room, sipping it steadily until it lulled me to sleep. But the resulting sleep was restless, my dreams moving in the same rhythm as Jared's chest as it rose and fell.

Escape from that stew of human need was imperative. He hadn't asked about our relationship again but I imagined his next attempt to pin things down would mean more pressure to move out of Noreen's together. It would be tempting, but in the long run, would create more problems than it solved.

I gave Tess a smile calculated to look pleased, but without glee and without communicating a sense that she'd done as much as she possibly could. She had not. Her own issues had surely gotten in the way. Suddenly she was afraid to break the rules and hesitant to exert her influence. A senior vice president should have very few people signing off on something that skirted the existing structure. It wasn't as if out-of-cycle raises were unheard of, they just had to be pushed through by someone who was a fighter, someone with her documentation in place to justify the request. If an employee threatened to leave the company to work for a competitor, there would be no objection to an unplanned increase. In fact, it wasn't truly unplanned — budgets allowed for such things. The problem was, the threat of going with the competition worked very well for an engineer. For a project manager, not so much. Although it should. Companies think only the engineers provide intellectual capital. They don't realize that without the creme de la creme in support functions, none of their precious engineering performs well in the marketplace. It was Tess's job to communicate that to her superiors.

"I'm really sorry," she said.

I studied her eyes. After a moment, she glanced away, looking toward the door to see whether anyone had come in who might dissolve the uncomfortable moment. As she looked back at me, guilt was visible in the erratic movement of her eyes, searching mine for reassurance. Guilt was good. Guilt would keep me at the forefront of her thoughts.

My body had cooled down from the treadmill and the AC

was set too high for such a large, unoccupied room. I rubbed my arms. The skin was cold and dry.

"I'll try again next quarter," Tess said.

I turned away.

"Don't sulk," she said. "It's unprofessional."

"I never sulk."

"It sure looks to me like sulking."

"I didn't ask for a raise. You offered it, so my expectation was set differently, that's all."

"I said I was sorry."

I stood there, looking at her, my arms hanging at my sides, not folded in defense, my feet planted about twenty inches apart. It was an intimidating stance without a shred of uncertainty.

Tess rubbed her hands together, grabbed the handles of the weight machine again, and began lifting the stack of iron blocks — one hundred pounds. She ran through ten reps without a break in her rhythm. She let go of the handles and rested.

I went to the leg machines and settled into the reclining leg press. I could do leg presses all day. It's soothing and doesn't require the concentration demanded by some of the other machines. I mindlessly bent and straightened my legs, trying to figure out how to push her harder.

33

When I came into the house after *girl time* at Tess's gym, my mind was still circling around how I was going to find a way to either make Tess fight harder for me, or go around her to find another ally. What I'd reminded her of was the absolute truth, and she shouldn't have brushed it off as if it wasn't important — I had not asked for the raise, she offered it. I'd re-configured my budget and calculated my exit from Noreen's loony bin based on Tess's confidence.

Noreen was in the kitchen wearing a little yellow apron with a red bird on it. As I stepped into the great room, she turned toward the fridge and I saw the sash tied in a big puffy bow. I hurried toward the hallway but my heels made too much noise on the tile, even with my effort to take gentle steps.

She came out of the kitchen, shot across the room, and blocked my way. "I made lasagna."

"Jared doesn't eat..."

"His diet doesn't matter. He's never here at dinnertime. I don't think he likes us." She waved a spatula coated in white cheese with streaks of tomato sauce.

She had part of that right. "And you're okay? Ready to let go of him?"

"No. I'm hurt. I have to figure out a new plan of attack."

"Why are you so set on a guy who's obviously not interested?"

"Let's talk about it over dinner. I bought two bottles of Pinot Noir."

The lure of wine, coupled with noodles full of carbs, overcame my reluctance to eat dinner with her. Besides, freeing my mind from trying so hard to come up with a solution for the Tess problem might allow the answer to emerge.

"Please?" She pouted. She held out the spatula, waving it under my nose.

"Bribery isn't necessary."

She smiled. "So that means yes?"

I nodded. I went into my room and dropped my purse on the chair. I kicked off my black patent leather pumps — a bit showy for the office, but Tess hadn't said a word. I hadn't detected more than one or two raised eyebrows in the hallways, from women of course. The men all loved the patent leather, although they wouldn't let on by giving my feet more than a passing glance, and they certainly wouldn't allow their mouths to twist into looks of hunger and curiosity.

Once my skirt and top were hanging in the closet, I peeled off my pantyhose and dropped them in the lingerie wash bag. I took off my bra and thong and added them to the mix. I stood naked in front of the closet, trying to determine my mood. Finally I settled on thick white sweatpants and a blue off the shoulder crop top, no underwear at all. This would be a total comfort evening. I almost looked forward to it. During my workout, I'd been so irritated by Tess's failure and lack of focus, I used heavier weights than normal and now my muscles were pleasantly weak and ready to be nourished with thick, fatty food. I put my hair in a ponytail and pulled the hair through the elastic again, creating a floppy knot on top of my head. I went into the bathroom and removed my makeup without the benefit of a mirror. I put on face cream that made me feel like I'd bathed in silk.

In the great room, all the lights were off. The dining table had a single white taper candle in the center. She'd put out beige woven placemats and off-white cloth napkins.

"This is a bit formal, isn't it?" I picked up the glass of wine on the bar separating the kitchen and great room. I took a sip. It was very good. I turned the bottle to face me — David Bruce 2013.

"I wanted it to be nice. You can sit, the food's ready." Noreen put a large ceramic bowl with lettuce, avocado pieces, red kidney beans, and small slivers of yellow bell paper on the table. It shimmered with an herbal oil and vinegar dressing. She'd heated the bread with butter and fresh garlic.

"I didn't know you were such a good cook," I said.

"You didn't give me a chance."

I sipped my wine. It wasn't true, she hadn't given *me* a chance — going from weird to batshit crazy in sixty seconds.

She served large portions of lasagna onto dinner plates and carried them to the table. I scooped out salad and placed two pieces of bread on the edge of my plate. I took a large bite of bread and drank some more wine.

"What do you think I'm doing wrong with him?" she said.

I took a bite of lasagna. "This is fantastic."

She giggled. "It's hard to mess up lasagna." She pushed her hair off her face and reached for the bread. Her fingers scrabbled across the golden brown crusts, looking for a slice that satisfied whatever criteria she was using.

"I suppose so," I said. "But this is better than most."

"You didn't answer my question."

"You're trying too hard."

"I don't like being alone."

"No one likes to be stalked."

"I'm not stalking him."

"Pretty close to it."

She sighed. She took a long swallow of wine. When she put down her glass, she was a bit emphatic and the candle flame wavered.

"Do you think he could be interested, if I played hard to get?"

"You shouldn't play anything."

"That's how it works."

In my case, she was close to the truth — there is a lot of playing, the game is thrilling, it's what gets me out of bed in the morning. But most people don't play games to acquire the things they want. They set goals, they pray and trust their hard work and intuition and all kinds of things I don't believe in. I play. It's more fun and equally effective. But it's a different kind of game and not what Noreen was looking for.

"Find something else to occupy your time. Give him a little space."

"That's what everyone says."

All I was doing was echoing conventional wisdom. Wisdom she apparently wasn't interested in following.

"I just like him so much. And I'm so lonely."

"Being alone can be a good thing."

She shook her head. "It's been awful since Brian left."

"So Jared's just a guy to slot into the place Brian vacated?"

"No. Don't make it sound so cold. I like Jared. A lot. He's cute and he's so nice, and he's…Brian hurt me."

"Maybe you need more space yourself, before you jump into another relationship."

"I don't think so."

"You could talk to a therapist, about why it's taking you so long to get over Brian."

I would never go to a therapist. They know crazy from first-hand experience. And their talking and listening and questioning is mostly bullshit. But it's a normal solution to recommend, and if you suggest it nicely, with a note of kindness, people interpret that as genuine concern. And in her case, I hoped a therapist could tone her down with a few well-prescribed meds.

"I don't think it's taking that long," she said.

My lasagna was nearly gone. I could manage maybe one more piece of bread. The wine bottle was two thirds empty. I refilled my glass and took a fourth piece of bread. I nibbled it slowly. "How long since he left?"

She shrugged. "Not sure. How long have you been here? He left a week or two before you moved in."

A week or two? How had I gotten the idea it was months, maybe a year or longer? She'd declared their shared investment to be her own home in less than two weeks' time? My earlier concern that he might not consider the house hers to rent space in returned with greater force. I studied her face in the candlelight. She didn't look insane, but madness isn't always visible.

"What's wrong?" she said.

"Nothing."

"Yes, there is. You have a funny look on your face."

"I just thought it had been longer, since he left."

"Why would you think that?"

"It's the impression you gave, but I suppose it doesn't matter."

It mattered a lot. Withholding that information felt like a lie. Not that I could judge her for lying, she did what she had to do to fill those rooms and get money flowing into the house. Or maybe it wasn't about money at all. Maybe it was about not being capable of living alone. She'd tried to get us eating together, tried to get Jared into her bed, tried to set up girl nights with me. She was a little kid, never developed past the middle of high school because she became an instant adult by moving out of her parents' house to be with her boyfriend. I'm not a psychologist, but it seemed to make sense. At the end of the day, she was needy and dependent, whatever the cause.

As if she'd read my mind, Noreen put down her fork. She pushed her plate away. "I didn't like being here by myself. Brian was angry when he left and I...I think he's planning to kill me."

I laughed. "I'm sure not."

She looked at me and said nothing. Her eyes seemed to be jittering inside her skull, as if there was something else she wanted to say.

"So we're your body guards?"

She looked down at her plate. She turned her fork over and pushed a kidney bean into a puddle of leftover tomato sauce. She pushed out her chair and stood up. She picked up her wine glass. "Come here. I want to show you something." She went to the door that opened from the dining area into the side yard. I splashed the last of the wine in my glass and followed.

Noreen crossed the yard to the shed tucked in the back corner, turned the combination dial, and unclasped the lock. She slid open the door and stepped to the side. She pulled out her phone and shone her flashlight app into the opening.

A tall dresser with six drawers, an armchair, an old fashioned shipping trunk, and a few other pieces of furniture, including a hospital-style bed, were stacked in one half, floor to ceiling. Another third was occupied by packing boxes. The only gardening supplies sat on a two-foot table near the front left and hung from a few hooks bolted to the metal wall.

"He didn't even take his stuff. So I know he's coming back."

Of course he'd come back, but not to kill her as she feared, spinning irrational thoughts out of nothing. The IKEA furniture and a few cardboard boxes were not the draw either. He'd be back for the several hundred thousand dollars sunk in the bungalow, money she obviously still owed him. "What's with the hospital bed?"

Noreen blinked and turned away. She stepped inside the shed. She went to one of the boxes. The flaps weren't tucked in place like the others. She pulled one back. "Come look at this."

I took a sip of wine and stepped onto the plywood floor. I went to her side.

Using just her fingertip, as if she was afraid there was a large poisonous spider lying in wait, she pressed the flap down so I could see inside the box.

On top of a stack of bills and other papers was a photograph of Noreen holding a beagle puppy. I assumed it was Terry. Precisely cut holes had been drilled through the stiff paper, removing Noreen's eyes. With her pale skin and solemn expression and missing eyes, she looked like a corpse.

34

Los Angeles

Reaching over the edge of that swimming pool, across a span of water eight feet deep, and turning Dianne onto her back was one of the hardest things I'd had to do in my twenty years of life thus far. The navy blue bikini covered with a sheer white top that clung to her sopping skin suggested it was Dianne. Her light brown hair, straight as blades of grass, cut blunt to the top of her shoulders drifted around her head. But I still had to see her face, to be absolutely sure. I was terrified of what I'd find, and terrified that seeing required me to kneel by the side of a huge pool of water and lean out over its life-swallowing depth to grab her ankle, risking falling in and sinking to the chalky bottom.

A better friend would have tried to drag her out of the pool, but I suppose we weren't really friends at all.

As the body turned, I saw her face, her empty eyes, her partially opened mouth, the tongue trying to push its way out. I scrambled away from the water like a crab. I half stood and stumbled to one of the poolside chaise lounges. Obviously the police should be called, but the murder game gripped my mind, hissing that I take my time to think things through. The longer I sat there debating with myself, the greater the chance of someone looking out of an apartment, seeing the horrific scene, and wondering what the hell was wrong with me. I wasn't crying. I doubt I looked like I was in shock. I was simply lounging by the side of the pool while a woman's corpse bobbed and drifted in the water a few yards in front of me.

Lisa was presumably still locked in a cold classroom taking a final exam, but I had no idea which one or what her exam schedule was like for the rest of the day. She might arrive in five minutes or another three hours, and I needed to talk to her before police started crawling around. What if they came and asked me questions and she showed up, clueless that Dianne was dead, and clueless about what I'd told them? I couldn't imagine Lisa lying to a detective, but neither could I imagine her voluntarily telling them about the murder game. It would be a simple lie of omission, but knowing Lisa, that would just as easily pierce her extremely alert conscience.

I pulled out my phone and typed a message to Lisa. *Need to talk asap.*

I almost typed more, and then thought about police and their investigative thoroughness, potentially wanting to view phone records. Vague was best. I deleted *asap* and hit send. Lisa and I rarely texted each other. The fact I was wanting to talk and the timing in the middle of finals would be enough to alert her that something wasn't right. The minute she was out of class, I'd hear from her. I cradled my phone in both hands, staring at the screen as if I could will her to respond.

After ten minutes, it was time to call the police. Waiting longer would stir up other problems. Maybe I could delay them by calling non-emergency, but no such luck. Eight minutes later, they were there. I was inelegantly led away from the pool area to a chair in the clubhouse where I couldn't see anything. A detective with a buzz cut and a platinum hoop in his ear, who looked as if he'd just graduated from high school, seated himself across from me. He asked my name. My phone chimed and I looked down.

"Please put that away for a few minutes," the detective said. "It can wait until we're finished."

I shoved the phone between my thighs, hoping Lisa realized today was not the day to bare her soul in an effort to ensure she continued on her path to law school with pristine ethics.

Once he'd calmed his obvious irritation that I prioritized my phone over a police officer, he moved onto a series of questions that were pleasantly innocuous. He wanted the first and last names of my roommates, the name on the apartment lease, the length of time each of us had lived there, and what I'd seen when I found the body. I admitted to turning Dianne on her back, figuring it would paint me as a painfully truthful, if careless person. He wanted to know what time I left for school, what building my final exam was held in, and what time I'd arrived back at the apartment. I fudged on the times. He wanted me to relate each thing I did before calling. Then, he asked me to describe Dianne's party habits. I said no drugs besides alcohol, as far as I knew.

The only tricky question was the last one. Tricky because I

didn't know what Lisa or Randy might say. Or Tom, for that matter. "Do you know anyone who might have wanted to hurt her?" he said.

"Do you mean kill her?"

He stared at me as if I was being deliberately dense. I stared back, holding his gaze until he looked down at the tablet where he was jotting notes. "Yes," he said.

I couldn't hesitate for too long. It would make him question my carefully constructed truthfulness. "Not off the top of my head." I gave him a sad smile.

He seemed satisfied. I was impressed with myself. Cool under pressure — that's me.

He stood up and I did the same. I glanced at the door leading to the patio. Lisa was just outside, talking to a uniformed cop. A moment later, she came into the clubhouse and I was told to leave.

Outside, I stood in an alcove by the soda and ice machines. I put my hands over my mouth and watched as the paramedics lifted Dianne's body out of the water and placed her on the concrete. They covered her quickly with a thick black tarp.

We weren't allowed in our apartment until they were done going through it, opening every drawer in Dianne's room and inspecting every hair and nail clipping in the bathroom. Two cops lingered around the pool. It was dinner time when they left and Lisa and I were finally able to compare notes. We dragged ourselves up the stairs, drained from standing around in the warm afternoon air for hours, sleepy with boredom. I opened a bottle of icy cold Pinot Grigio and poured two generous glasses. I sat at the table and sipped my wine while Lisa started making mac and cheese.

Neither of us spoke. After a while, the water boiled and she poured dry macaroni into the pot.

"It took you a long time to answer my text," I said.

"I was in my psych final."

"Really?"

"What?" She took a sip from the wine glass and stirred the macaroni.

"Did you kill her?"

She let go of the spoon and turned quickly. "Of course not! Why would you say that?" She slammed the wine glass down on the counter. Wine splashed onto the back of her hand. "I would never…"

"After what Tom did…"

"That was him! Not her, as awful as she was. And…"

"She was so casual about what he did to you. She must have known, don't you think?"

"I don't know. It doesn't matter. I would *never* kill a living soul. Never! Not even him, even if he deserves it."

"Calm down," I said.

"That's a terrible thing to say."

I didn't think it was that terrible. Certainly not worse than what he'd done. "Just asking the question. I thought maybe she put him up to it, so I wondered."

"No!" She picked up her wine and took a drink.

"And it was your idea."

Her face was red. Her voice rose to a screech. "My idea? What are you talking about? You're…"

"In the murder game. You suggested she should be drugged and drowned."

"It was a game!" She swallowed the entire contents of her glass. The macaroni boiled over. Thick, foamy water, like something toxic, spread across the stove and hissed on the burner. Lisa whipped around. She turned off the heat. The timer began chirping to announce the macaroni was done cooking. She shoved her hands into potholder mitts, picked up the pot, and walked to the sink. She heaved the macaroni into the waiting colander.

After she returned the pot to the gooey stovetop and rinsed the macaroni, she approached the table where I was sitting. She refilled her glass without topping off mine. She drank some. She spoke in a low, ragged voice. "I never wanted to play that game, if you can even call it that. I told you that from the beginning. I don't know why I let you and Randy pressure me into it. And now look. It's like we brought it on ourselves. Maybe we *are* guilty of killing her, because we talked about it and imagined it. The things we said were sick. I'm disgusted with myself." She swallowed more wine. "You better not have told the detective."

"Of course not. And I was just wondering. You'd be perfectly justified if you had."

"No."

"Tom didn't get that idea all on his own. Maybe she suggested at least part of it. She certainly set him against you."

"You don't know that. And even if she did, it's on him. And still not deserving of murder. No one deserves that."

"We all die in the end."

"No one gets to make the decision for someone else. They don't get to take it into their own hands."

I wasn't sure I agreed with her. Maybe next semester, I'd sign up for a philosophy class.

She started crying softly. "Please don't ever tell anyone the things we said."

I refilled my wine glass.

She returned to the stove and began making the cheese sauce. She pushed her hair back from her face and twisted it in a coil down the center of her neck. "You didn't promise."

"I can't promise to *never* tell *any*one."

"You have to. I can't live my life knowing something so awful might come back to bite me."

"So you don't really care about slipping away from your moral compass, you're more worried about the detective thinking we did something wrong, or your future political career getting derailed by the revelation of a youthful indiscretion." I laughed.

"Don't laugh. And that's not it. Of course I care about those things, but I care more that I did something reprehensible, that I took life so lightly, that I said such wicked things about Dianne. And now she's dead." She let out a soft, pained cry.

"I'm hungry. Is the macaroni almost ready?"

"Sometimes I think you're an animal."

"I'll take that as a compliment, since animals are smart and self-sufficient, although I don't think that's how you meant it."

She didn't say anything else.

We ate dinner without talking much. After dinner, we opened a second bottle of wine and I rolled a joint. We went out on the balcony.

"Do you think it's safe?" Lisa said.

"What?"

"Smoking pot. Maybe the cops are still hanging around."

"I don't think so. The only thing they want now is to talk to Randy. And Tom."

She nodded.

I lit the joint, inhaled, and handed it to Lisa.

We smoked in surprisingly companionable silence for a while. Then we speculated about where Randy was, and whether or not Dianne might have gotten herself wasted and drowned without any help at all.

35

Aptos

After Noreen's bliss-inducing lasagna and the shock of the eyeless photograph, I'd made a half-hearted attempt at helping her clean up the kitchen. My contribution consisted of covering the lasagna with plastic and wrapping the bread in foil, while she loaded the dishwasher and washed the sauce pans, turning them upside down on the counter to dry. We sat on the couch and finished the wine. When she started to nod off, I escorted her to her bedroom door, assuring her I'd wash the wine glasses. I rinsed them and left them on the counter.

The wine hadn't made me sleepy at all. I sat in my armchair, feet propped up on a suitcase, watching a video of a pregnant shark. There was a soft knock on the door. I opened it and Jared stepped into my room. As I closed the door, he picked up my tablet, closed the cover, and set it on the nightstand. He climbed into my bed, holding up the covers like a yawning mouth, waiting for me to join him. Once our bodies were wrapped around each other, he put his mouth by my ear. "Let's run away together."

"Let's stay right here and get rid of these clothes." I

reached for his belt buckle and pulled the end out of the metal ring. I unbuttoned them and eased the zipper down. As I tugged them off, he whispered. "I'm tired of being quiet, tired of hiding this. Why won't you leave with me?"

"Shh," I said.

"I want you. I need you like air. I..."

"Shh."

"Who cares? It doesn't matter if she knows."

"It does." I pushed his shirt up and got on my knees. He raised his arms and I pulled it over his head and dropped it on the floor.

If Noreen found out, she might decide to restart the roommate search. I hadn't signed an agreement. It wasn't impossible to believe Noreen might change the locks without warning, or do something even more aggressive to force me out. She wanted Jared and if she knew I had him. The more I thought about it, the more I realized there might be something a little crazed in her eyes — a slight blankness and a look of confusion, as if she was never quite sure where she was. Maybe that's why her ex removed her eyes from the photograph. If he truly was her ex. I was no longer sure about that either. And there was that mirror, reminding me every time I stepped into the bathroom that she had minimal control over her emotions, and a tendency toward violence.

Jared grabbed the front of my shirt. "Slow down."

"You're the one who knocked on my door."

"I wanted to be with you, not just have sex and go back to my room to sleep alone again."

I sat up. "What do you have against sex?"

He laughed softly. "Nothing."

I put my finger to his lips.

He pulled me down so my head was close to his on the pillow. He turned and whispered. "We never talk."

I sighed. I thought I'd made it clear I didn't expect sex to come wrapped in a pink bow and glitter. I knew he wanted to talk, he'd said it enough times. He wanted a relationship, but still… Late at night, with Noreen in her room, possibly drifting in a light sleep, maybe not sleeping at all, was not the time for a deep conversation. Whispering more than a few words at a time is painful. It strains the vocal chords.

"I don't want to sneak around," he said. "It's stupid. We're adults. I feel like I'm fourteen, whacking off in my bedroom, one ear tuned for my mother's footsteps."

I laughed.

"It's not funny. Why don't you want to talk to me, have dinner with me?"

"I already told you. Haven't you ever had a friend with benefits?"

"We're not even friends," he hissed.

"I'm hurt."

He pinched my hip.

"I thought you were practicing self-restraint? Letting go of attachment. Just go with the flow," I said.

"Meeting you blew that all to hell."

I sat up and put the pillows behind me. If he wanted to talk, I could indulge him. I was curious about him. He had money from a source that he'd never revealed. He walked away from a career with a lot of potential and was pursuing a somewhat esoteric spiritual practice while driving an expensive car — a man of contradictions.

I kept my voice low. "Okay. Let's talk. What made you decide to become a Buddhist?"

He settled next to me and kept his voice equally soft. The pleasure of thinking he'd won emanated from his skin like cologne. "I wanted control over myself. Which I'm failing at miserably. But when you and I get straightened out, I'll get back to it."

"I can straighten you out right now," I said.

He pinched my hip again. I pinched his.

"I'm serious," he said.

He went on to tell me that all his life he felt controlled by other people. He began to realize he didn't even control his own inner self. As a child he played soccer and baseball. When he suggested to his father he didn't really enjoying kicking and batting balls, his father laughed and assured him — *of course you do*. The note of confidence in his father's voice made Jared doubt his own desires. Eventually, he mentioned his ambivalence to his mother who laughed and reminded him that all boys liked sports. When she repeated this unarguable fact in front of Jared's father, his father chuckled that soon Jared would be in junior high school where sports would make or break him. In junior high, he wouldn't be whining to mommy any more. Team sports paved the way to high school friendships and college acceptance. Even if team participation didn't generate actual cash for college, there would be a comforting wall around him, corralling the right circle of friends and ensuring he didn't wander about on his own without a solid identity.

College turned out to be one big stew of groupthink. The goal was to study business, paving the way into business school itself, where you studied the deeper inner workings of business. The world ran on business. Or rather, business ran the world. If you weren't in business, you couldn't make a living. There were engineers and businessmen, but far more of the latter. A man needed to make a lucrative income, securing the future, providing for a family, making sure he could afford a home in a good neighborhood where the kids could play on well-established soccer and baseball teams.

He was funneled out of business school into a high paying position.

A year or so ago, he'd wound up reporting to a Buddhist manager named Ren.

"That guy didn't think like anyone I'd ever met. He was in complete control of himself. It was there in his eyes, a total lack of concern over how others viewed him. Ren didn't care whether he led the pack. He didn't care whether he was viewed favorably by superiors or even got credit for his work. He was like steel. The true man of steel. Above it all. He glided through life knowing who he was, unruffled, focused and calm, even when everything around him was fractured or taking an opposite course. He didn't play sports, but he was completely fit because he did yoga and walked everywhere. That guy walked ten or fifteen miles every day. It was phenomenal."

"Why did you quit?" I said.

"This was before I quit. Ren left Cisco and started his

own company."

"Why didn't you go work for him?"

He was quiet for several minutes, providing some space that allowed me to listen for Noreen. I heard nothing. Which meant nothing. She might have been standing outside my door for the previous twenty minutes, straining to hear every whisper. I turned on my side and bit gently on his nipple. "You're not going to tell me?"

"I guess I wasn't a good fit for his venture."

"So you bolted?"

"Sort of."

"Into the arms of Buddha?"

"It's not like that."

"Are you ever going to return to your career?"

"I don't know."

"At some point, don't you sort of need to have a job?"

I waited for his answer, but he remained silent. I touched his face. His eyes were closed, although maybe he closed them when my fingers drew too close. I moved on top of him and touched my lips to his. He held my head in both hands and we kissed for a long time, our bodies pressed together, aching for each other, but not wanting to finish that kiss. There was something he wanted from me and I didn't think it was just a relationship.

He wanted to swallow me whole, drink my essence so he could become me. It wasn't obvious to him that's what was going on, but it was quite clear to me. He thought he wanted a relationship, and that was part of it, but he also wanted what I have — the detachment from not behaving according to others' rules and beliefs. A disregard for polishing an admirable reputation. A steely inner strength that nothing can touch. Buddhism might be able to give him that, after years, decades, of study and practice. Maybe he was jealous that I had it without effort.

Analyzing him while he was sucking everything he could out of my mouth was rather cold. He was there in the kiss as if his life depended on it and I was somewhere else, thinking I shouldn't have allowed him into my room after all. Thinking about Noreen and becoming more and more convinced the reason the house was so quiet was that she was standing outside my door, wanting him and considering how to be rid of me, contemplating worse things than defacing a mirror.

It wasn't as if I was destitute. I had enough money to live adequately if I went back to the motel. But I was supposed to be on an upward trajectory toward a nicer living arrangement, not groveling around a motel with people living on public funds or panhandling or pot sales or sex.

If Joe was still around, I could move to the Ocean Breeze with him, but that would take a bit of doing. And it would spoil the thrill between us. I'd be in a position of need, giving him the advantage and I didn't like that. The complete equality was part of what drew me to him.

No, it wasn't a choice. I had to keep Noreen happy until I could work out the raise and save for a few more months. Then I'd look for a nicer place with people who didn't need me so damn much.

36

It was becoming clear to Jared that Alexandra was more interested in keeping Noreen out of her face than she was in seeing what might develop with him. He understood the concern, and he wondered how long he was going to remain living in an unsettling house, waiting for the distance between him and Alexandra to grow smaller.

The only promising change was that Alex had finally agreed to have dinner with him. *Nothing fancy, though.* She'd said that before he could even register her acceptance, before he could open his mouth to suggest The Crow's Nest. It was a relatively casual place, but she wouldn't perceive it that way. The white tablecloths pushed it too close to *fancy.* He suggested the Paradise Beach Grille in Capitola, and once again, the moment he finished speaking, she dictated the terms, informing him she'd meet him there after work. Of course she would. She wouldn't want Noreen to see them leaving the house together. It was exhausting and childish. Alexandra acted as if she owed something to Noreen. Maybe she did.

His thoughts circled again around the possibility that the two of them were playing some kind of twisted game with him — hoping to make him believe one girl was on the brink of madness and the other took on the appearance of a goddess because she demanded nothing from a man. But what would be the purpose? Was Alexandra trying to prove to him that a woman who didn't want the entanglements of a relationship wasn't all that much fun after all, despite a frequent male fantasy to the contrary? Was he supposed to get so frustrated with Alex's untouchable nature that he fell for a needy, clinging woman like Noreen? But why would they do that?

It made no sense. It was simply the luck of the draw. Two very unusual women.

Unfortunately, he was in love with Alexandra. He couldn't tell her that, not yet. She'd think he was ridiculous. He didn't even know her. But the strange thing was, he felt he did. He felt that whatever he didn't know about her would eventually reveal itself to be pure delight, her soul opening to him slowly, every day showing more of herself, and there wouldn't be a single piece of her history that failed to fascinate him or a single aspect of her personality he didn't adore.

He'd lost his mind.

He found a parking spot two blocks away from the Esplanade. Parking was easier to find on a Tuesday night. Looking for a spot on the weekends involved thirty minutes or more, driving narrow streets and rounding tight corners, waiting for beachgoers to toddle across the street at will, flip-flops slowing their pace. In the summer, it was pointless to bring a car to Capitola at all.

He walked to the restaurant and went inside. He scanned the room and the bar area. She wasn't there. He wove among the small tables in front of the bar to the door leading to the deck. It was after seven. He felt a chill, wondering if she'd changed her mind, set him up to look like a fool, if only to himself.

He returned to the area near the door and glanced out at the street. The hostess asked whether he had a reservation and if he wanted to be seated. He hesitated for several long seconds while she stared at him, tapping the podium with a purple fingernail. Sitting alone wouldn't bother him under normal circumstances, but Alex wasn't a normal girl by any standard, and his feelings and behavior had veered far north of normal the past few weeks. If he waited outside, the restaurant might implement the fifteen minute rule and give away his table. "Okay. I asked to hold a table on the deck."

"And you got it." She picked up two menus and a wine list and swept past him, headed toward the back.

Alexandra was only twenty minutes late. Not unforgivable. If he wasn't so anxious about her to begin with, if she hadn't turned down so many invitations, it wouldn't have bothered him at all. As it was, he felt off center and he didn't like it. She seated herself across from him. Her dark hair was woven into a complicated braid across the top of her head. She wore sunglasses even though dusk was on its way. Her arms were bare, lightly tanned next to her loose white top that dipped in front. When she moved, a thin piece of lace from her bra revealed itself, disappearing each time she straightened. He couldn't stop watching for it, as if they were playing a game of hide and seek.

They ordered a bottle of Chardonnay and bowls of clam chowder.

"I'm not that hungry," she said. "Chowder might be all I want for dinner."

He nodded.

She reached for a slice of sourdough bread and spread butter across it, sliding the knife back and forth several times even though the entire surface shone with creamy white.

She talked about her job.

When the chowder came, she refilled their wine glasses before the server could take the bottle out of the chiller.

She took a sip of wine. "I just remembered, I never told you what really happened with the mirror."

"What about it?"

"She attacked it with a butcher knife."

"That's..." He shuddered. "Did she say why?"

"She's jealous of me, and I guess her feelings got the best of her. Or something."

He wanted to ask her whether she was planning to find new housing, but that might lead to blurting out the suggestion they find a place together. She would say no.

He hoped he didn't appear weak for putting up with Noreen's bullshit. Alexandra didn't seem interested in his reasons for staying. Possibly she was more concerned about her own situation.

There was so much he didn't know about her. Everything. Her job must pay well, all high tech jobs did. Maybe she lived hand to mouth anyway. She had a lot of clothes. It must be that she blew through every paycheck and this was the best she could do. Maybe she had family obligations.

"It was such a bizarre thing to do, scratching it up like that. But she explained it so casually, it actually came out sounding like something rather ordinary. As if she was telling me she was upset and not paying attention and accidentally broke a wine glass."

He thought about the rat. He wouldn't mention her thong. "There was a dead rat in my room. Under my bed."

She laughed. "That sucks."

"I think she put it there."

She took a sip of wine and dug into her chowder.

"Do you think we made a mistake?" he said.

"We?"

"Renting rooms from her. I...she's creeping me out more every week," he said.

"Look. She has a thing for you. She's jealous of me, worried you're interested in me, and she's playing silly games. It's nothing."

He put down his spoon and reached across the table. He touched her wrist.

She pulled back slightly.

"What's wrong?" he said.

"I'm trying to eat."

She scooped up a spoonful of chowder and put it in her mouth. She chewed carefully, her jaw hardly moving around the tiny bits of clam and soft potatoes. She made it seem as if the soup was the center of her life, as if she was eating something pure that transported her beyond mere taste to an intense pleasure that dominated every part of her body. It made him want her. He pushed his bowl away.

"Aren't you hungry?"

"In a minute." He took a sip of wine. "So you're not worried?"

"About what?"

"I don't know, that she'll take her butcher knife and stab us in our beds."

"Like Psycho?" she laughed.

"That was the shower."

"I lock my door. Don't you?"

"Yes." He couldn't make sense of it — Alexandra was absurdly concerned about Noreen overhearing them, finding out they were having sex, but she was completely nonchalant about the possibility that Noreen might be demented to the point that their lives could be in danger.

Any normal man would take this opportunity to announce he was looking for another place to stay. But her lack of commitment, her seeming disinterest except when they were having sex, or the most banal conversation, made him certain she would respond by wishing him the best, picking up the tab for their chowder and wine, and walking out the door. He'd never see her again, aside from a silent nocturnal good-bye in his bed. He'd wake and she'd be back in her room, the door locked, and that would be the end of it.

He should give up. She wasn't interested and he was making a fool of himself. But it was impossible. He couldn't stop looking at her, couldn't stop thinking about what it felt like to touch her skin, the things she did to his body. His face grew warm. He picked up his wine glass and held it close to the side of his face as if the chill of the glass would drift across his enflamed skin. He lowered the glass and took a sip. She'd taken absolute control of his being. Although he could never remember the details, he knew that his dreams were filled with her. He was possessed even when he was unconscious. Her dark, heavy hair was soft and alive. When they were in bed, it fell across his skin and made him feel she was weaving silken blankets around his body. Her eyes glowed like the opening to a dark, quiet cave, pulling him toward her, magnets preventing him from looking anywhere else.

He closed his own eyes, tying to calm the ache in his bones. He wanted to take her away from here so no one else in the restaurant could look at her, no one else could hear her voice. He wanted to kidnap her out of her office and prevent anyone from talking to her or taking one single moment of her time. If he could, he'd find a secluded cabin by a river that wound through a quiet forest, and they'd live in solitude until they died. He shook his head.

"Are you okay?" she said.

"Sure." He pulled his bowl back toward him and stirred the soup, burying the skin that was trying to form in the cooling evening air. "I just don't understand you."

"Maybe that's deliberate." She smiled in a friendly way, but her tone was threatening.

"I like you a lot, and I want to hang out. I want to get to know you better. I know almost nothing about you."

"You know every crevice of my body."

"I want to know *you*." He tapped the side of his head.

"I don't have a lot of data on you, either. Aside from your disinterest in sports and your religious quest. Maybe you should go first. Maybe once you trust me with more, I'll trust you. Let's start with how you can afford to live without even thinking about work."

"I'm not trying to hide anything. I just don't like to talk about it. My first gig after biz school was a startup, okay? The company was purchased by Cisco."

"And?"

"Do I really need to explain it?"

"How much did you get?"

"Well I'm living in a run down bungalow that's hanging off a cliff with a mad woman as a landlord, so I think you can infer I'm not rolling in it. I have a decent enough nest egg to not think about work for a while. A long while, if I'm careful."

She smiled as if she'd won a contest of some kind. Was it that she got him to reveal something and she continued to sit there, an inscrutable smile on lips that shimmered, despite drinking wine and eating a bowl of chowder? Was it something else? Would he ever be able to call her his own? But the more she pulled back, the more he refused to give up, digging in deeper every day.

37

Los Angeles

Twitter is a fascinating phenomenon. It seems to me, people don't really get the power of it. You can talk to *anyone* in the world, a person you'd never in a million years stumble across in a bar or at work or even on an international trip. It's possible to meet and strike up a conversation with any living soul on the planet. Of course there are language barriers, so it's not completely open to the entire human population, but the feeling of possibility is there. You might find your twin, you might find your soulmate. It feels like the first step toward physical transportation to any place you want to go, like they did on Star Trek. That was decades ago and we're all still waiting. Twitter connections aren't limited by passports and airfare. They aren't limited by the odds of coincidence that a particular person you'd connect with psychologically leaves the bar ten minutes or ten hours before you arrive, instead of sitting beside you the moment you open your mouth and order a vodka martini. It stretches the imagination to consider how amazing it is. I think about this a lot.

Three hundred million Twitter users, give or take, scattered across the planet, shouting about what they think and how they feel. Three hundred million people expressing their opinions, complaining about the weather, lamenting their food cravings, shrieking about politics and injustice and fear, and broadcasting their sometimes successful attempts at wittiness. The flood of messages and images feels as if the entire planet really is simultaneously talking to each other, or at each other. A massive tide of words capable of poking a new hole in the ozone with its heat. Of course, all those voices represent only four percent of the people walking about on the earth. That's a lot of noise coming from a very small portion of the human population. I suppose the rest of them are screaming inside an echo chamber.

Of those three hundred million, how many are real? I have two Twitter personas, neither of which bears my name. It's possible to have five personas. Or ten. Or a hundred.

Because of that easy anonymity, without fear of law enforcement watching his feed, Randy tweeted from @Slacker81 to @GirlStuff29 twelve days after Dianne was found face down in the pool. The cops might be watching @RandyF100 and @ALX342, if they watched at all. They needed access to my digital world to do that, and my digital doorway was always a coffee shop.

@Slacker81: *Got time for a toke? Just you and me.*

I'd never seen the @Slacker81 ID before, but knew immediately it was Randy. Pretty obvious from what he tweeted. And even more obvious from his ironic identity — Dianne's mother called him a slacker and Dianne had shared the compliment with Randy.

@GirlStuff29: *Tell me where and when.*

@Slacker81: *Majestic Park. 10pm Thursday.*
@GirlStuff29: *You won our game.*
@Slacker81: *Yep.*
@GirlStuff29: *People want to talk 2 U.*
@Slacker81: *Guess I'll lose you after all :(*
@GirlStuff29: *After all?*
@Slacker81: *C U there.*

38

Aptos

Tess and I were sitting in the coffee shop drinking our Monday morning lattes, talking about the upcoming week. The week would be dominated by a 3-day engineering review. These reviews had nothing really to do with me, but she liked me to attend so I could *gain a sense of the big picture* of the product portfolio and understand where new products fit in with the rest of the line. The reviews were boring beyond description. I'm sure the engineers were on the edges of their seats, but it was all so much nonsense and terminology and acronyms floating over my head. The only flow I followed were the discussions of software bugs and their ability to delay a product launch and the raised voices regarding the late discovery of said bugs. That was fascinating, mostly because of the raised voices, and the way the bugs managed to remain anonymous until late in the game.

Occasionally the discussion veered into other territory I understood — marketing and sales. Those discussions had their moments. It was interesting to hear debates over sales compensation or how to move the needle against the competition. There was a surprisingly steady flow of jokes that were sometimes quite funny. Laugh out loud funny.

Tess finished her latte and stood up. "I need to get going."

I put the lid back on my half full cup and pushed back my chair. I took one last sip. I hadn't secured the lid correctly and latte splashed onto my chin and dribbled down the lapel of my pale green jacket. "Shit."

Tess laughed.

I looked up at her. The laughter stopped abruptly.

"What is it?" I wiped my chin and stood up.

"I'm going to lose my mind if I don't remember where I've seen you or your photograph before. It's really annoying that you won't help me figure it out."

I turned and carried my cup and the dripping lid to the trash bin. I dropped them in, grabbed a napkin, and wiped my fingers. I stuffed the napkin in the trash. There was no way she'd seen me anywhere and I was starting to wonder whether it was possible that through some against-all-odds fluke, she'd seen the pictures Charlie took of me.

We left the coffee shop and started walking the two blocks back to CoastalCreative.

"Why won't you help me with this?" she said.

"How am I supposed to know where you think you've seen me?" I laughed. "That's an impossible puzzle."

"You can help by telling me where you might have had photographs appear — online, in a magazine — I don't know."

"What does it matter?"

She stopped and turned. She hoisted the strap of her

leather bag higher on her shoulder. "It makes me think I shouldn't trust you as much as I do. That you're hiding something."

"So you *think* you've seen me, or my picture, and because I can't read your mind back through the past five years of your life, or more, you don't trust me?"

"I have this weird sense that you're deceiving me. Playing me."

I stared at her, not blinking, waiting for her to hear how ridiculous she sounded, waiting for her to drop my gaze. She didn't.

"It's Jared too." She looked down.

"What does he have to do with it?"

"There's something not quite right about you."

I started walking again.

She hurried to catch up. "There are a lot of little things."

"You're my boss, you don't get to dictate my sex life."

"I'm not. But you're so cold about it."

"You don't know me as well as you think you do. You can't judge whether or not I'm cold."

"That's how you come across."

I felt my pay increase, and possibly my job security itself sliding through my fingers like egg yolk — slippery, impossible to hold, ridiculous even to think I *could* hold on. I took a deep breath. "If it's that important to you, I'll try to think where you might have seen my photograph. It's just hard to know where to start."

"Facebook. Twitter. A blog?"

"I don't use Facebook. I use Twitter, but I don't have a photograph."

"See. That's what I mean that you're hiding something."

"What?"

"Everyone uses Facebook."

"That's a bit sweeping."

"Nearly everyone."

"I like Twitter better, and I'd feel like I have a split personality if I go on all these different social media sites and try to keep people and conversations straight."

She stopped walking again and nodded. "It's not that complicated, but I guess I see your point."

I let out my breath slowly. She seemed slightly less worked up. "I don't have much of a public presence, so I really can't think where…"

"It's when you spilled the coffee and you looked up with that extremely irritated expression on your face. That's what I remember. And your eyebrows, of course. They're perfect."

"You have quite a memory."

"It's semi photographic. Didn't I tell you that?"

I shook my head. "If it's photographic, won't it come to you?"

"Yes. But it's your refusal to help that almost bothers me more than the actual details. It seems like you don't want me to remember."

"I'll try harder."

"And Jared…"

"What about him?"

"If you don't like him, you shouldn't dangle him like you are."

She had no right to delve into my personal life, but I'd opened the door, so I couldn't really complain. Before, I'd thought her personality had gone through a rather sudden and unnerving change from a hard-driving, singularly focused woman bent on getting to the top and staying there, but now I wondered if I'd misread it and she hadn't changed at all. She was a control freak, and being in control of the work life of her employees wasn't enough. She was so smart, she needed activity for all that excess brain matter, so the natural thing was to venture into other arenas. And I *had* invited her, trying too hard to bond as females rather than just colleagues. I never expected her to start advising me on how to live my life, and I wasn't about to listen. "I don't think I ever said I don't like him."

"He wants more than you're willing to give."

"He does."

"It's not fair. By seeing him, you imply you might want more, in the future."

"I'll give it some thought."

She actually smiled. It was all about control. She was happy now that I planned to spend my after work hours considering her advice, letting her influence creep further into my life. Maybe the raise wasn't denied. Maybe she was withholding it because she thought she could buy me, make me belong to her entirely.

But the photographic memory was more concerning. She'd eventually remember, and if it was one of Charlie's pictures, what did that mean? It had to be one of his because there just weren't any other pictures of me out there, floating around the world. I avoid photos so carefully, I didn't even show up for my senior portrait and didn't appear in my high school yearbook.

If he'd passed it around, under what context had he distributed it?

39

Mountain View

Charlie and I were eating chicken enchiladas at a Mexican place, drinking martinis, much to the despair of our server. It wasn't the best martini, but better than a margarita, ever. Popping an olive in my mouth, I suggested it would be fun to get high on Friday night, do a few shots, or whatever. I'd sleep over. If we were too wasted for sex, there was always the next morning. Charlie lit up. I'd never spent the night and his ego prevented him from thinking he'd ever be too wasted for sex. He was busy imagining several repeat performances. His eyes glowed with the images passing behind them.

I dipped a chip in the salsa and held it up to his lips. He opened his mouth and ate it in one bite.

On Friday night the air was cool — winter was coming fast, ripping dead leaves off trees and sticking its sharp, cold fingers into condos constructed with dicey attention to detail. We sat on the balcony bundled up in leather jackets. I wore a silk scarf to keep my neck warm. I spent several long minutes considering whether or not I should use the scarf to lead Charlie to his final breath, instead of one of his lovely king-sized feather pillows as I'd planned.

If you didn't have a full-blown party, you could get away with smoking a joint on your own balcony at our complex. Clearly Charlie thought breaking the law regarding smoking dope was perfectly acceptable, while sharing your rented condo with a friend so you weren't living half a paycheck or a serious bout with the flu from homelessness, was not.

We sipped vodka tonics and ate from a bowl of fish crackers. Charlie told stories about risqué law school parties. I smiled and gazed at his face, watching his mouth move, his eyes dart about as if they could see anything in the darkness. Each time he handed the joint to me, I put it to my lips and leaned forward slightly. I rubbed the insides of his thighs, gliding my fingers higher with firm, steady pressure. He closed his eyes and I held my breath for a moment, then released it as if I was blowing out a stream of smoke. He never noticed the joint hadn't decreased much in size after I finished with it.

When the joint was gone and he was nicely buzzed, I took his hand and led him inside to the couch. I got his bottle of Grey Goose out of the freezer and a shot glass out of the cabinet. I set them on the glass coffee table. I took off my jacket and scarf. I removed his jacket, tossing it on the chair. I knelt and untied his shoes and took them off his feet. He sighed and leaned back.

I closed the blinds and pulled a deck of cards out of my purse. "Shots or strip."

"What?" His eyelids drooped and he looked at me hungrily but with inertia.

"We'll play Blackjack and whoever wins each hand gets to

tell the loser to strip or take a shot."

He grinned and his eyes opened slightly, but his pupils were huge, bleeding out toward the whites of his eyes. "Sounds good."

The game went as expected. After twelve hands, I'd had one shot and was wearing nothing but a thong and my boots. That sequence had been a hassle — he'd made me take off my leggings after my first loss, and put the boots back on. I'd worn a few extra layers to make sure he had two or three shots to my one.

It was time for the next game.

I'd discarded the idea of using my scarf, best not to risk leaving an imperceptible fiber behind.

We went into the bedroom and I pushed him onto the bed. I removed the rest of his clothes slowly. His breathing turned rough, inching toward the edge of snoring. I slid his boxer shorts ever so slowly down his legs, brushing my fingers over the thick hair. I gave a sharp tug to one of the hairs to see how out of it he was. He didn't respond. I dropped the shorts on the floor.

I had a pretty good idea it wouldn't be all that easy to smother someone. The autonomic nervous system takes control, the body fights for its oxygen even if the conscious mind is essentially dead. But someone who likes sex with cuffs is a whole lot easier.

In the drawer of the nightstand was a pair of handcuffs that I was familiar with. He was right-handed, so that was the hand I secured to the slatted headboard. I used neckties from his dresser drawer to secure the other wrist to the headboard and both of his ankles to the footboard. I moved to the side of the bed and climbed on. I got on my hands and knees and crept up toward him. I swung my leg over and straddled him. His dick was moderately firm, but he seemed unaware of that fact. I inched up slightly, putting most of my weight on his hip bones. He didn't complain or move. I leaned across and picked up the large, downy pillow.

First, I lowered the pillow gently over his face. He didn't react. After a moment, he groaned and turned his head slightly, but he made no move to push away the pillow. I pressed gently. He tried to turn on his side, but the cuffs and ties prevented him rotating more than a few inches. He groaned and coughed.

It was now or never.

I pushed as hard as I could. The results of all those bench presses and curls, the triceps work, the lat pull-downs, the squats and shoulder presses, came into play. He groaned and coughed, his body thrashed, but there wasn't enough freedom to allow movements violent enough to throw me out of position.

Before my arms grew tired from the effort, it was over.

I took a folded trash bag out of my purse and put the pillow inside. I lifted his head and dragged the other pillow underneath. I picked up his phone, powered it down, and dropped it into the bag with the pillow. I went into the living room and dressed quickly.

For the next hour, I wiped down every door, table, chair, counter, and piece of glass I'd touched. I cleaned the handcuffs and flushed the joint and the ashes down the toilet.

Although I'd wiped it down, I grabbed the bottle of vodka at the last minute, tucked the deck of cards into my purse, and let myself out.

40

It was clear that I had to immediately leave the condo I shared with Maria, without saying good-bye to Sylvie and her brownies, not to mention my very solid roommate. The police would question everyone in our building. Charlie and I weren't a couple with an established relationship, but we'd been seen together at the pool often enough. Maria knew we went out to dinner and that I hung out at his place on a somewhat regular basis. She knew we slept together. What she didn't know was very much about me.

In the photo used for my gym membership ID, I was blonde, with a pixie haircut. The blue shadow on my eyes and the lipstick that was too dark for my complexion made me look a little cheap. Maria wouldn't be able to tell them my previous address, my employer, or anything about my relatives. She didn't know. It's amazing how a few weeks of bonding over fitness and diet, chatter about guys and clothes, can make a woman feel like she's your best friend. She was so anxious to get a roommate for help with her mortgage, and believed she knew me so well from the gym, she let sensible caution dissolve in favor of foregoing a bunch of unnecessary paperwork.

On the Saturday morning after Charlie died, I pleaded a

hangover and told Maria to go ahead to our usual yoga class followed by a full workout. I cleaned her condo more thoroughly than I had Charlie's — bleach and a disposable cloth on every surface, including the inside of the refrigerator and the medicine cabinet. The place reeked with the burning sensation bleach produces. I filled my two suitcases and packed the rest of my clothes loose on their hangers in the trunk of my car. I filled boxes with shoes and purses and with make-up and shoved them as high as the ceiling on the back seat. Fifteen minutes before Maria was due back, I did one last walk through. I wrote a short good-bye note on a scrap of paper. I left cash for the first half of next month's rent, just to be nice.

Before I climbed into my car, I wiped Charlie's phone. I set the phone on the pavement and drove over it until it was a pancake of glass and metal. I stopped at a Target store, opened the lid on one of the dumpsters, and dropped the phone inside.

Of course, leaving abruptly made me more suspect, but it was cleaner.

While I'd been contemplating the end of Charlie's life, I'd landed the job with CoastalCreative and quit my former position in Silicon Valley. I was thrilled to find Noreen's ad, and thrilled that I could move in so quickly.

It's not that I'm completely invisible. I have a passport. I have a driver's license and a social security card. You need those things to get a job, but the woman people know is not the woman in those documents. And who, beyond the Security or HR department at a company, ever looks at those images or processes that information? It's just numbers and bad photos. I never use credit cards. I don't even have a debit card. I use disposable phones and gmail at internet cafes. All my music is uploaded from CDs and people are generous about sharing their streaming accounts with friendly, easy-going roommates.

Leaving Sylvia and her cute kids without saying good-bye was disappointing. Remembering her brownies left me feeling deprived. She'll never know I saved her life, but I don't need her to thank me or anything self-serving like that. I just want her to be able to do what she needs to do in peace, to become a strong, self-supporting woman who isn't vulnerable to a takedown by a guy who doesn't know shit.

41

Aptos

Tess opened my office door, stepped inside, and closed it firmly behind her. "I figured it out." The triumphant, superior tone in her voice ran into my ear and pressed against the soft tissue inside my skull, causing a sharp pain.

"I saw your picture on Twitter."

I smiled regretfully. "My picture hasn't been on Twitter."

"Yes it has."

"There are upwards of three million photographs a day on Twitter. How on earth would you remember one that looked like me?"

"I explained what my memory is like."

"You did, but you'd have to focus specifically on that photograph, not just see it passing by."

"Why are you arguing with me?"

I smiled. "I don't think I'm arguing."

"As I've said, your eyebrows are perfect." She settled back in the red guest chair, crossed her legs, and folded her arms the opposite direction of her legs. "They're a lovely shape. A perfect palette for dramatic eye shadow."

"Thank you."

"And that scowl. When you're angry, it's so easy to read. I hope you don't play poker."

I brushed my bangs away from my forehead, exposing my perfect brows. I may utilize expressions that appear angry if it fits the circumstances, but I don't get angry. Inconvenienced is a better word. Disgusted by the sluggish pace of evolution. Determined to do what I can to eradicate misogyny. And right then I was very inconvenienced and trying to foresee where she was headed with her discovery. I was disgusted all over again with Charlie for taking my picture when I'd asked him not to. What makes a person think they have the right to bulldoze right over a request for respect?

Tess had no clue about any of that, so she wasn't as good at reading me as she thought she was. I let her keep verbally patting herself on the back.

"Your picture was retweeted by a woman I follow. Corporate_Bitch2."

"I'm not familiar with her."

"I'm surprised. She tweets about gender issues in the workplace."

I nodded.

"She retweeted a guy she's friends with. He tweeted a picture of you. Your expression was identical to the look you had when you spilled your coffee — pissed as hell. You were wearing a bathing suit. I remember exactly what he wrote."

"What's that?"

"He said, *Hot chick. I thought I could love her but she's such a bitch.* Then he added, *#MostHotChicksAre*. Then, Corporate_Bitch2 commented that he needed to get in his time travel machine to the twenty-first century."

I gave her a slim smile.

"Aren't you going to say anything?"

"Like what?"

"That he was a jerk for putting that on Twitter," she said.

"It goes without saying."

"You're not upset that he was so crude?"

It depended on what else she was so proud of. It sounded as if the story of her sleuthing wasn't finished yet. I rubbed my knuckle. I curled my fingers over my palm and looked at my nails. The polish was a dark gold. Suddenly, I was tired of it. As soon as she was finished crowing, and I could legitimately sneak out of the office, I'd see if they could take me for a manicure as a drop-in.

"There's more," Tess said.

I put my hand on my lap and smiled, waiting.

"He's dead."

"Who's dead?"

"The guy who tweeted your picture. A few weeks after that…"

"How do you remember all of this? Do you spend all day trolling twitter?"

"I told you I have a…"

"Semi-photographic. Got it." What a waste, using the valuable resource of a semi-photographic memory to store the often mindless drivel from a Twitter feed.

"Corporate_Bitch2 tweeted about his death. She wrote — *Such a loss. Such a mystery.*"

"What's a mystery?"

"His death was being investigated. Police believe he was smothered, but they haven't identified a suspect, or found the weapon. They were checking into a former girlfriend."

"That's a lengthy discussion for Twitter."

"We did it with short phrases."

"Okay." I picked up my phone and rubbed the screen to wipe away the smears my fingers leave after I've used hand lotion.

"Are you worried?"

"About what?"

She looked at me with a smile at the corner of her lips. I stared at her, not blinking. She gazed back and didn't lower her lids or turn to the side. "He tweeted something nasty about you and then he's dead and then they're looking for his girlfriend."

"I'm not his girlfriend, if that's what you're thinking."

"Then why was he taking your picture in a bikini?"

"We lived in the same building, I saw him at the pool."

"That's all?"

"That's all."

"Hmm." She unfolded her arms and placed her hands in her lap. "It all sounds a little...I don't know. It's a strange story."

"Not really."

"You don't think so? That he called you a bitch and now he's dead?"

"You've never been called a bitch?"

She laughed. "Of course I have."

"Well, then."

For the first time since she'd glided into my office, she looked uncertain. The things she was saying finally penetrated her own mind.

"I'm glad you were able to remember," I said. "I know it was bothering you a lot. I thought with your kind of memory, your recollection would be instantaneous."

She laughed. "Not always."

"Hence the *semi*-photographic and not photographic."

"I'm not sure anyone has a truly photographic memory," she said.

I shrugged. "I don't know a lot about it."

"We're off topic," she said. "I'm just curious. Are the police looking for you?"

"Of course not."

"Why was it so important to conceal it from me?"

"I didn't conceal anything. I don't have a semi-photographic memory, and I'd forgotten all about that picture. I'd almost forgotten that guy. I hardly knew him."

She re-crossed her legs. "I guess if you didn't even know he tweeted it, you'd have no way of helping me figure it out where I'd seen you."

"That's right," I said.

"He does seem like a bit of an ass, tweeting your picture and saying nasty things about you, without you even being aware of it." She sat for a few minutes. She put her left index finger with it's colorless nails to her lips and touched it with the tip of her tongue. She started to nibble at the cuticle, then let her hand fall to her lap. "You didn't have a thing with him?"

I studied her hands, now clenched into fists.

"He said he could fall in love with you. That sounds like more than some guy you saw at the pool."

Something about it bothered her, but I couldn't figure out what. It seemed as if my body was giving off a scent, rewarding her constant sniffing with an odor of...what? Not fear, I wasn't afraid. I was simply calculating what had to be done to redirect her. I nibbled the edge of the cuticle on my own index finger, showing her I had my own occasional bad habits. We were friends. If not that, we were surely colleagues with a close friendship.

I pouted slightly, stared at the wall behind her until my eyes grew glassy. "I don't understand why you think so badly of me." I looked back at her face. "He was stalking me. Saying things about me because I asked him not to take my picture. He had no right to invade my space like that, to assume I would politely smile and give that part of me to him just because he decided he wanted it. Wouldn't that make you furious? Like he thought he could take what he wanted?"

She nodded. "Absolutely. Still..."

I waited a moment before filling the space she'd left. "The temperature is supposed to be in the mid-seventies this weekend. Would you want to go hiking? I've been wanting to check out Henry Cowell since I moved here. Do you know it?" Of course she knew it, she'd tweeted about it a few days earlier. She loved that place and went hiking there every chance she got.

The change in her eyes said the unwanted photograph of me, and Charlie's unexpected, unexplained death had slipped below the surface of her thoughts, replaced by redwood trees and wildlife. For now.

"I love that place," she said.

"So? Are we on?"

"Sure. I have a tennis tournament in the afternoon, so it would have to be early."

"I love early. Seven? And meet for breakfast first?"

She nodded. She shifted in the chair, obviously not yet ready to leave me to my manicure. I'd decided to go colorless, just like her. That would be best for hiking anyway.

"Are you trying to change the subject?" she said.

"Why would I do that?"

"I don't know, Alexandra. Something is bothering me about this. You seem to want to avoid giving any details."

"It sounds like, for whatever reason, you don't trust me. Maybe this position isn't a good fit for me after all, now that we've gotten to know each other."

She looked guilty. "We don't know each other that well."

I relaxed the muscles around my mouth and looked down at my desk. I turned slightly so I could see the parking lot spread out beyond my window, then looked back at her. "I thought I'd proven myself as someone you can depend on. Someone you can trust completely, personally and professionally. I'm not sure what happened. I…"

"You are." She uncrossed her legs and leaned forward. "I don't know what's bothering me. Sometimes trivia gets stuck in my head and it's like a piece of sand inside your sock, rubbing on your foot and even though it's tiny, after a while, it's all you feel. It's the only thing you can think about. Please don't go looking for another job." She stood up. "It's Twitter, for god's sake. It's a bunch of mindless chatter most of the time, no different from sitting in a coffee shop and listening to all the conversations around you, only hearing pieces of each one, trying to guess what's going on. There's no context. I didn't mean to question you. I think because I couldn't immediately recall where I'd seen you, I made it into something bigger than it is. Hiking will be fantastic."

She went to the door and stood looking through the glass panel into the hallway. Without turning, she said, very softly so I almost didn't catch the words, "It's really nice to have a female friend at work. They're hard to come by. Male friendships at the office are never equal. Never." She opened the door and stepped into the hallway without looking back.

42

Los Angeles

When Randy tweeted @GirlStuff29 that he wanted to meet up at Majestic Park, my first thought was I would have preferred a private place where we could also get naked after we got high. I guessed he had other things on his mind. Like finding out how certain they were that Dianne's death was not an accident. Like finding out how much effort was being put into locating him, if any. Like trying to determine whether he needed to disappear. I hoped he wasn't planning on asking for my help.

As I walked toward the picnic tables where we agreed to meet, Randy looked in my direction, stiffened, and took off running. I sat on one of the benches and waited for him to return. Twenty minutes went by and I was getting cold by the time he came sauntering into the picnic area, acting as if he didn't see me. He was seriously paranoid.

He sat beside me. He spoke in a whisper. "No one followed you? I saw a guy, I think, he…"

"What is this a spy movie?"

"Did they?"

"How would I know?"

"You didn't check? You didn't keep your radar on alert?"

"I always pay attention to what's going on around me, but I can't guarantee no one followed me."

"Do they want to talk to me?"

"Yes."

"I thought so. I need to hit the road, so this is good-bye." He pulled out a joint and lit it, took two hits, one right after the other, and handed it to me.

"They'll find you."

"Finding someone is not as easy as it seems. If I don't use credit cards, don't get in touch with the fam, etcetera, it's much harder. Almost impossible, I think."

I blew out a narrow ribbon of smoke. It hung for a moment in front of me, then faded. I handed the joint to him. "So far, it seems like they think it was an accident. But I don't know for sure." I leaned against the edge of the picnic table. It stabbed my back, but my shoulder ached from the extreme weight of my purse during the six-block walk to the park after I got off the bus, and another half mile or so to get to the decrepit picnic area.

"They can't prove I was the one who gave her the roofie. Anyway, they have to find me first."

"How are you going to get cash?"

"I have some on me. I hit the ATM a bunch of times before this all happened." He laughed. "See, I'm more educated than you might think. College wasn't wasted on me, even though I haven't managed the degree yet."

"I guess you won't now. So you won our murder game. Was it worth it?"

He took a hit from the joint and held in the smoke for an extraordinary long time. Apparently he'd thought about the short term need for cash and getting away on his bike, but not the rest of his life.

"I did."

"It was never really a game," I said. I sucked on the joint, but kept the smoke in my mouth instead of pulling it into my lungs.

"It wasn't. Dianne's a whore, any way you look at it."

I pulled my purse closer. I unzipped it and slid my hand inside. "Explain."

"Oh, come on. She sleeps with me and charges me rent for sharing her bed? I get with you and she charges me more. I guess that makes her more of a pimp. A whore and a pimp. Owning the whole business, no middleman." He laughed. The sound was rough and loud. "And then she moves Tom in? With the same financial set-up? Unbelievable."

"I don't think that makes her a whore. Men do shit like that all the time."

"No they don't."

"Maybe not exactly the same, but the point is, they conduct their sex lives without anyone calling them whores."

"If the name fits."

"Her mother was trying to dictate her entire life. The only way to get some control was to have her own money."

"Then get a fucking job. Don't be charging your boyfriends."

"It's a nice apartment. It seems fair to charge a little for using it." I wasn't really on her side, but she didn't deserved to die for extorting a bit of cash.

"Quit making excuses for her. She's a whore. Lisa agreed. Lisa called her that to her face. So Dianne sicked Tom on her."

I hated him. I hate that word. I hate that it even exists. I hate that there's no male equivalent. I hate the smug attitude when guys use it. I hate that women who are just doing what they have to do in order to survive, women who are giving men what they want, are shunned. The woman gets shamed even though the guy is an equal participant! A man can have sex with anyone, whenever he wants, and he's admired and considered a stud. A woman does the same thing and she gets slapped with a filthy label that's custom-made for women. It's epically unfair and degrading. There were a lot of things wrong with Dianne, not the least of which was her controlling mother. Dianne was arrogant and cruel. She was self absorbed and entitled. She shoved Lisa and me into sleeping bags when we were paying rent for a nice room, holding us hostage. But she wasn't a whore. It's an ugly, undeserved word.

Before I took the bus to meet Randy, I'd spent a lot of time thinking back on how unconcerned he'd been that day Tom picked the fight with Lisa and dragged her off to humiliate her. I'd started to wonder whether Randy knew something about it.

My fingers felt around inside my canvas bag. They stroked the metal container filled with ice and enough vodka for both of us. They moved lower, touching my wallet and keys, sunglasses and a zippered leather bag with makeup. They traveled over loose coins and lip gloss and receipts I hadn't bothered to file in my wallet.

"What are you rummaging around in there for?" Randy took a puff on the rapidly shrinking joint, of which he was enjoying three or four hits to my one.

That was fine with me. After all, it was his joint.

"Chicks and their purses. Did you really need to bring the whole goddamn bedroom closet with you?"

I pulled out the travel mug. "Want some vodka?"

"Oh yeah." He sucked on the cigarette and held the smoke inside for a brief moment, then let it out in a thick cloud. "That sounds good. I'm thirsty. Do you have any snacks in that suitcase?"

I held the container in both hands, feeling the icy chill that came from its contents. It was so cold, it felt as if it was burning my fingers.

43

Aptos

The Saturday morning of our hike, Tess and I met at Bojo's Coffee Cafe at six-thirty. The minute we sat down with our turkey sausage links and fruit plates, Tess started gushing about Henry Cowell's. She'd had been going to the state park since she was a child. She had an almost mythical affection for the place because her memories were of rigorous father-daughter hikes. During these hikes, her father pushed her to improve her endurance, to learn not to complain about the heat or aching legs. Once, when a wasp attached itself to the space around her, pestering, humming, her father coached her to stay calm. The victory she felt for her stoicism when the insect left her alone without her dissolving into panicky, useless slaps at empty air, stayed with her all her life. It was a simple but empowering moment.

Her father transferred his love of the natural world to Tess, and through their casual talks, taught her about survival in the male business world. During the father-daughter hikes, Tess's two brothers were out of the picture and her mother was nowhere to be heard. Tess felt like the most important person in her father's life, the only one allowed into the world of his first love. She felt he was proud of her, admired her almost, for how well she listened to his guidance and how many miles she could hike, learning by the age of eleven to never whisper a word of complaint. Apparently her brothers were quite whiny during their hikes — another point of victory for Tess.

After the go-around in my office over the tweeted photograph, I was a little surprised that she suddenly opened up. In some ways, she seemed nearly as unstable as Noreen. At least Tess had taken her neuroses and channelled them into a successful career, making them pay, while Noreen seemed to be sinking inside herself, afraid to breathe without someone holding her hand.

We drove to the park, paid the entrance fee, and left the car under a canopy of trees, hoping the shade would keep it relatively comfortable until we returned.

Tess wore bona fide hiking boots, thick white socks, and khaki shorts that showed off legs tan and strong from tennis and hiking, not to mention her regular gym visits. She wore a white tank top and had a white sweatshirt tied around her waist. Despite my closet full of shoes, I didn't own a pair of hiking boots. I wore heavy-soled walking shoes. I'd also chosen khaki shorts, shorter than Tess's conservative mid-thigh pair, and a turquoise spandex workout cami over a black sports bra.

The route she'd chosen — a level walk to the Redwood Loop Trail, passing the San Lorenzo river in places — would get us back to the parking lot by eleven-thirty at the latest, according to Tess. We started out, and within fifteen minutes

I realized I was right to not bother with a sweatshirt tied around me like Tess had. The temperature of the air and the steady walking left me comfortably warm, even with the rising sun still nestled behind thick redwood growth. It was really beautiful, but difficult to enjoy since I was so focused on the agenda outlined in my mind. I needed to follow that script more carefully than I had to keep to the trail that wound through ancient redwoods with its musical score of cheerful birds.

After talking about the trees and plants surrounding us, commenting on the variety of bird calls, and how far we felt from the technology and traffic and relentless movement of Silicon Valley, we fell silent for several minutes. The sound of our feet on bark and pebbles and dirt was steady, our breathing soft.

I moved slightly behind Tess so she couldn't read my face when I spoke. "Whatever happened with Steve Montgomery?" I said.

"What about him?"

"When you lost your temper...and he let you have it for being irrational and emotional?"

She heaved a loud, lengthy sigh. "It's a losing battle."

"What is?"

"The male-female dynamic."

"What would your friend CorporateBitch2 have to say about that?"

She ignored the reference. "Never yell at a customer. He was right." She walked faster, leaning forward as if it would make her progress more rapid.

"He's never raised his voice at a customer? A man raises his voice, but a woman yells? All you did was insist on finishing your thought."

"Maybe we are."

"Maybe we are, what?"

She slowed and turned to look at me. "Maybe we are shrill."

"Are you serious?"

"A woman's voice is higher pitched."

"Is that what you think? That the natural sound of our voices deserves mocking?"

She shoved her hands in her pockets. Her hiking boots thudded on the path.

"Why does he get to define what's appropriate? Raising your voice when someone talks over you is perfectly reasonable. Men do it all the time. You know that."

"Yes."

"So what's the problem? He's marginalizing you for something men do every fucking day. He's trying to take away your power." I took a deep breath to calm myself. I needed to stay even-kneeled and let the rage build inside of her, in contrast to my understated response. If I got wound up, she would work to remain calm.

She stopped suddenly. I plowed past her a few yards, then paused and turned.

"I shouldn't let him. I know. It's just that…"

I spoke softly. "You need to take back your power. You should do something outrageous and ask him to support your effort. That's what a man would do to reassert himself, don't you think?" I was right, but she would feel superior that I expressed doubt, looking to her authority and experience and intelligence — a triple play.

"Do we really have to turn into men?"

"No. But in this case, if you're competing with a man who's beating you with male games, you have to engage with male weapons."

She laughed.

I smiled. "It's true, and you know it."

"It's just..." She started walking again.

"You'll show him you aren't cowed if you demand something, demonstrate your confidence. Tell him you have a critical need and you require his support to ask for more headcount for your team, or..."

"Or a pay increase for you?"

It had been easy to lead her up to it. And guilt is a strong driver. It causes all kinds of irrational behavior. I'd been fortunate that I'd avoided the guilt strand in my genome. "Whatever you think would work. You'll feel powerful and in control and that will make him respect you...he'll sense your power."

"What are you, some kind of life coach?"

"I could be."

She smiled, but looked uncertain.

"What's wrong?"

She turned slightly so I couldn't see her face. "I've trusted you before. I suppose I can trust you. I *should* trust you — you have my back."

"What's wrong?"

"There's another complication."

"Yes?"

"I had sex with him."

"So?"

"He pretty much has the upper hand."

"Why?"

"It makes me look bad, sleeping with a peer."

"No!" My voice was loud. A crow I hadn't known was perched in a pine tree up the side of the hill shrieked and took off with a rapid, heavy beating of its wings.

"Calm down," Tess said.

"It does not make you look any worse than it makes him look."

"You can pretend the world is balanced, Alex, but it's not."

"He risked as much as you did. And so what if two colleagues want to hook up? It's not as if he's your boss, or above you in the overall hierarchy."

She shook her head and smiled. "I trusted you, okay? You wanted trust, I gave it. Do not tell any one about this."

"Absolutely not. I would never do that." I wouldn't. Unless I needed something from her. Even then, I wouldn't actually spread the information. It was simply nice to have the leverage.

44

When Jared woke, he knew immediately that Alex wasn't in the house. There was a flatness in the atmosphere, a lessening of tension or electricity. Something. Maybe the wall between their rooms was cooler. Maybe there were indistinct sounds that normally came from her room, and without them, her absence was palpable.

It was dark. He pulled his phone toward him and tapped the home button. Four-forty a.m.

He rolled onto his back. He lay there for several minutes, then realized he needed to take a piss. He felt fully awake. It might as well be seven-thirty. He would try meditating. Not that it had been fruitful in a very long time, but his teacher continued to assure him that failure was part of the process. *It's a journey. The point is observing the flow of thoughts, not necessarily taming them. You watch a leopard and observe its behavior, you don't bind its legs and put it in a cage.* Sitting was what mattered. Remaining seated on your cushion with a storm inside your mind *was* the practice, trusting that sitting had value. The important things were consistency and never giving up. Never. That mantra applied to Alexandra as well.

He threw off the covers and put his feet on the floor. He yawned and stood up. He went to the door, turned the knob, and pushed. The door remained solidly closed. The force of its immovable position sent a jolt of pain up his arm. He jiggled the knob and pushed again. It refused to yield. He tried rattling it in its frame, but it wiggled only a fraction of an inch. He stepped back.

"Jared!" Noreen's voice came through the partially opened window. "Come here."

In the few steps it took him to reach the window, he was sickened by his robotic obedience to her voice.

"Open the window wider and let me in," she said.

"What the fuck is going on?" He pulled the cord and opened the drapes.

"Does Buddha allow you to say that?"

"What are you doing out there at four in the morning? What…"

"It's almost five."

"What's wrong with my door?"

"Let me in and I'll explain."

"You can explain right where you are."

"Come on. It's cold."

"Tough shit."

"I didn't realize you used so much bad language."

"What's blocking my door?"

"I attached a bolt."

How had she attached a bolt without him hearing? It would have required drilling. He didn't want to know, it didn't matter. She must have done it when he was out of the house. Late at night, in the darkness, he hadn't noticed. "Unfasten it."

"But I need to talk to you. It's important."

"I have to take a piss! Open the fucking door."

"Calm down. You can hold it for a few minutes. I couldn't get your attention with my body, or my food, I had to do something."

He stepped back and slammed the window down. He yanked the cord. The drapes raced across the track, swinging madly. It was an ineffectual display of anger. If he was forced to climb out the window and go around to use the bathroom, he'd have to see her. Now, he'd look foolish, relenting and pulling the drapes apart, pushing the window open again, allowing the sound of her pleading to wind its way into his room, inside the circuitry of his brain. He moved toward the bed and sat down. He reached behind his head and rubbed the muscle between his shoulder blades. There must be a way to get control of the situation, but if there was, he couldn't see it.

Noreen pounded on the window. Her shouting sounded far away through the closed window. "Please, Jared. I'm sorry. I'm so scared. I need someone to talk to."

He went to the window, pulled back the curtains, and opened it. "How about a psychiatrist?"

"Please. I'll explain everything."

He slid the window open. "I need to piss. Go unlock my door and we'll talk."

She nodded, her eyes protruding as if her brain were pressing on the backs and they were about to burst out of her skull. She disappeared into the darkness. He pulled on his jeans and a t-shirt, went to the door, and waited. A moment later, he heard the bolt slide. He yanked open the door and stalked across the hallway without looking at her.

He flipped the light switch and slammed the bathroom door. The damaged mirror glared at him. The first time he'd seen that deck hanging out over nothing, he should have realized the precariousness of the situation. He'd known she was wacky, or flat out nuts, and done nothing to get away from her. He wasn't locked in his room by Noreen's ridiculous bolt, he was locked there by Alex and her refusal to let him get anywhere near her. He pressed his knuckles to the scratched mirror, wanting to smash his fist into it. All that prevented him was the thought of glass tearing apart his skin.

When he finished using the toilet and washing his hands and face, he opened the door. She was standing right there.

"Don't ever do anything like that again," he said.

"I know, I'm sorry. It was an impulse. But you keep sneaking out of the house. And you come home so late. I…"

"Ever given any thought to why that might be?"

"You don't like me."

"That's…"

"You like her."

He didn't answer.

"I'll make coffee. Or tea?"

He shrugged.

"And oatmeal?"

Betraying his desire to be stoic, his stomach growled.

She gave him a weak smile. "See, you're hungry."

He followed her to the kitchen. Anger roiled his stomach more than hunger, but he was mildly curious to see what she had to say. He stood near the counter. The tile floor was cold and so unyielding the small bones of his feet ached. He watched as she filled the coffee carafe with water and scooped coarsely ground beans into the filter. He would have preferred tea, an offer she'd clearly forgotten the moment she made it.

When the coffee and oatmeal were on the table, they sat across from each other. Noreen squirted maple syrup into her oatmeal. Jared's stomach turned over and he pushed away the container of brown sugar after a adding a single teaspoon to his own bowl. He stirred the sugar and oatmeal as he dribbled in a bit of almond milk. Noreen used his almond milk rather than her own carton of cow's milk, but he didn't point that out either.

"This isn't going at all how I'd planned," she said.

"What do you mean?"

"Our living situation."

He agreed with her, but her version of what was wrong would be vastly different from his own, far from reality. "It's not perfect…" He thought of the dead rat. It seemed so long ago, its importance diminished. "The bolt is intolerable. If anything like that happens again, I'm gone."

She pushed her bowl to the side and rested her forearms on the table. She leaned forward. Her hair fell over her cheekbones and brushed against the edge of the table. "I thought we'd hang out together more."

"I told you I'm not…"

She held up her hand. "I get it. I'm not stupid. But I still thought, because it's a small place, because…I don't know…"

Her eyes filled with tears. She wiped them away with the ring finger of each hand. "I'm scared. I need company and I thought we'd eat together, hang out in the evenings, at least some of the time. I realize everyone has their own life, but it's like we're staying in a hotel."

"We have nothing in common. We're just renting rooms."

If his use of the plural upset her, she didn't let on.

"What are you so worried about?" he said.

"Not worried. Scared."

"Of what?" He wasn't sure he wanted to know.

"I saw something. It terrified me."

"What did you see?" He was tired of dragging things out of her. Why couldn't she get to the point? Had she seen him and Alex? He wasn't sure how that was possible. Maybe she'd seen one of them enter the other's room, but that would be all. His bowl was almost empty. "What are you trying to say?"

She sat up and took a long, slow breath. She seemed to hold onto it for a moment. "The mirror. I scratched it up because I saw something, and it scared me." Her eyes filled again, but she left them alone. "I was cleaning the sink and I looked up and I saw a face…in the mirror."

He laughed.

She let out a little shriek. "Don't laugh at me. I need your help. Alexandra won't help me, she dismisses my feelings, but you seem kind and generous. Maybe there is something to Buddha." She blinked rapidly. "It wasn't *my* face."

"Whose was it?"

"It only flashed there for a second, so I…"

Did she really expect him to believe she'd seen some kind

of apparition? "You're upset about something and you're imagining things. If the bathroom was steamed up and your mind was elsewhere and you looked up quickly, you might be startled by your own reflection."

"You must really think I'm dumb." She picked up her coffee mug and took a sip.

"I don't."

"I saw a woman's face. More than once. I don't like being here alone at night. It seems like you and Alex stay out later and later. Especially you, I thought having a man around would be...I don't know, more comforting."

"We didn't rent your rooms to be your bodyguards or your live-in companions. I'm sorry if that's what you were hoping for. You should have been more clear about it up front."

"But then you wouldn't have taken the room."

"That's right."

"So I had to keep that to myself."

He shoveled two more spoonfuls of oatmeal into his mouth, pushed the bowl to the side, gulped down his coffee, and stood up. "I'm going to head out."

"You don't have anything to say?"

"About what?"

"The face...And getting to know each other better. Supporting each other. That's what communal living is all about."

"Not what I signed up for."

"But you're into all that stuff...meditating and vegetables..."

He thought about his bold statement to Alex — the assertion that living in close quarters with other human beings would develop his awareness of Buddhist principles, keep him rooted in the tangible world while he explored the intangible, the interior universe, through meditation and yoga and lectures from visiting gurus. Now, as his words echoed around inside his head, they sounded arrogant. Somehow he'd thought it would be easy, fun. Living with two women would offer interesting insights into the parts of his personality that needed polishing. He'd imagined cooking together and sharing meals, small conflicts over water usage or musical tastes, and possibly a few spats between the two women that he'd be required to mediate. The garden was supposed to get him in touch with the earth and allow him to impress them with the fresh, healthy food he brought out of the ground. They'd be grateful for the rich taste of naturally grown food, allowed to ripen while it was still attached to the earth, taking in the maximum amount of nutrients from the soil and sun. He hadn't even gotten around to purchasing seedlings! But in general, he'd assumed they would each go their own way, live separate lives, the time together casual, not fraught with the aching, consuming emotions of intimacy. "If I wanted to live in a commune, I would have looked for one," he said.

She stared at him.

"I can't help you with panic attacks that cause hallucinations, or whatever it is. I was serious earlier — you should see a psychiatrist."

"That's not very nice."

He carried his dishes to the kitchen, rinsed the bowl and mug, and placed them in the dishwasher. "Thanks for the oatmeal. And coffee."

"I know you prefer tea. I forgot."

He shook his head rapidly, trying to dislodge the scratchy fuzz of confusion that resulted when she spoke, as if she were engaged in a completely different conversation.

"What's wrong?"

"Nothing. I'll see you around."

"So you have no sympathy that someone might be... haunting me. Or tormenting me?"

"I think any torment you're dealing with is inside your head."

"Why don't we all plan to go out to dinner? The three of us."

He walked around the table and took a few steps toward his bedroom.

"I'll set it up," she said.

It was a mistake to leave it open, but responding would send her reeling off in another direction. He'd deal with it later. Maybe before any dinner plans came to pass, she'd realize she needed to take his advice regarding psychiatric care.

45

Los Angeles

Randy was zoned out, staring into the thick grove of trees surrounding the weather-battered picnic tables where we were seated. I leaned my head against his shoulder and wrapped my arm around his thigh, hugging his leg like a life preserver.

We sat in buzzed silence for quite a while — his buzz. I simply waited, breathing softly as I might if I were stoned. My bones and blood, my stomach and lungs and heart burned with fury when I heard the word *whore*, so often accompanied by an unconscious sneer. The word is used so easily. Worse, is the frequency with which women use it to refer to women they don't like, or women who threaten them in some way, however minor. Women who don't follow someone else's rules are labeled whores.

It's not okay for a woman to have sex whenever she wants — that's whorish behavior. Of course, many would argue, insisting that it's the acceptance of money for sex that's the issue. But it's not. Women who have sex whenever and with whomever they please are called whores or sluts. Men who do the same are called — men. Boys being boys. The irrepressible male sex drive. A woman who does take money for sex is considered the lowest form of human existence, and so the word gets thrown around at anyone who isn't behaving herself.

The night was getting colder. We hadn't seen another soul.

There were no lights in this section of the park. A newer, more spacious picnic area had been established near the children's play structure and swings. The tables where we sat had been there since the sixties. The wood was rotted and stained dark as if it had soaked in the discarded cells of every human being who sat on the benches and ate off the tables. Even people who came to the darker sections of the park to drink or get high didn't favor this area, despite how well hidden it was. It gave off an atmosphere of decay. It was the type of secluded, overgrown space where you often stumbled across hypodermic needles and limp, wet condoms littering the ground. The possibility of finding a severed hand, maybe an entire corpse, wasn't out of the question. The trees grew together overhead, obscuring the sky and even in the daylight it was cold and dark. Squirrels rarely darted across the ground and the only birds in the branches above were crows.

"How about that vodka?" Randy said.

My fingers felt as if they'd frozen onto the metal container. I moved it slightly. Ice rattled as I lifted it out of my bag.

"I'm thirsty," he said.

"You should have brought a sleeping bag."

He laughed. "How would that help me not be thirsty?"

"So we could get friendly."

"Oh. Ha. Ha. I'm kind of wasted. Are you gonna give me

a drink or not?"

I unscrewed the cap and handed it to him. He took a long swallow and handed it back. I replaced the cap and set the container on the bench between us.

"Aren't you thirsty?" he mumbled.

"Not really. Maybe later." I handed the container back to him and stood up. I walked toward the trees.

"Where are you going?"

"Just checking out the area."

"There's nothing to see, not to mention it's impossible to see." He laughed with a soupy, confused sound as if he'd already forgotten what he was laughing about.

I walked into the grove of trees. Most were pine, the branches high above the ground, too high for me to even brush with my fingertips, much less grab onto and hoist myself up. I walked farther. It smelled damp and musty.

Randy called after me. "Hey! Come back. It's not safe."

"Just a sec." I pulled out my key ring. It had a tiny plastic egg-shaped trinket that shone a red light when it was squeezed. I'd found it a few weeks earlier in the student lounge, stuffed between a cushion and the side of a chair, a broken chain attached to it. It was an ingenious little gadget and somewhat addictive. I squeezed it often, and wondered how it worked, whether the light would eventually die out. So far, it was as strong as ever.

Straight ahead was a barren fruit tree of some kind. All its leaves were gone. There was a huge gnarled bulge near the base of the trunk and another smaller one near the top of the trunk where it split out into two thick branches and several smaller ones. I grabbed the largest branch. Despite the dead appearance of the tree overall, the branch was firm and didn't give when I lifted my feet off the ground and let it hold my full weight. I climbed onto the bulge and reached up to the other large branch about eight feet off the ground. It too was sturdy. I slid down off the gnarly bulge.

"Alex? Where are you?" Randy's voice was faint, not because I'd walked far, but because he must have been sipping steadily at the roofie-laced vodka tonic. A guy falling under the influence of a date rape drug — a whore's revenge.

I put my bag on the ground and pulled out a long, one-inch thick rope. I tossed it over the lower branch and wrapped one piece around the other until I had a tidy noose. I'd studied the proper construction of the knot online at the University library. I stood for a moment, contemplating a suicide note. Finally, I decided it wasn't worth the effort.

The story that would be inferred from anyone who knew Randy was that Dianne had cast him aside and he'd never gotten over the heartbreak, or the damage to his ego. He'd decided if he couldn't have her, no one would. It's a clichéd story, retold many times every year, throughout the world. Once she was dead, he was filled with remorse — for his own loss, not genuine regret over taking her life.

I returned to the picnic table. Randy was lying on the bench facing the sky, his eyes closed. The thermal mug sat on the table. I picked it up. A few sips and most of the ice cubes remained. I stuck it in my bag. I put my hands in his armpits and unceremoniously dragged him off the bench. His feet thudded as they hit the ground.

It took about fifteen minutes to drag his nearly unconscious body to the tree I'd chosen. I was sopping wet under my arms and across the back of my neck and all the way down my spine. I took a sip from the water bottle in my well-stocked bag and walked back to the tables. I grabbed one end of the closest table and began dragging it across the hard-packed dirt, scraping through the pine needles and pieces of bark.

When it was finally in place beneath the noose, I pushed and bent and shoved Randy's sleeping body until he was back on the bench. I got onto the table top and dragged him up onto it. I looped the noose around his neck and tightened the knot. I sat down to catch my breath. Randy groaned. He tried to speak, but the words sounded like something out of a Furby with a dying battery.

I finished my water, stuffed the bottle in my bag, and stood up. I kissed his very fine lips, but there was no pleasure. They were loose and floppy with unconsciousness. I shoved him as close as I could to the far end of the table then walked around the other side. I rubbed my hands together and took a deep breath. I squatted, grabbed the bar connecting the benches to the table, and with every ounce of strength I could summon, I yanked the table. As the table crashed toward me, I rolled out of its path. It scraped my arms and one of the bench corners jabbed at my thigh, making me cry out.

When I stood, Randy was where he belonged. He was grunting and gagging, making horrible noises, his feet kicking as they tried to find solid ground, but his eyes remained closed. His body started to shudder and I turned away, offering him the dignity of privacy as he died. Not that he deserved it.

46

After sex with Joe, the desire to have Jared in my bed waned. Sex with Jared was decent, very good, in fact. But remembering Joe's body, thinking about the way he touched me, the charge that came from an equal level of power between us, played a big part in how quickly and thoroughly I came when I was with Jared, rather than Jared himself. The equality I felt with Joe was difficult to explain. I don't know if it was because we'd started off simply chatting, flirting in a very disconnected manner. Neither one pursued the other. Neither of us wanted something the other couldn't give or didn't possess. There was no first move. We were simply two bodies, expressing whatever passed through our minds in that moment. Smoking cigarettes together contributed to the balance of power, as the rhythm of our breathing aligned, as the smoke filled the space between us when our voices fell silent.

It's impossible to make sense of desire. Much smarter and better educated people than I have tried, and for the most part, failed to gain significant insight.

None of that stopped me from opening my bedroom

door when Jared knocked. I no longer went to his room, but he didn't seem fazed by my lack of pursuit. The hunger in his eyes was ravenous, so out of proportion to mine, I had to look away, embarrassed by his need.

While Jared undressed, I lay on the bed, my head propped on my elbow, watching. He yanked off his shirt, dragging it over his head inside out. He unbuckled his belt, lowered the zipper, and stepped out of jeans and boxers in the same movement. He came to the bed. After all the eager stripping off of his clothing, he looked hesitant. I moved over to make more room for him. He continued to stand there.

I smiled.

He sat on the bed, his back turned toward me. I ran my finger down the knobs of his spine to the spot where it curved and the bones became less prominent. He didn't react. "Come down here," I said.

"I wanted to tell you what Noreen did."

"Aww. Not now."

He complied and we began kissing. After a few minutes, he pulled away. "You really should be aware of this."

"You sure know how to kill a feeling."

"Just be patient for two minutes."

I wondered where the ravenous look from a moment ago had gone.

He tucked my hair behind my ear. "She thinks she's being haunted, or something like that. She told stories to both of us."

"Stories?"

"About the mirror. Neither story about the damage was

true. She destroyed it because she thought she saw a woman's face in it."

I laughed. "Of course she did. I also see a woman's face when I look in the mirror."

"That's what I told her. She said it wasn't her own, so I suggested it looked unfamiliar because of steam, or her mind was elsewhere and she startled herself."

"Of course."

"She insisted it was not her face."

"Whose was it?"

"She didn't say."

"She's just trying to create drama. Where were we?" I flatted my hand and ran my palm across his chest.

He trembled, but took hold of my wrist and stopped the progress of my hand. "I told her to see a therapist."

"Good idea. Now can we…"

He let go of my wrist. "She thought the three of us would spend time together, that this was to be some type of quasi commune."

"She told me the same thing. That's not what I'm looking for."

"Me neither, but…"

I took his head in my hands and turned his face toward mine. I ran my lips across his brow, brushing them over the creases of skin, lowering them to the fine hairs of his eyebrows, kissing them until the muscles relaxed. "Let's talk about Noreen another time."

"I'm concerned."

"She's just lonely and horny and needy. Ignore her."

"I don't think we can keep doing that."

I started kissing him. After a few minutes, his body forgot about Noreen's mirror.

My body was on the precipice, ready to let go, when there was a loud crash. Another followed quickly. Jared pushed me off him as a third crash shook the room. He scrambled to the side of the bed as the door shuddered in its frame.

Noreen was screaming. "I know you're in there, you disloyal bitch."

The door trembled. Her blows weren't having much impact on the solid wood, so substantial and effective for keeping sound out, and in. Obviously solid wood was also nice in case of a full-on assault with some kind of weapon.

"Stop it!" Jared pulled on his pants. "Whatever you're doing, stop."

"Why are you getting dressed?" I said.

He paused as if he hadn't considered exactly what he was going to do. Opening the door might be worse than enduring the crashing until she wore herself out. The door made a cracking sound as she struck it again. Maybe it wasn't as sturdy as I'd thought. Or maybe the frame was splintering.

"Open the door," Noreen said. "Both of you are terrible, selfish human beings."

The label didn't bother me. I'm well aware that all human beings are selfish, some of us recognize it, others don't. Noreen should have considered her own selfish traits — starting with the belief that collecting rent gave her the authority to dictate our roles in her life.

Jared didn't look as comfortable with the suggestion of

selfishness. A spasm of guilt crossed his face. "Let's see what she wants."

"We know what she wants. You."

He laughed, his voice tinged with hysteria.

I scooted to the edge of the bed and pulled on my jeans and a sports bra that was sitting on the shelf of my nightstand. I went to the door. "It's not a good idea to destroy your own house, Noreen. And I don't really see that there's anything to discuss."

"You knew I liked him." The door shook. I stepped back. The splintering sounds suggested she had a blade of some kind. "You were supposed to stay away from him, and now you're in there doing it right under my nose."

A knife clattered onto the tile floor. Noreen fell against the door with a thud. "I know I seem crazy, I know what it looks like, but you don't understand. You both seemed so nice. I thought you were my friends. I thought Jared might be looking for someone like me. That he thought I was — not pretty — but interesting, soulful, maybe. I thought…" Her voice dropped. "I thought so many things that were wrong."

Jared and I stood side by side, staring at the door. Our breathing was short and fast, our bodies still warm from sex, fired up by the adrenaline of Noreen stabbing the door like the crazed character in *Psycho*.

"She's harmless," I whispered.

"Do you really believe that?" He took my hand and squeezed it hard.

For several minutes, the house was silent.

Jared let go of my hand and returned to the bed. I took a step toward the door. "Noreen?"

She let out a fierce sigh and something thumped the door
— the palm of her hand? The side of her head?

"I just wanted company. Friends," she said in a dull voice.
"I'm scared. I…please open the door. I won't do anything."

Jared shook his head.

I put my hand on the knob. "Slide the knife under the
door."

She was silent.

"Noreen?"

"Don't you trust me?" she said.

"No."

For several more minutes, there was nothing. Then, the
knife blade appeared beneath the door, the tip pointing up
slightly as it moved from the tile in the hallway to the
bedroom carpet. She pushed harder and part of the handle
appeared. I grabbed it and picked it up. I handed it to Jared
and he slid it under one of the pillows. I opened the door.

Noreen looked at us, her eyes washed almost colorless
with tears. I stepped back but she didn't move to enter the
room. "I'm scared of BJ, but I miss him too. It's so
confusing. I've been with him my whole life. I thought things
would turn out differently."

"Who's BJ?"

She stared at me as if I was mocking her. "Brian."

"Oh."

"I call him Brian because that's who he was when I met
him. But recently he started going by BJ — Brian Joseph."

It felt as if I'd swallowed a gallon of ice water.

"Sometimes I look out on the deck and I think I see him,

grinning at me. And when I look in the mirror…" she glanced at Jared.

"What does he look like?" I said.

She turned. "Why is that important?" She stared at me. Slowly, she raised her hands and stroked her hair away from the sides of her face. She raked her fingers through her hair toward the back of her head, dragging them down to the ends. Loose hairs came out in her hands. She spread her fingers and let the hairs fall onto my floor. "Have you seen someone?" she whispered.

"A guy named Joe was asking about you. He drives a Boxster."

She tipped her head slightly and gazed up at the ceiling. "Boxster?"

"It's a type of Porsche. I thought Brian, BJ, drove a motorcycle."

She shrugged.

"Well what does he look like?"

She behaved as if she couldn't quite hear me, or understand the language I was speaking, or was drifting to sleep standing up. She whispered. "He's tall. Thin." She slid her fingers into her hair and left them, lifting it slightly of her scalp.

"Do you have a photograph?"

"Somewhere. On Facebook."

The description was uselessly vague and she either had no idea what a Porsche was or she didn't know he owned that car, but I didn't need a photograph. I knew. Why else would he refuse to give his name for so long? Why else would he keep coming around? He'd said he was unaware Noreen had an ex-boyfriend. Did that mean he thought they were still together? But why wasn't he living at the house if that was the case? She seemed to think he'd left her.

I don't like being lied to. It's hypocritical, I know, since I adjust the truth to create whatever story benefits me the most at any given moment. He hadn't technically lied, simply withheld key information. But I don't like being played. He put me in the middle of something I'd wanted to steer clear of.

Still, even now, my desire for him hadn't faded.

47

At six-forty a.m. on Monday, I sent a text message to Tess. *Sick as a dog, can't meet for coffee.*

She texted back in less than three seconds. *You can't be!*

I am.

This is the day I meet with Steve. Remember??!

Yes. Can't be helped. Puking my stomach lining.

Take something.

Like what?

I need to run my plan by you.

How very nice that a senior vice president was leaning on me to strategize the reshaping of her reputation and image. Facing Steve without the crutch of my preliminary support would increase her perception of my value — when she faced him, she'd be thinking about how I would handle each gesture, each verbal exchange. I smiled at the thought, then adjusted my expression to one that would consume my face if I were kneeling over a toilet bowl, my stomach weaving and thrashing, wishing more would come up because then the sickening motion would stop for a short while. I needed to keep my messages brief, desperate. Smiling would lead to excess verbiage in my text messages, creating suspicion about how sick I really was.

Ur on your game.

I need a sounding board.

Ask for moon. Who speaks first loses.

Sigh. I know. Feel better.

You'll do good.

She sent a thumbs up icon and a moment later, my screen went dark.

Noreen was banging around in the kitchen. Since she'd caught Jared and me, she and I hadn't spoken. Or rather she hadn't spoken to me. Before that, I hadn't initiated a conversation in a long time. Her desire for me to approach her, to apologize for being a cheating, disloyal slut, begging to know what was scaring her, pulsed through the house, taking up more space than all three human beings.

I jumped in the tub, let the warm water run, and spent fifteen minutes shaving my legs. When they were silken, I turned the dial to direct the water into the shower head. I spent so long standing with water streaming down my back, occasionally gliding my hand up my leg to feel how slick it was, that Noreen finally pounded on the door.

"You're wasting water," she shouted. "If the water use hits tier two next month, you'll owe the extra."

I longed to be living somewhere else by next month, but in reality, it would be two or three months. I turned off the water.

"Thank you!"

I dried myself and toweled my hair and wrapped a second towel around me. I went to my bedroom and closed and locked the door.

After applying all the appropriate deodorant and lotion, I put on a black bra and black thong. Bending my knees to a slight plié in front of the mirror, I dried my hair, captivated as the warm air transformed it from sopping wet, to damp, to satin strands. The position was tiring and irritating but benefited my calves and quads, so at least it was a good use of my time. With the help of a heavier than usual styling cream, I rid my forehead of my cute bangs and the accompanying illusion of naïveté.

I dressed in faded skinny jeans, a black shirt that was tight around my middle and loose and off the shoulders at the top. I slid my feet into silver flip-flops and touched up my burgundy toenail polish. Long, thin silver chain earrings completed the casual, hanging around the house look — more or less. The earrings might have been a bit much, but the shirt required them.

I settled in the armchair and listened for Noreen's progress through the kitchen, back to her room, and out to the garage, her final departure signaled by the hum of the Jetta as she backed out of the driveway.

My Toyota was parked prominently in front of the house, announcing to Joe—Brian—BJ, whoever he wanted to be today, that I was home. All by myself.

Seven minutes after Noreen putt-putted down the street and turned the corner, there was a knock on the front door. I walked into the great room. He saw me through the eight-inch glass panes that made up the front door. He didn't smile or wave or do anything goofy, just stood there, looking at me, sending mental vibes of *I want you now*. My vibes responded and I crossed the room. I unlocked the door and opened it. He stepped inside.

We didn't kiss in the great room, not because of decorum, but wanting to prolong the moment before the initial touch. It seemed his manipulative behavior toward me had enflamed my desire. And I'm always a sucker for a hot car, so there was that.

In the seven minutes between Noreen's departure and his arrival, I'd scooped up armloads of shoes and discarded but not-yet-ready-for-the-wash clothing, dumped them on Jared's bed, and closed the door. The rest of my space was tidy. When he stepped onto the soft carpet and I closed the door, he looked around with admiration. The window was partially open, and the white curtains I'd bought to give some flair to the industrial-looking metal mini-blinds floated on the breeze. The dresser was swept free of cosmetics, with nothing but a glass tiger and a small pewter bowl. The nightstand was similarly uncluttered except for the elbow lamp with its tiny purple glass shade and my iPad.

He turned, looking at the framed black and white photograph of a white tiger. The wall beside my bed was decorated with a fringed black silk shawl tacked up with a dramatic fold in the center. "Nice," he said. He didn't hesitate as if he'd almost said more and had to stop himself, didn't give any indication that he'd seen the room before or that my decorating was an improvement.

He came toward me. We kissed until our clothes seemed to slide off our bodies of their own accord. All we noticed was the touch of the other's hands on our skin. We fell onto the bed and spent the next two hours exploring each other's bodies. We slept, wrapped around each other, until two in the afternoon. We woke starving. After throwing my clothes back on in a slightly less organized fashion than the first time I'd dressed that day, Joe—BJ—Brian drove me to a barbecue place.

Without looking at the menu he ordered baby back ribs, potato salad, coleslaw, and two beers. We sat at a table in the back corner of a rather nondescript room. The tables were picnic style, covered with vinyl blue checkered cloths. There was a small platform at one end where local musicians played blues on the weekends.

In the middle of the afternoon on a Monday, we didn't need a secluded table in the corner. There was only one other patron — a withered man with a shaved head and an expertly trimmed beard. He was eating Tri-tip cut into small pieces, resting on a bed of white rice, one small piece of meat at a time. He placed his fork on the plate between each bite. Every few minutes, he sipped from the cola can sitting in front of his plate. He didn't look at us, didn't seem to notice he was no longer alone in the restaurant.

Six ribs, a small bowl of potato salad, a few bites of coleslaw, and half a beer later, I was ready to take a break from food inhalation. I put my forearms on the vinyl table covering, despite the somewhat tacky feel. I leaned forward. "So, why did you switch from Brian to BJ to Joe?"

He smiled slowly, the change in his expression moving like a wave from his mouth to his eyes, as if he'd been expecting the question. The photograph of Noreen with her eyeballs drilled out passed through my mind. It was surprising I hadn't thought about it while I was getting dressed that morning, or any time since. Now, a chilling sweat formed on the back of my neck. I squirmed on the bench and lifted the beer bottle to my mouth.

"You know who I am," he said.

I waited.

He gnawed at the last rib, looking at me. He made no effort to tidy up his eating simply because he was being studied so closely. When he'd cleaned the bone to a polish, he placed it on the pile of other equally smooth bones. "I don't want Noreen to know I'm looking for her."

"Too late."

"Why is that?" He took a long swallow of beer.

"She thinks you want to kill her."

He nodded.

"Do you?"

"Do *you*?" He smiled and licked the top of his bottle, slowly and seductively. Or at least that's how it seemed to me.

I laughed.

"I thought so," he said.

"I suppose you aren't going to tell me if you're seriously planning to murder her," I said. "She seems quite frightened."

"She can't just take possession of the house."

"It's half yours?"

"Twenty percent."

"Why did you leave, then?"

"It's a long story."

"We have all afternoon."

"Okay, that was an avoidance tactic. I don't want to tell you. Not right now."

"Because then, if she turns up dead, I'll know it was you, and I'll know why you killed her." I finished my coleslaw, ate the meat off one more rib, and took a few sips of beer. He watched me, not moving or eating.

We ordered two more beers and took them outside to the narrow porch that ran past the front window of the restaurant. We sat on comfortable wooden chairs watching traffic and drinking beer. It was hard to know whether he was serious. The damaged photograph suggested he was. Noreen was so erratic, her fear could be silly paranoia or something very real.

I didn't understand why someone who had part ownership in a house would walk away as he'd done. Noreen tried to blame it on their dog's horrible accident, but it had always seemed as if there was something else going on. And now, BJ seemed to be brooding about something more than the ugly end of his pet's life.

48

Now, Jared understood — Alexandra respected men with balls. All women did. Why had he let his fascination with her suck the life force out of him? He'd been too nice, too accommodating to her stated desires rather than thinking about what lay beneath her cool exterior. Hadn't she proven many times there was a raging fire inside of her? She was the kind of woman who would respond to decisive action. She wanted to be dominated, as long as he didn't go to far.

Knowing this, he'd searched for housing and found the perfect spot. She obviously had limited funds, and the place he'd found was fifty dollars a month cheaper than what they were paying Noreen. He'd considered offering to subsidize the rent and handle all the utilities himself, but he'd have to proceed cautiously with that. She was likely to rebel against the suggestion she needed his help. It was much smaller than Noreen's place — seven hundred square feet. It was a cabin of sorts, a second structure situated on a one-acre lot, a few hundred yards behind a spectacular glass and redwood house on the bank of Soquel Creek. The cabin mirrored the six-bedroom main house in style — one wall consisted almost entirely of an enormous window looking out into the forest. The elevation was good, ensuring the property was safe from the occasional flooding that arrived during El Niño cycles. It was secluded and quiet, surrounded by trails and two-lane roads that were perfect for Alexandra's daily run. It was closer to her office than Noreen's bungalow.

Surely after the knife attacks on the mirror and Alexandra's bedroom door, coupled with Noreen's expectation that they function as her body guards, Alex had had enough. Noreen was unstable at best, and possibly dangerous. Her stories and her moods shifted minute to minute and there was no telling what the next change might be. She'd quickly yielded the knife and returned to her sad, needy persona, but she'd made that transformation before. It wouldn't last. She was still furious at Alex for the perceived betrayal.

Alex would share his bed in the small cabin, but he would make it clear that didn't imply they were establishing a relationship with its expected obligations. Safety was more important than relationship definitions. They had great sex and they needed to get away from Noreen — that was enough for now.

Tonight, he'd bring a bottle of wine to her room and they'd spend a little more time together, talking before they succumbed to kissing and slithering out of their clothing. Now that Noreen knew about him and Alex, there was no worry about being overheard, although they faced a much greater risk of physical danger as Noreen's anger simmered toward an inevitable explosion. Alex would see that they couldn't wait any longer to make other plans. She'd appreciate him refusing to brush it aside for another day, another week. She'd appreciate him putting effort into finding a place. He'd downloaded the four photographs provided online so he could show them to her on his phone without jumping around the website. He also had a picture of the main house and estimated costs for utilities.

The bottle of wine and glasses were in his room, waiting. It was dark now. Her car had been parked out front when he arrived home, but she was nowhere around. It was possible she'd gone for a longer run than usual. Still, it had been two hours. How many miles could she run in one go?

Twenty minutes later, time spent reading the same page repeatedly in a book on the nature of breath, he heard the front door open. He stepped into the hallway and walked toward the great room.

Alex closed the door, locked it, and turned. She dropped her keys in her purse. She wasn't dressed in running clothes or work clothes — she wore skinny jeans and a sexy top that fell off one shoulder. Her feet were bare and she carried silver flip-flops in her left hand.

He smiled. "Playing hooky?"

She dropped her flip-flops on the floor and stepped into them. "Hi, honey. I'm home."

She didn't smile so he wasn't sure how he was supposed to interpret her greeting — Joke? Annoyance? Affection? Something he couldn't guess at?

She walked toward the kitchen. Her flip-flops slapped the tile. Without turning, she said, "Is Noreen around?"

"Are you looking for her?"

She laughed. "Hell no. Just asking." She turned on the light and opened the cabinet. She removed a wine glass and set it on the counter.

He came up behind her. "Hey. I thought we could share a bottle. I have a nice Zin waiting in the bedroom."

"Mine or yours?"

"Whichever you prefer."

"Yours is better." She paused. "Oh, I, uh…"

He smiled. "I saw. Cleaning out?"

"I just tossed stuff out of the way so I could vacuum and change my sheets. I forgot to move it back."

"No worries," he said. "I folded everything. There's a stack in my closet."

She kissed his cheek. "Thanks, honey."

It was unnerving. Her ironic tone was sharp — was it affectionate irony or bitter?

"I need to take a shower," she said.

"Not now."

She shrugged and fiddled with her earring. They went into his room. She kicked off her flip-flops. She removed the earrings from the holes in her ears and dropped them on his bookcase. She scraped at the hardened wax spots with her thumbnail.

"I was going to get to those," he said.

She went to his meditation cushion and settled herself on it. She folded her legs easily into a lotus position. Unbelievable. He'd worked since the day he'd bought the cushion, and could barely manage to force his left foot onto his right thigh. Forget the right foot. She put her hands on her knees, forming a lovely teardrop with her thumbs and middle fingers. She closed her eyes. "Ohm."

He hoped she wasn't mocking him. It didn't seem that way, but it was impossible to read her sometimes. Most of the time. Maybe he couldn't read her at all. He poured a liberal amount of wine into each glass. She lifted her arm, holding out her hand for the glass. Apparently she planned to drink her wine while sitting on the cushion. He wasn't sure how he felt about that, it seemed sacrilegious. But why? It was just fabric and stuffing. He handed the glass to her. Kneeling beside her, then sitting on his heels, he touched his glass to hers. "TGIM."

She laughed.

Knowing he'd elicited that laugh dissolved his worries about some of the things she said, or didn't say. He relaxed and shifted into a cross-legged position facing her. He took a sip of wine. "What were you up to all day? How come you skipped work?"

"I needed a break."

He put the wineglass close to his nose and inhaled the aroma, waiting for her to say more. He shouldn't have asked two questions on top of each other. He clenched his jaw. She made him feel as if he were prepubescent, asking questions that made him appear stupid, clueless about how to talk to a girl. No other woman had had this effect on him. With other women, he'd always been in control. He absolutely needed to take charge, but he wanted her so badly he was terrified of taking a wrong step. He moved the glass away from his face. "Did you hang out at the beach?"

She shook her head. She put down her glass on the carpet, re-formed the lotus position with her left leg on top, and picked up the glass.

"A secret rendezvous?" He laughed.

She smiled.

"You sure can sit easily in that position. Have you ever meditated?"

"Doesn't everyone meditate when they're sitting and thinking? I don't see why it has to be an event."

"Meditation is more like thinking about nothing, or not thinking at all. It's about working to quiet your mind while watching the endless flow of mental judgement and analysis and complaining, rehashing the past, contemplating the future…"

She took a sip of wine. "Huh. Interesting."

"How are you feeling? After that go-around with Noreen and her knife?" he said.

"She seems quite frightened of her ex…"

"Maybe." He stood up and went to the dresser. He put the bottle of wine on the carpet and sat down again. "Or she's afraid of her own mind."

"That too. She showed me this photograph of herself with holes poked through the eyes. She said Brian, or BJ, whoever he is, did it."

"Do you believe her?"

"Who knows. She does seem genuinely afraid…or genuinely…something." She laughed.

He pulled his phone out of his back pocket.

"Do I get a refill?" she held out her glass.

He put down the phone and splashed wine into both glasses.

"It's only a matter of time before she loses it completely," he said.

"She does get off on the drama."

"But we don't know."

"True."

He liked it that she responded as if they were making plans together. Partners. A couple, maybe. It was a good sign. "It's a bad situation." He picked up the phone. "Check this out." He tapped on the exterior shot of the cabin and turned the phone in her direction.

"Nice."

"It's small, but it's a great location, and the price is right." Holding the phone so she could see it, he scrolled through the interior shots and the picture of the main house.

She sipped her wine. "Are you thinking of renting it?"

"It's large enough for both of us."

She sighed. "Are you deaf? Or just hard-headed?" She unfolded her legs as gracefully as she'd arranged them. She finished the wine, put the glass beside the bottle, and stood up. "I told you I don't want a relationship. The sex is great, but I'm not playing house with you."

He stood up. He had to prevent her from leaving. "I know you don't, and I'm not suggesting it. Just...we need to get out of here. I'm trying to protect you." The minute he spoke, he knew it was the wrong thing to say.

She laughed. She stepped around him, picked up her earrings and flip-flops, and went to the door. "Thanks for the wine."

"What about friends with benefits? Roommates with

benefits," he said. "We're just sharing a cabin and we can have sex, or not. Whatever. We don't have to…"

"I'm not sure I want to be friends." She gave him a smile that softened the words, slightly. She opened the door and was gone before he could take a complete breath.

49

The Thursday after I stayed home *sick*, Tess came into my office without knocking. She sauntered up to my desk and put both hands on the edge. She leaned forward. "Got it." She straightened and crossed her arms, grinning.

The appropriate response was thank you, so that's what I said, although most thanks rightfully belonged to me, because if I hadn't kept nudging her, she would have dropped it. That isn't something to point out to your boss, to anyone, in any situation. It was knowledge I'd have to enjoy alone.

The energy snapping in her eyes said she was riding an adrenaline high from winning, pride in knowing she'd done something to reward me and that she had power to impact my life. She tapped her phone and handed it to me. An approval email filled the screen, announcing a $4,328.23 annual increase for Laura A. Mallory — almost three hundred dollars a month after taxes. It's not clear how they calculate such an awkward sum, and it wasn't quite what I'd hoped for, but hoping and expectation versus actual cash aren't the same. It was another small step toward the kind of life I envisioned. A life with a luxurious car, high end clothes, an elegant, spacious, well-decorated home…some travel…and all the creature comforts I craved.

"Tell me how it all happened," I said.

She slouched in the chair and stretched her legs out in front of her, crossing her narrow ankles in the same way a man might. She tossed her head back.

The experience had been heady even though it started out badly.

Before Tess could even begin making her pitch, Steve had tried to dominate. First, he'd winked at her and pulled out a chair, holding it while she sat. He put his hands on her shoulders and squeezed gently, increasing the pressure as if he was about to give her a massage. She'd told him to have a seat and he chuckled. It was the kind of chuckle that tells a woman she's cute and charming, an object designed to amuse the man, not a business peer.

Despite the queasy feeling in her stomach, fearing that she was seeing evidence she'd never recover from her dual-headed mistake, she took a long, slow breath. She stiffened her back and told him not to touch her. Inside, she was quivering, certain that all he saw was her naked body, that the brief hour they'd spent in bed consumed his thoughts, that she would never be on an equal footing again. She worried she was making an even worse mistake trying to get his support for expanding her team and recognizing its importance. The meeting felt like a flimsy, transparent attempt to stake out her territory. He would hold the indiscretion over her. Possibly, he'd suggest they continue on a regular basis if she truly wanted to enlist his support. If she reacted, he'd point out again her lack of control over her emotions.

While she sat worrying, he rambled on about his Sunday golf game. She smiled and nodded as he described his best putts, his shockingly long drives, his analysis of the mental aspects of the game and how well he'd mastered them.

As he talked, she suddenly realized he had no idea she wasn't really listening, and in the same moment, realized also he had no idea she was consumed by self doubt — her failure existed only inside of her own head. He might be hoping they could continue, but it was equally possible he was terrified she'd do something to damage his career, and the winking and squeezing were designed to keep her under his control, to turn the blame on her and influence her behavior.

She interrupted the play-by-play golf tournament to tell him that before she got to the purpose of the meeting, she wanted to discuss the incident where she'd raised her voice at the customer. She said she didn't appreciate his criticism, that he was out of line — he didn't understand the background of the situation.

It seemed as if Steve physically shriveled before her as she told him the sales team had gone on to win a $1.4 million, three-year contract with that customer after she'd raised her voice. The customer had an aggressive company culture and the reason they were all speaking over her to begin with was a result of that culture's influence on the meeting. They'd been using their interruptions and confusion over the terms of the support contract as a tactic to get a better deal for the contract renewal. When she raised her voice, they gained respect for her.

She informed Steve she wouldn't tolerate him questioning

her abilities and her suitability for her role ever again. Constructive criticism was fine, but he'd implied she'd lost control. She had not. He was out of line and in danger of harassment with his comments about *typical female behavior*.

Half of what she described was bullshit, of course. The team had won the million-dollar contract, perhaps because of, but easily in spite of, her outburst. All that nonsense about company culture and negotiating tactics was a flamboyant embellishment.

Then, she'd taken the sex bull by the horns, so to speak. She'd decided that instead of acting as if she'd done something wrong, she'd treat it as if he was the one who should be worried. She told him it was a pleasant little encounter and she hoped he didn't think it meant anything. She'd been concerned he read more into it, that he'd think they would end up in a relationship and she was simply not interested.

By the time she circled around to asking for his support in approaching their management for my pay increase and additional headcount for her team, Steve was looking at her with a curious and surprised expression of respect.

As she told me the story, her face grew more animated. She appeared to be having the time of her life, reliving each word. The air in my office hummed with her strong, articulate voice.

It was obvious why customers liked listening to her, why she was so persuasive, and why she'd done so well in her career. That voice was mesmerizing, every word perfectly pronounced, a clarity in her tone that made the listener want to take a bath in the pure musical beauty of the English language.

For someone who had risen so effortlessly to a rather high position in a male-dominated world, I was surprised that she'd let him get the better of her to begin with. Maybe all that self-doubt about living out of a backpack or suddenly signing up for motherhood had thrown her whole system out of whack. It's funny how a bunch of things inside your head can start to make the entire world appear to shift around you.

She sat up straight and crossed her legs.

I smiled. I folded my hands together and rested them on the desk. "This won't prevent me from getting an increase during the regular performance review process, will it?"

"No. And by the way, Steve really went to bat for you."

"So did you," I said.

"Yes, but he fought like the company was in danger of going under without you." She laughed. "The email he sent with his recommendation for why he agreed with my request was almost embarrassing."

I turned slightly and looked out the window. I thought about Steve Montgomery and his tall, lean runner's body, his fine brown hair, and dark blue eyes. Those eyes took in a lot. He was always watching, always calculating. He'd fixed those eyes on me during meetings. When my eyes met his, he quickly looked away. His office was on the floor above mine, at the opposite side of the building. Yet I'd seen him walk past my office at least three or four times in the space of a few weeks. Possibly he was on his way to a conference room on my floor, possibly not.

Tess stood up and tugged her jacket hem. "Anyway, he asked me to let you know how much he values you. That the increase is well deserved."

I stood up and reached out my hand to shake hers. I held her hand for a moment longer and held her gaze equally long. "I'll be sure to express my gratitude."

Tess let go of my hand and left.

I sat down again and looked out the window. It wasn't too early to think about how I'd approach getting more than my fair share of the pot allocated for pay raises during the annual review process.

50

Los Angeles

Letting Randy hang from a tree, assisted by a roofie, is how I committed my first murder. It was easier than I would have thought.

Randy was a coward of the worst kind. The day Lisa returned from her ordeal with Tom, Randy couldn't be bothered to find out whether she was okay and it got me thinking, maybe he put Tom up to it. Tom had a good looking face without a lot behind it. He could vent his spleen on Lisa, but coming up with the whole idea for bullying and shaming her was a bit more complex.

When Lisa wept out the story of how Tom humiliated her, she'd mentioned something else — *Tom said I fantasize about murder. That I want to be all peace and justice for the people, but I'm a hypocrite. Why would Randy tell him about the game? He promised no one would ever know.*

It was more of a lament, I don't think she really wanted an answer, and I didn't give her one. She just wanted to express her feeling of utter betrayal, betrayals layered on top of each other.

I knew then, Randy was behind it. When he tweeted at me

that he was losing me *after all*, I think he believed Dianne was planning to tell me what he'd done to Lisa by proxy. He feared losing me and killed Dianne to stop her talking. When he realized the police were looking for him, he saw he would lose me after all. He didn't get that he never actually *had* me.

Even so, the murder game was never really a game. Lisa felt that in her gut. Randy and I knew it. He wanted to kill Dianne for the way she treated him. When he thought she was going to reveal his ugly secret, it fired him up enough to actually do it. But she didn't deserve to die.

He needed to be taken out of circulation — for what he did to Lisa. For killing a woman who was simply trying to get away from her mother's iron grip on her life. Calling Dianna a whore fired *me* up enough to actually do it.

What I did might horrify quite a few people. Murder is the worst crime of all, a crime against life itself, taking the ultimate something that doesn't belong to you. There's taking a parking space and taking cuts in line and taking two bucks someone left in the women's restroom without bothering to find out who it belongs to. Then there's taking nail polish or hair dye from a discount store, lingerie or a bathing suit from a department store. Stealing someone's lover. Mugging and armed robbery. Kidnapping. And finally, murder. How many people have stolen a parking space when another car was clearly waiting? How many have dashed to the newly opened checkout line, leapfrogging over others who had been waiting longer? Taking something that's not yours is a sliding scale.

The world is better off without some people. No one denied that the world was rid of a heinously evil scourge when Hitler died, when Osama bin Laden was taken out. Unfortunately, those men, and so many others like them, resembled those seemingly innocuous but horrifying wolf spiders — when the female is smacked, a hundred spiders burst out, spilling into every corner of the room. There's no hope of finding and killing them all.

Women have been shackled and shoved in corners and treated like shit by too many men for too many centuries. Words have been invented for the sole purpose of shaming women for wanting and having sex. *Whore. Slut. Hussy. Strumpet. Floozy. Hooker. Tart. Trollop. Harlot.* Where are the mirror images of those words for men? *Gigolo? Toy boy?* Even then, it's implied the woman is the one pierced by the slur, an object of pity — she can't get a man without paying him to accompany her. Besides, how often is the word gigolo bandied about? It doesn't show up in the Twitter stream. Pimp? He's considered a businessman, an entrepreneur, in some circles.

It's not like men have a super special sex drive that deserves honor while a woman is ambivalent or supposed to keep hers under wraps. And she'd better not wear a top that's cut too low or a skirt too short or she'll face blame and shame if she's raped. She can wear jeans and a sweatshirt and she'll still be blamed for going somewhere she *shouldn't* have.

Women are mocked and ridiculed for fussing over makeup and getting their hair and nails done, and sneered at if they let their hair grow as it will and leave their faces naked. They're covered head to toe in heavy fabric so they don't tempt men. They're chastised for not smiling at a man's whim and criticized if they're too friendly at the wrong time in the wrong place.

When their hormones affect their mood, women are categorized, dismissed, and told they're incapable. When a man's hormones drive him to punch a guy in a bar or launch a bombing strike on the other side of the world…well, they're strong and defending what's right.

Fuck that.

51

Aptos

I hadn't seen Jared for three days and I felt like I could breathe again. He didn't seem to recognize that he was almost as scary as Noreen. He wasn't erratic and full of obvious lies, but he lived in some sort of alternate reality. Inside his head, he and I were a couple, bonded by sex, drawing closer to each other, fighting against potential danger from Noreen, setting up housekeeping in a cozy, if sleek, little cabin by a lazy creek in the middle of a forest, making love and preparing and eating our meals together. Heading into the sunset, hand in hand. Us against the world.

Listening to him stirred up a desire to grab his neck and squeeze the breath out of him. Vicious, yes, but speaking and not being heard is tiresome. He acted as if my thoughts were insignificant or unimportant, water dribbling unnoticed from a leaky faucet. Not being heard suggests you don't exist. Being talked over, ignored, dismissed eats away at your soul. If you don't dig inside and find the will to make yourself heard, you absolutely will disappear altogether.

Noreen was crazy, but she wasn't going to hurt us. She liked waving that knife around, playing with our heads. She didn't have the courage or the strength to cause serious injury.

Now that I was alone in the house with her again, I pushed Jared out of my thoughts. Without his fears tripping me up, there was a chance I could get some information on what went down between Brian and Noreen.

I went to the French doors and looked out, picturing the eroding cliff below the deck. The tree brushed its heavy branch against the railing. Beyond, the world was an endless splash of blue sky and water. I opened the door and stepped onto the deck. The wood planks seemed to give ever so slightly beneath my feet, but I swallowed and moved forward until my hip touched the railing. The sun was nearing Pleasure Point at the opposite side of the bay, headed down for the night. I'd never ventured onto the deck at night and I wondered what it felt like, if there was the same sense of being suspended over nothingness, or if not seeing meant a greater sense of security. Once you know there's nothing beneath you, I doubt it's possible to remove that knowledge from your mind, so even without visible evidence, I expected it would be equally unnerving.

I leaned against the railing with more force. It seemed to shift at the pressure of my body. I stepped back, unsure whether I'd imagined it. I returned to the house, closed the doors and locked them. I don't know why we were careful to keep those doors locked. The deck was inaccessible from any other side. Perhaps the lock gave a false sense of security. Maybe we all secretly feared sleepwalking, and needed to know there was a barrier to simply pressing the handles down and stepping out into nothingness.

The sound of Noreen talking on the phone drifted out of her bedroom. I couldn't make out the words, but her door had to be open if her voice was audible in the alcove near the deck. I went into the kitchen and got out the vodka and vermouth, shaker and glasses. I picked up one of the glasses and went to the doorway of her room. I tapped my fingernail on her partially open door. She turned, listening now instead of talking. I raised the glass. She smiled and held up her thumb, then replaced it with the peace sign to indicate two minutes. Nothing like the offer of a martini to make her forget I'd betrayed her.

In the kitchen, I got out the jar of olives and filled the shaker with ice. I poured vodka into the shot glass and then into the shaker. As it glided over the ice cubes, they crackled under its relative warmth, even though the vodka was cool from being stored in the freezer.

When the drinks were ready, I went to the back doors and looked out. We'd never sat on the deck, never done more than step out there briefly to feel its menacing presence. The evening was warm enough. Why not enjoy our drinks out there? Two iron chairs were in the corner closest to the tree, tucked up against a small round table. I unlocked the doors and went out. I moved the table slightly to make more room for us to sit comfortably. The ocean was far enough away, smooth as glass, free from the threat I feel when I'm on its level and able to feel the advance of the water.

Noreen didn't object to sitting outside. We toasted the sunset and took simultaneous sips of the soothing liquid.

Without preamble, I said, "What's going on with Brian?"

"What about him?"

"I'm a little unclear about whether you two are still together, whether he's planning to move back in here."

"That will never happen."

"Isn't he a partial owner?"

She sipped her drink and looked out at the water. "It's mine. I bought it with my grandmother's money. I told you that."

"I thought…"

She placed her hands flat on the table. "It's mine. You don't know anything about it, 'kay?"

For several minutes we sat in silence. She took several small sips of her drink. I waited for the alcohol to smooth over her tension, loosening her tongue. The sun dropped closer to the tree line draining the sea of color. Her drink was almost half gone.

"Are you hungry?" I said.

She shook her head.

I leaned forward so I was more fully within the range of her peripheral vision. I tucked my hair behind my ears, sincere and vulnerable. "Look, Noreen. You're in danger of losing your roommates. Do you realize that?"

She turned. Her lips parted slightly. The upper lip trembled. "Why?"

"You're acting crazy."

"No worse than you two."

"Actually, it is. The knife on the door. Locking Jared in his room. The mirror. The rat."

"You're the rat. It was wrapped in your thong. So there

you are."

"Okay." I took a long swallow of my drink and scooted my chair to my left so I was directly facing her. "That's demented, don't you see that? Leaving rodent carcasses in his room isn't the way to attract a guy's interest."

"Obviously I can't attract him at all, so what difference does it make? Only girls like you can do that."

"You're scaring him."

"What about you?"

"I don't scare easily," I said.

"Well he's not as scared as I am."

"Why don't you tell me what's going on. Maybe if we understood…"

"You're the last person I'm going to confide in."

I finished my drink and popped both olives in my mouth. "Do you want another one?"

She shrugged. She looked near tears. I picked up the glasses and went inside. When I returned with fresh drinks, she gave me a soggy, limp smile. "Thanks."

"We should drink these more slowly." I laughed. "We don't want to trip and fall off the deck."

Noreen shivered, convulsions passing through her body repeatedly as if she was having some kind of fit. Finally, she rubbed her arms and settled down, slumping lower in the chair. She poked her finger at her olives but didn't take a sip.

52

I left Noreen on the deck, poking at her olives, reminding me again of the decapitated heads I'd envisioned the first time we drank martinis together. I went back inside and returned with a plate of tiny crackers and thinly sliced cheddar cheese. I sat down and ate one. "You have to trust someone. And I think I'm a good candidate. Better than most."

"You have no reason to think so highly of yourself."

I shrugged. "Jared will leave if there's not an explanation."

"So I'll never get a chance? Maybe I don't even care." She took a sip of her drink. "I think I'm still in love with Brian, on some weird, sick level. How can you love someone who wants to kill you?"

"Are you sure you're not just a little paranoid?"

"You saw that photograph."

The photograph was disturbing. But it was also meaningless. When I was a kid, we used to erase the eyes of models in magazines. When the ink was gone, the eyes blazed white, giving them a soulless, other-worldly quality. It was the same impression conveyed by the empty-eyed photograph of Noreen. But maybe Brian, if he was even the one who did it, was just fooling around. Like we'd done with our erasers. A childish thrill at altering another's appearance.

"Are you sure he's the one who drilled out the eyes?"

"Who else would do it?"

"Did he say why?"

"I found it after he was gone."

"And you haven't talked to him? You have no idea what it means?"

"I might." She took several sips of her drink. Her eyelids were heavy and her demeanor was finally, gradually, uncoiling itself.

"Who would I tell? Except Jared, and he should know. If you want him to stay."

"It's worse than you think. I might be in trouble."

"Pregnant?"

She laughed. "No. I mean serious trouble."

The sun dropped away from the sky and a cool breeze sprang up. Before the sun disappeared, the deck had grown quite warm. The breeze was a relief. For now.

"So you do know why he damaged the photograph?"

"He didn't like what I was seeing."

"What was that?"

"In the mirror."

"I don't understand."

"When I looked in the mirror, I saw a woman's face."

I laughed softly.

"Not my own. His mother's."

"Does she look like you?"

She shook her head.

"Then why...are you taking medication, or anything?" I

wondered why I'd never considered it. That would explain her bizarre behavior. And maybe she wasn't taking a prescription, maybe she was using a hallucinogenic and we hadn't noticed. It's not like we'd spent much time around her.

It annoyed me that I was starting to think in terms of we, as if Jared and I were a unit after all. But when it came to facing our psychotic landlord, I suppose we were. When he showed me the picture of the classy little cabin, I felt as if he'd thrown a net over me and was slowly pulling a rope, tightening it ever so slowly while he whispered that everything would be okay, his soothing tone mimicking the trainers that capture escaped wildcats and try to coax them back into a cage. He made too many assumptions, assuming sex meant more than it did, assuming we were friends, assuming I wanted to chain myself to another human being, assuming he understood me, or that he understood women in general and there was no variation in desire from one woman to the next. He seemed to think all women wanted the same things.

I'd bolted from his room, although I was sorry not to look more carefully at the pictures of the small house. It looked new, very nicely constructed with dark hardwood floors and a small, but gleaming kitchen featuring charcoal gray granite counters and buff colored cabinets.

Noreen sipped her martini and didn't speak for several seconds. "He thought I was making it up —seeing her face in the mirror — trying to upset him. Playing mind games."

"Why would he think that?"

"It's a long story."

"I think you should tell me. Maybe I can help."

"It's too late for that." She plucked an olive out of the glass and ate it, her face turned toward the horizon so I couldn't read her expression.

53

The martini glasses were empty and Noreen still hadn't spoken. I needed her to tell me what was going on. I didn't care if she decreed it *too late*. What did that even mean? I played my ace — "I met Brian."

She jerked her head toward me. "No you didn't."

"He came by a while back, when you were at your parents."

Her voice rose and turned shrill. "Why didn't you tell me?"

"He didn't say who he was."

"Then how do you know?"

"I figured it out eventually. The point is, I could ask him about the photograph, and about whatever it is you don't want to tell me."

"He won't say anything."

"I bet he would." I smiled with a brief twitch of my lips.

She glared at me. "You wouldn't." She made a whimpering sound. "You wouldn't seduce my...You're a..."

I stood up. "Do you want another drink? And then you need to tell me, or Jared and I will be moving out this weekend." There was no doubt Jared would be willing. I wasn't sure I was, but I wanted to know what was going on with Joe...Brian. Asking him was not the ideal solution, and I wasn't entirely sure he would tell the truth. Noreen seemed to be moving closer toward truthfulness, at the end of her rope, in some ways.

She let out another whimper, the sound faint and faraway, like a dog outside a solid wood door, the cry so faint you have to stand motionless and strain to determine whether you'd really heard it. I took her meek noise as a *yes* to a third drink. My mind was pleasantly floating. Three martinis in a relatively short span of time can really knock you over, but it was a warm, relaxed, unworried feeling and it was what I needed, with the ocean growing darker beside us, white caps starting to emerge.

After mixing the drinks and carrying them to the table on the deck, I refilled the plate with cheese and crackers. I returned to the house, picked up one of Noreen's gardenia candles and a lighter and brought them outside. I set the candle on the table, clicked the lighter, and held the flame to the wick. The sky was a deep inky blue and a few stars had popped out like eyes opening brightly, equally curious about Joe. The moon was a thin slice, crystal clear in the cloudless expanse. There wasn't even a whisper of fog along the shore and the lights of Capitola sparkled on one side, Monterey on the other.

Candlelight flickered across Noreen's face, bleeding off more of the color from her already pale skin. When she lifted her arm and reached for a slice of cheese, the light fell across her arm, making it appear more frail, a thin flash of white. She wore a black sleeveless top and a gold chain with a gold letter *N* hanging from it. There were purple and gray shadows under her eyes. It looked as if she hadn't slept much over the past several days.

"Why did he leave?" I said softly. "It wasn't because your dog died so tragically."

"No."

She pinched the stem of the glass between her thumb and index finger. She slid her fingers up and down the length, staring into the liquid. "Nothing in my life turned out the way I thought it would."

"I think most people feel that way."

"Do you?"

"I never considered it. I have a long way to go. So do you. It's not like you can't shake things up, change direction." I kept my voice low and soothing, hoping that between a gentle hypnotic tone of voice and the dulling of the alcohol, the story would begin to ease its way out of her lips. I could feel it right there. She was aching to tell me, to tell someone, but there was a dense lump of fear filling her throat, sealing it off.

"If you think he might hurt you, isn't it better that someone else knows about it?"

"Why?"

I didn't know why, I just said it because I was trying every angle to get her talking. The more she held it inside, the more my curiosity gnawed at the insides of my skull, taking tiny bits of bone in its teeth, getting more anxious and demanding.

I wanted to take Noreen's narrow, breakable shoulders and shake her until her teeth rattled and those large, bulging eyes jiggled around in their sockets and the story fell out of her head.

It was difficult to imagine Joe…Brian…committing an act of violence. He had an easy, languid style about him. Even when he was having sex, he wasn't vigorous and driving, his movements were controlled and fluid, very certain. It was disconcerting to realize that he might have been using me for some purpose related to Noreen that I couldn't figure out. Jealousy didn't seem likely, unless he planned to reveal our relationship later, holding it for the right moment. Watching her house, biding his time before he approached her was an odd way to handle whatever issues he wanted to resolve with her. Why didn't he simply hire a lawyer and get his fair share in the usual way? Killing her, if that was a legitimate possibility, would accomplish nothing in terms of getting his money out of the house, unless she had a will granting the whole thing to him. But when someone is murdered, all that changes. There is no easy access to what they've left behind. And who has a will when she's not even thirty years old? I'm sure there are anal, financially astute types that have already recorded their last wishes, but I couldn't imagine Noreen fitting that category.

"Why is it better if someone else knows?" she said.

I picked up my glass and took a sip. "So he can't get away with it."

She pushed her glass toward the candle. "I don't know if I should drink any more."

I put my hand on her arm, feeling the bone hard and sharp through the nearly fleshless skin of her forearm. "Tell me."

"I suppose it doesn't really matter that I can't trust you. I can't trust anyone to do what they promise. And whatever happens to me — it's probably too late."

I nudged her glass back toward her. She picked it up, took a sip, and started talking.

54

Noreen's face looked as blank as one of those stiff, thin plastic masks with painted features. She spoke as if she'd sunk into a cavern inside of her head, and rather than remembering the events, she was actually seeing and hearing the people and things she began to tell me about —

Six months after we moved to Aptos, Brian's father died of a heart attack.

Before that, his mother had been in and out of the hospital for several years with anorexia. I always thought of anorexia as a teenage disease, that it's caused by pressure from pop culture, wanting to be accepted by the group, obsession with your appearance. But Cheryl had it. When I first met her, I thought she was stylishly thin. She had great clothes, not what I would choose, of course, but very expensive fabrics and perfect for her age. She wore lots of white and beige, and she always looked sleek and elegant — tunic tops and longish dresses with baggy sweaters and that sort of thing, so I didn't notice right away that she was just bones.

About two months after Brian's father died, she was admitted to a new program. When she came out, they didn't want her to go back to her home by herself. She needed

support, someone to make sure she ate. Not that she did…
eat. She was so frail, she was bedridden. So she came to stay
with us. She stayed in the room you're renting now. Brian
bought a hospital bed so she could sit up, hopefully to eat.
For a while, a nurse was coming by to prepare meals, feed her,
turn her so she didn't get bedsores. The nurse gave baths and
did all of that stuff.

I hated having Cheryl in our house. We're young. We were
supposed to be a couple. I wanted my own place where I
could cook what I chose and make a home for Brian, grow
vegetables, decorate in the style we preferred. All the things
you want with your first house — any house, really. But
especially the first one.

Cheryl was like this ghost in the other room. Always
listening, always there. I couldn't do anything without her
trying to pin down where I was in the house. She'd call out to
me — *Noreen? Dear? Where are you? I can't hear you. I need to
know where you are.*

She was like an old woman but she was only forty-eight.

After a while, Brian decided we didn't need the nurse.
Having someone come in was expensive. Every time he paid
the bill, he thought about cash leaking out of his eventual
inheritance. He realized the things the nurse was doing didn't
require an RN. There were no injections, just monitoring her
diet, which he figured was not rocket science and besides,
after watching for several weeks, we knew what the nurse
advised her to eat, we could figure it out. I was already
starting to help prepare her meals. I had a good handle on the
appropriate diet.

He decided that since I was around the house all day, without much to do, in his opinion, I could take care of Cheryl. I told him I didn't feel comfortable taking her clothes off and bathing her and trying to get her dried off properly. And carrying the bedpan into the bathroom without spilling it, dumping her pee and her shit, although there wasn't a lot of that since she still didn't eat more than a few spoonfuls at a time.

It was horribly unfair. It wasn't my job. He reminded me that his mother took me in when my parents threw me out of the house. But they didn't throw me out. I left by choice. Sure I needed a place to stay. I wanted to be with Brian, that's all, but he twisted it around to make his mother out to be a saint for letting me live with her family, cooking for me, doing my laundry. He seemed to think his mother was a saint.

Anyway, I didn't have a choice. The nurse was gone, Brian was at work, and the woman wasn't mobile. I was her slave. She'd ring this stupid copper bell on the nightstand. Sometimes I think she waited for me to settle down on the back deck with my knitting before she'd ring it. Cleaning her up was awful — wiping her butt. She drank shakes with a straw, the glass sitting on a tray across her lap so the only strength required was to put the straw in her mouth. To get her to eat solid food, I had to spoon feed her.

Brian acted as if he was some sort of hero because he moved her to a sofa in the corner and changed the bedding every few days. But guess who washed it?

It was hard watching her. And infuriating. Pity and fury in a single moment which left me disoriented. She was so weak, but she'd done it to herself! She was still doing it to herself. It wasn't as if she had cancer or some other terrible disease that took over her body against her will. She just refused to eat. She was vain and wanted to be thinner than all her friends, as if that was some sort of prize. And then she got addicted to not eating. I know anorexia is a disease, there's something wrong in the minds of people who diet until they're sick, but it's not the same as a real disease. And it was so fucking unfair! I hated her. I hated him.

Sometimes I wondered if he was punishing me because of what happened to Terry, him dying in such an awful way like that. Brian blamed me and now he was going to make me suffer. As if I didn't suffer as much as he had when Terry died.

Finally I figured out that I didn't need to respond to the damn bell quite so fast. I could let her shout at me, because that's what she did no matter if it took me seven seconds to get in there, or seven minutes. I started lengthening the time it took to go into the room by a half a minute every day. She sort of got used to me not jumping the minute the clacker hit the side of the bell. She complained to Brian and he gave me a lecture about being kinder to someone who was suffering. By that point, I didn't care what he thought. He could lecture me all he wanted. It wasn't as if he could fire me or dock my pay.

Once I got her acclimated to a forty minute response, I started sneaking out of the house every few days. Sometimes I'd just go for a walk on the beach, stick my feet in the cold water and forget there was a woman screaming down at me from the top of the cliffs. It kept me from killing her, I really believe that. Some of those days, I'd drive to a cafe and have a glass of wine, extending my absence to almost an hour. Often, when I returned, she was asleep. I think she wore herself out shaking the bell as hard as she could, as if that would make it ring louder, make me run faster. It was funny she had enough strength to shake that damn bell but not to lift a spoon up to her mouth. She exhausted her lungs calling for me. She didn't have the strength to spend fifteen minutes shouting.

She should have been in a care facility, but Brian viewed that as sticking her in a warehouse.

Then, she started falling out of bed. She would sort of topple to the side and just slide off. The first time it happened, I went in to feed her lunch and she was on the floor, crying. Some of those hospital-type beds have railings on the sides for just that type of situation, but this one didn't. I guess we bought the bargain model.

It wasn't impossible for me to pick her up in my arms and put her back on the bed, she hardly weighed anything. But it made my back stiff and I developed a constant pain right at the center of my lower back.

At least when she fell she didn't shout at me. I think she was embarrassed and when I picked her up in my arms like an infant, she felt so foolish, it made her consider what she'd done to herself. Not that it gave her any self-awareness of what she'd done to Brian and me. Especially me. But she didn't tell Brian about the falling. I'm not absolutely sure why, maybe it was the shame. To me, having to use a bedpan would be the worst shame, but the falling is what did it for her. They say everyone has their own rock bottom which you have to hit before you realize you have a problem. Why they didn't get her to that point in the program she was in, I have no idea. I thought that was the purpose.

Knowing she might fall out of bed, especially when she got herself riled up shouting for me, kept me from going out for several weeks. Then I got an idea, but it turned out to be the worst idea of my life.

It's impossible to completely describe how trapped I felt. I couldn't take a shower without turning off the water and hearing Cheryl shouting my name. I couldn't pee without hearing the bell ringing.

In the mornings, I made buttered toast and coffee for myself and loose scrambled egg beaten with milk for Cheryl. I sat by her bed and fed her one piece of fluffy egg at a time followed by a sip of tea that had to made from loose tea leaves, not a bag. She held the egg in her mouth, puckering her lips around it as if she might vomit any minute. After a while, she'd suck on it, moving it around with her tongue, not chewing. It would slowly turn softer and slightly dissolved and she'd swallow with a gagging sound. She never finished the whole egg. Tea dribbled down her chin because she refused to swallow if I let her sip it before it cooled enough to suit her preference. I'd wipe her face and take the dishes to the kitchen. I'd clean up the pan and put the dishes in the dishwasher.

After breakfast, I gave her a sponge bath and dried her off. I even lifted each arm and rolled on deodorant for her.

Touching her body sent chills down my own arms and legs. Her skin was dry and loose. I felt each bone, and could see every single tendon when she moved. I put a clean nightgown on her, brushed her hair, and turned on the TV for her. Then I'd take my own shower, already tired at nine o'clock in the morning. Once a week I'd hold her cold, clammy feet and clip her toenails, take her bony icy hands into mine and trim her fingernails.

The vegetable garden died. I didn't have the energy or the time for it. My day was consumed by preparing, feeding, and cleaning up her meals, washing her clothes and sheets, keeping her body from decaying right before our eyes.

I hated Brian.

I hated our house. I didn't want to look at my dead garden.

If I didn't start going out again, my mind would rot and I'd end up a blathering moron. Brian was working six days a week with his landscaping business, so the only day I got even a partial break was Sunday, and most of the time he complained he was tired from physical labor all week. I still had to feed her. I had to bathe her because he said it wasn't right for a man to see his mother naked.

And she wouldn't eat! She would not fucking eat more than a few bites. I wanted to smack her face. It seemed as if she liked being taken care of. She liked being frail and weak. She liked watching me do all the work.

Then, a friend of mine from high school called to say she was in town. She wanted to hang out at the beach, grab lunch at a taqueria. The invitation seemed like something from another life, another woman's life. I hadn't been that carefree in a thousand years.

So I implemented my terrible idea. After I fed Cheryl her lunch, I tied her to the bed. She objected but I told her she couldn't risk falling again and breaking a bone. I didn't tell her I was leaving. I figured she could scream until her lungs burst. I'd deal with it when I got back home. All I wanted was to lie on the sand and listen to the waves and drink beer and talk to my girlfriend.

It was glorious. We brought our tacos to the beach and sat on a towel with our feet buried in warm sand while we ate. We both had two beers and gossiped about people from high school. We did some body surfing and drank another beer. I was gone for hours and felt like a normal person, almost happy.

When I came home, I found Cheryl. She had thrashed around like a trapped rat, gotten herself completely tangled in the rope, slid over the side of the bed, and strangled.

They ruled it suicide. The police officers that came when I called 911 said the position of her body defied the laws of physics. It was impossible that she'd managed to choke herself like that without deliberately putting herself in that position. I was sobbing, inconsolable with guilt but secretly, so relieved. I was free. They assumed it was grief. It's funny how people assume you have the same emotions they do.

After Brian came home and they'd taken away her body, he said he didn't believe it for one second. He didn't break down. He just started packing up his things.

I did laundry and cleaned up the hall bathroom. I was

scrubbing around the base of the toilet. I stood up and glanced in the mirror and she was there. I started crying. I closed my eyes, trying to make her go away, but when I opened them she was still there. I knelt down and put the bedpan and the pads I'd used on the bed to catch urine overflow into a plastic garbage bag. When I stood up, I couldn't help glancing at the mirror. She was there again, her lips formed into a circle as if she were calling my name. I dropped the stuff on the floor and ran out of the room.

When I told Brian what I'd seen, he got really pissed off. Angrier than I'd ever seen him. He accused me of making it up, trying to torture him. He said I twisted the story to make it look like she'd committed suicide and would never find peace. He refused to believe his mother would kill herself and leave him behind. That she would abandon him, no matter how weak and sick she was.

He grabbed me around the neck. He said he wanted to kill me, but he let go and said he'd decide to wait, so I would suffer like his mother had. Like Terry had.

He put his things in the shed and left with just the clothes that fit in a duffel bag. He said he'd be back to take care of me.

A few days later I found that horrible photograph.

The face continued appearing in the mirror and I thought if other people were living in the house, she would leave me alone. I know it's not really her, it's probably my guilt, or some weird psychotic breakdown because of all the stress of taking care of her. I don't know. But she's still there. Every time I look. Once the mirror was destroyed, it's harder to see her, but she's still there.

I've been waiting, and I know he's coming. You and Jared can't really protect me. I know that. I expect he'll be here tomorrow because it's the anniversary of Terry's death. He thinks I kill helpless creatures and he's certain it's only a matter of time before I do it again.

I didn't kill anyone. I didn't want Terry to die. It broke my heart. I was in the wrong place at the wrong time, maybe. With his mother, I shouldn't have had to do all of that care. She was Brian's responsibility, not mine. But in some ways I don't think I'll mind if he stabs me while I'm sleeping or something like that. It would be better than seeing that woman's face every time I look in the mirror, for the rest of my life.

55

There was no doubt Noreen had issues, big issues, huge issues, possibly insurmountable issues. But the things Brian had inflicted on her made me think we couldn't be talking about the same man. Joe is an insanely common name. It was absolutely believable that the Joe I'd had sex with was someone else. A casual acquaintance of hers. He could be Noreen's brother — I'd never asked her brother's name. A cousin, former co-workers, high school classmates, neighbors. Hell, maybe the Joe who captivated me was a friend of Brian's.

Beneath my surface attempt to rationalize, I heard my brain lying to itself, not wanting to face the horror that the same man could be a charming, teasing, expert lover, and a despot. He made Noreen a virtual slave, leaving her to clean up the mess of his mother's life. Literally.

No one but her ex would stake out her house with such care, watching, coming close enough to talk to a roommate lounging in the front yard, then pulling back. When I first saw him, I'd thought he could be Noreen's twin. But it was something else. There was a similarity in their psyches — two people locked in a battle for their souls came to resemble each other. The fierce glaze in their eyes, the burning hatred for the other, transformed their mannerisms and facial expressions into mirror images.

Only a lover bent on revenge — a man whose passion had turned to hatred — would have the tenacity to move in circles, ever closer, with such a willingness to wait for the right time. I knew deep inside this wasn't a guy from her past who wanted to give her a pleasant surprise. It was a guy with a plan. It wasn't a guy who wanted to remember old times, catch up on the details of her life. It was a guy on a mission.

I was also on a mission. I had a plan.

My plan formed itself around the newfound assumption that Noreen wasn't completely unhinged. Her fear was based in truth — Brian wanted to avenge his mother. The holes drilled through Noreen's eyes in the photograph were permanently lodged in my mind's eye. Each time I recalled the image, I thought about how the removal of eyes turns a human being into a horrific monster. We proved that in childhood with our erasers. Removing the eyes lays waste to the entire face. It transforms a human being's face to the world into a lifeless, disturbing, inhuman mask.

I took the day off work and I didn't bother faking illness. I told Tess I had personal business to deal with.

Noreen had gone to work in her cornflower blue scrubs and white running shoes with touches of pink. Her hair was yanked back as she always wore it for work, tied in a ponytail and then braided. She didn't mention the anniversary of Terry's death. I'd expected her to plead with Jared or me to stay around, convinced Brian would arrive that evening. Maybe since I hadn't mentioned plans to go out, she assumed

I'd be there. Or, for all I knew, Brian had already contacted her and she was resigned to the inevitable. There were so many possibilities — he wasn't coming after all, or she'd enlisted Jared as her body guard. She had a fair amount of guilt swimming around inside of her and despite the way she protested the things Brian had forced her to do for his mother, a deeper part of her believed she deserved whatever punishment he decided to deliver. She had issues.

Or, she had a plan of her own. I thought of her favorite butcher knife, already utilized on the mirror and the door to my room.

After Noreen left, I drove to the gym and completed a weight lifting circuit that took forty-five minutes. I drove home sweaty and changed into clean workout clothes. I chose black capri length spandex pants, a black sports bra, and a black t-shirt cropped to the bottom of my ribs. I took the house key off the ring and tucked it into the zipper pocket on the back of my pants. I did my hair in the same style Noreen had worn to work. I ate a turkey sandwich on rye bread with German mustard and lots of lettuce. I spent the early afternoon watching weight lifting technique videos, drinking water, and straightening my room. I wandered around the house and checked out the shed, where Brian's things were packed as efficiently as Tetris blocks. I studied the eyeless photograph and ran my hand down the length of the hospital bed. I surveyed the collection of tools hanging near the front and made sure they were arranged on their proper hooks. I went through the house and onto the back deck, needlessly studying the layout.

At three o'clock, I drove to the Safeway parking lot. Since the store was open twenty-four hours, no one would notice my car was parked there longer than it should be. A car had to sit there for days, gathering dead leaves and pine needles in the windshield wipers before anyone even thought of reporting it as abandoned.

I ran two miles back home at an easy pace and reached the house well before Noreen was due home around five-thirty. Jared's car wasn't there. I put on a dark blue hoodie and went onto the back deck. I nestled myself in the corner behind the table and chairs. I leaned forward and dragged the table and chairs closer so my presence was less visible. I bent my knees and hugged my lower legs. It was possible I'd have to maintain the position for several hours, but there's nothing like fury to provide superhuman control over your body.

There were two gambles. One was that Noreen would notice the unlocked doors and expect to see someone on the deck. But it was equally possible she would be so agitated, she wouldn't give it a second thought. The odds were much longer for the other gamble — if Brian came to the house looking to punish her on the day of Terry's death, he might not choose the deck. But thinking about Terry, as well as the strange manner of his mother's death, it was a highly probable educated guess that he would appear on the deck before he was finished.

At first my body was a little warm, wrapped up in a thick sweatshirt with the sun casting its rays across the deck, drenching the back of the house in light. Once the sun dipped to the tree line on the far shore, the air grew cool fast.

I hugged my knees tighter.

From where I sat, I couldn't see the water. To most people, the expanse of water was glorious while I had to put effort into not keeping my eyes on it for too long or it would sweep my thoughts toward the danger it posed. Most people longed to enjoy the view of the shimmering ocean, but the precarious nature of the structure chased them into the house, clinging to its solid concrete foundation. The weathered boards of the deck, the tree branch constantly knocking against the railing, and the knowledge there was nothing below terrified them. None of that bothered me. I have no fear of heights, no twisted desire to throw myself off cliffs or tall buildings like some people worry they might, as if it's programmed into the depths of their minds. But the ocean is another matter.

As I pulled on my hood, I heard Noreen's Jetta purr into the driveway.

The sounds of Noreen entering the house and moving about, presumably in her bedroom, changing clothes, weren't audible from the deck. After a while, the kitchen light came on.

I sat there for another half hour or so before I heard the rumble of Brian's Boxster. The engine died. A car door opened and closed. Then, nothing.

56

Behind me, the house was eerily silent. I realized that below my conscious thoughts, I had heard the subtle sounds of Noreen moving around after all, possibly a door closing, a plate on the counter, a chair scraping the floor. Now, it was the silence of an abandoned building. Surely if Brian had done something to hurt her, I would have heard a scream, or some other, more shocking sound. The Boxster would have announced their departure if he'd taken her somewhere else.

Another twenty minutes passed, maybe more.

I waited.

The French doors crashed open, each hitting the interior wall on either side of the alcove. Brian laughed. "You and that crazy fucking knife. You won't do anything."

She had a plan after all. Instead of needing everyone to take care of her, she was up for defending herself. I felt a tremor of pride.

Brian stepped out the door, stumbling slightly as he misjudged the lip between the alcove and the deck. He backed up toward the railing. "Bring it on!" He held up his left arm that had been blocked by his body from my line of sight. Wrapped in a coil from his thumb and around his elbow was a white rope. "You'll dangle over the side like

Terry, kicking your legs into empty space. I only regret I can't humiliate you with a ridiculous outfit first." He folded his arms across his chest as if he wanted to protect the rope. "You'll thrash around without anyone to help you, until you choke to death like my mother."

"I'm surprised your mother didn't choke on her own vomit," Noreen shouted. "That's how she spent her time, right? I made delicious meals to entice her to eat and she gagged and spit it in my face."

"She was grieving."

"Oh, bullshit. She wanted to be skinny. Like me. She was jealous of me. She wished she could be young again. I felt it the whole time I lived in her cold, dead house."

"Stop talking shit about her!" His voice was loud and thick with rage. The deck seemed to vibrate in response.

For the first time, I realized that if the entire deck went down, I would go with it. The base of the structure was relatively solid, though. All floorboards have some flex to them. I hoped my thoughts weren't wishful thinking, lies to myself about the stability of the gradually falling house. The railing alone was meant to be weak. Brian alone was meant to fall to his death.

His list of sins was short but grievous —

Imprisoning his girlfriend to care for a woman whose frail body and diseased mind required a team of doctors and psychologists if she was to have any hope of a normal life.

And leading me to believe he was a man who respected women. Hell, the guy didn't even respect his own mother enough to buy her a bed that would keep her safe. He couldn't be bothered to get her the help she needed. If anyone was to blame for her death, it was him.

I don't require a lot from a man I want to have sex with, but he better not be someone who thinks I exist solely for his pleasure. He better not be the kind of man who believes women are there to do the cooking and cleaning and laundry and give them the shivers.

It was irritating to know he was better at the game than I was — adept at concealing his true nature.

Noreen stepped out the door, the knife raised, like a warrior goddess. There was no way in hell that small, delicate Noreen was going to accomplish what she wanted to with that knife.

She charged at Brian. He stepped toward her and grabbed her arm. There was a snapping sound and she screamed. She wriggled frantically but he held the arm with the knife immobilized. She kicked at his shins. He laughed and stepped to the side. The knife wobbled in her hand. Slowly, her fingers uncurled and it fell over the side of the deck. Screaming, she flung her entire body at him. He twisted slightly to the right and fell back against the railing. There was a crack, much louder than what had come from her arm as the force of his grip fractured the bone.

The railing gave way and Brian fell, taking Noreen with him.

A howl like the cry of a wild animal leaping at its prey drifted up as they plunged to the rocky cove below.

My back and legs were thick with sweat, as if I'd been part of the struggle. I stood up and tore off my sweatshirt.

My legs trembled. I turned and picked up the sledgehammer I'd used to damage the railing that afternoon. I carried it through the house and out to the shed where I hung it from the two prongs, perfectly spaced to hold the iron head.

The only thing left to do was go through the things in her room to find Jared's rental application. His would be filled with truthful information. I'd take mine as well, although it really didn't matter.

Entering Noreen's room gave me pause. I hadn't planned her death. I wanted to save her, but like she'd said, maybe it was too late. Maybe she preferred to be with Brian. I began opening drawers.

57

Jared had put down the deposit and first month's rent on the cabin. He refused to believe Alex had been serious that she didn't want to be his friend. Of course she did. The way her body responded to his touch screamed that she wanted him. She liked her space, that was all. He'd pushed too hard, and hadn't made it clear that he had no expectations, for now. Once she saw that it would give them a tranquil environment where they could make love, free from Noreen's watery eyes and pleading lips, Alex would be eager to move with him. Other than that, she could come and go as she pleased. They didn't need to eat meals together or hang out in the evenings. Whatever she wanted.

Once she was secure in her freedom, despite the small space, she would let go of her resistance and be drawn closer to him. She was like a wild animal. He needed to step back and let her approach *him* as her trust developed and she saw he didn't pose a threat.

It didn't take him long to pack up his things. He didn't have much. Noreen hadn't been around all day, which helped him breathe a bit easier.

As if he'd planned it, he was tucking in the last flap on the final box when Alex knocked on his door. He opened it. Her hair was brushed smooth and dark around her shoulders, reminding him of a cape. Her bangs were thick, combed over her eyebrows like she'd worn them the day he first saw her. There wasn't a touch of makeup on her skin or color on her lips. She smiled and it was beautiful — natural and pure and hungry, for him.

"I changed my mind." Her voice was soft. "It's not too late, is it?"

"For what?" His heart thudded against bone and his ribs ached. Following his instinct was satisfying. He'd known she wanted him to take control, to recognize her need for space. He wasn't obliged to explicitly tell her she'd have all the freedom she wanted in the tiny cabin. Simply steering a wide path around her for the past few days had been enough.

"The cabin you found is charming. And not too far from my office. Lots of roads and trails for running."

Charming didn't seem to fit her, but there was so much more to her that he needed to learn. He swallowed the grin trying to force its way onto his lips. He wouldn't be giddy, over-excited. He'd take a cue from her and remain aloof. "Your timing is excellent. I put down a deposit and signed the agreement."

"I'm feeling uncomfortable here." She pushed her bangs to the side of her face. "You were right, something is terribly wrong. I think the sooner we get out, the better." She stepped into the room and closed the door. She glanced around and lowered her voice. "You're packed?"

"I said your timing was perfect."

"Will you help me pack?"

He followed her across the hall. She opened the closet and dug around inside. A moment later, she hauled out a stack of eight or ten flattened boxes tied with twine.

"You saved your boxes?"

"So did you."

"I had, umm…four." Looking around her room, he felt a sharp thorn in his throat. There was no storage shed and no garage at the new place. He couldn't picture where her boxes would go in the seven hundred square foot cabin. He shook off the feeling of dread regarding the erosion of the simplicity he sought. He picked up the first sheet of folded cardboard and began reconstructing the box.

An hour later, they were finished. "When should we tell Noreen?" he said.

"I saw her on the deck, waving her butcher knife. She was ranting at Brian."

"Shit. That's scary shit. Talking to someone who isn't there."

Alexandra's eyes were wider than normal, filled with moisture. "Frankly, I'm scared. I think we just need to get out of here."

"We can't fit all of this in one trip."

"How far is it?"

"About twenty minutes."

She nodded. "Then we better get busy."

"What's the rush?"

"I just told you…"

"It's not like she's going to come into the room and stab us right now." He laughed, then his voice dissolved into his throat. Maybe she was. For Alex to express fear, meant something. He didn't like the anxious tone in his laugh. Everything was going as he wanted. Why was he delaying?

58

Two hours later, the far corner of the great room in the cabin was stacked with moving boxes, making the tiny space appear even smaller. During the daytime, the cabin's mild sense of claustrophobia was offset by an enormous window that occupied most of one wall, allowing light to fill the open-beam room despite the tightly clustered oak and pine trees with thick undergrowth between the cabin and the main house. Down a slight incline, but not visible from the cabin, was the languidly moving water of Soquel Creek. Occupying one side of the great room was a granite counter with a sink large enough to bathe a small dog, a two-burner gas cooktop, and a refrigerator. Opposite the kitchen area were adjacent doors, one leading to a small bedroom, the other to a bathroom.

"It's fantastic," she said. "Better than the pictures."

The smile she gave him eased his concern over the number of boxes. He walked up to her and put his arms around her waist. She held him for a moment, patted his back, and stepped out of the circle of his arms.

Something about the way her gaze darted from the kitchen area to the window to the bedroom made it seem as if she was making plans. And he didn't have the impression her plans had anything to do with rearranging the furniture already in place, nothing to do with considering where she might store her belongings. She pulled her purse off her shoulder, removed her wallet, and opened it. "What do I owe?"

"For the deposit...well, I can cover that. So seven-fifty for half the rent. And once we get utility bills, I'll let you know the rest."

She pulled out a fistful of bills.

"You can't Paypal me, or write a check?"

"Nope." She held out the bills. He took them reluctantly.

They set to — unpacking toiletries and the clothes they'd need for the next day. It was close to eleven when they settled into bed. Lying beside her was bliss, knowing he'd wake and she'd still be there.

The purpose of meditation was learning to live in the present moment. He wouldn't think about their frantic departure from Noreen's, Alex's insistence on paying him cash, the boxes crowding the main room, eating together, shopping for food, or any other details about how this would all work. He put his hand on her thigh, feeling her soft warmth. He took ten long, slow breaths, not thinking of anything.

And then he was asleep.

59

I'm not like other women. I think most women feel that way. And really, when you stop to think about what that means, it's absolutely true. None of us are alike. Of course we share desires and there's an overlap in beliefs regarding society and philosophy, but beyond that, there's infinite variation. Seven billion different permutations, and counting.

Of those seven billion, approximately forty-nine and a half percent are female. Glorious, strong, smart human beings. Women think and read and form opinions. They lift weights and run, they dance and play golf, soccer, basketball, and poker. They cook and eat. They partner with another person to raise children. They smoke and drink and fuck. Just like men.

Yet a despairing percentage of men treat women as if they are sub-human, existing only for male pleasure and comfort — whores and Madonnas, if you will. Some view women as punching bags and vessels for the disappointments in their own lives. They talk over women and bully them. Weak men, to be sure.

Strong, confident men don't behave that way. But those men, who can't feel strong unless they demean a woman, deserve to die. It's a harsh statement, but it's the truth. The law of evolution decrees that weak animals will not live to their life expectancy. The herd is trimmed whether we like it or not, whether we approve or not. It's how the planet's ecosystem works.

Randy Flynn was my first and I'll never forget a single moment — shaping the noose, listening as his tongue grew thick and inarticulate from the combination of pot and vodka and the roofie, while I recalled the warmth of his body against mine, and remembered how we laughed and tripped out over the murder game. I won't forget how he sounded as he thrashed at the end of the rope in a drugged stupor. But neither will I forget what they did to Lisa simply because they wanted to define the place a woman is permitted to occupy in the world. At the same time, I won't ever forget about Lisa's graduation from the UCLA School of Law. Last I heard, she was planning to run for the Inglewood city council. Her first step. Occasionally, I call her from a disposable phone. She still feels guilty about the murder game, but she mentions it less frequently since she graduated from law school. I think studying law taught her there's a little more blurring between *right* and *wrong* than she originally believed.

I haven't been in touch with Sylvia, but I trust that without Charlie, she's working hard, raising her puppy-cute kids, and baking brownies. Once her kids are teens, maybe she'll lace up those brownies with a bit of herbal relaxation.

Moving into Noreen's house was an act of desperation because I had to wipe out my existence in Santa Clara county. I'd left an indistinct footprint, so it wasn't difficult. It's not a problem to erase pieces of my history, but I don't like making changes from a place of desperation. I like to plan, I like to think things through. Desperation leads to mistakes.

The day after Noreen and Brian plunged to their deaths, I drove back to the Safeway and ran back to the cliffside bungalow. I spent three hours cleaning all the surfaces Jared and I had touched. I vacuumed and swept and dusted. I used a damp mop and cleanser to chase down every loose hair and fingernail clipping.

The broken railing yawned off the back deck. I went out to clean the table and chairs and the area where I'd crouched waiting for them, but I didn't look down at the rocks and water below. Presumably the surf had taken their bodies, but it was likely the current would also return them at some point in time.

Escaping to the cabin, despite it's classy charm and secluded environment and my fascination with the massive house that also sits on the property, was another act of desperation. I had to get myself out of Noreen's bungalow before bodies washed back up on the rocks or a curious neighbor came to investigate. I had to get Jared out of there before he realized what had happened.

Someday, I'll have a spacious home filled with easy silence. When there's noise, it will be my choice, filling it with the crashing and complex music I love. It will have gardens and skylights, Italian tile floors and a magnificent kitchen. It will have a jacuzzi tub and a three-head shower. Every piece of furniture will be custom made and hold my body like a precious jewel. It will have its own weight room.

The house I'm in now might turn out to be an even

tighter prison than Noreen's, but one small step at a time.

It's a huge disappointment knowing I'll never flirt with Joe again. I'll never see his body, taste his kiss, smell his desire. He was a beguiling man in so many ways. Without a doubt, he's the best lover I've had so far in my life. Part of that was the mystery of concealing ourselves in equal measure. I had no idea that would be such an aphrodisiac. Or maybe it was simply that we saw inside of each other and liked the stillness we found there. That's what I first thought was so captivating about him.

As it turned out, maybe I only saw a reflection of myself in the mirror of his face.

Acknowledgements

An ocean of gratitude to Don Grant — my First Reader and Editor. He waits eagerly for each novel to make its first draft appearance, devouring the story with all its rough edges. He reads the book again, offering suggestions on tweaks to the plot and characters, pointing out where I've droned on for too long and where I obliviously skipped past an important scene. In the end, he painstakingly proofreads — twice.

Without his always available ears, his belief in my writing, and his sense of humor, I might never have found my voice.

A Note for Readers

Thanks for reading. I hope you liked reading about Alexandra as much as I enjoy writing her stories.

I'm passionate about fiction that explores the shadows of suburban life and the dark corners of the human mind. To me, the human psyche is, as they say in Star Trek — the final frontier — a place we'll never fully understand. I don't look for heroes to root for, I look for characters who are damaged, neurotic, and obsessed.

From the time I first learned to read, I could always be found with my nose buried in a book. I loved Margaret Sutton's Judy Bolton series as a child. During my teens, I devoured Agatha Christie's and Erle Stanley Gardner's novels. To be honest, the criminals in these books thrilled me more than the detectives. As an adult, I've fallen in love over and over with Ruth Rendell and John Updike, Joyce Carol Oates and Ian McEwan, Gillian Flynn and Tom Perrotta, Patricia Highsmith and Philip Roth, along with countless others. I love to hear from readers. You can email me at Cathryn@SuburbanNoir.com or find me on Twitter — @CathrynGrant. Sign up for my quarterly newsletter if you want to be notified when the next Alexandra Mallory novel is published.

CPSIA information can be obtained at www.ICGtesting.com
Printed in the USA
BVOW08s0216130916

461958BV00003B/75/P